The Angel Hair Conspiracy

A multi-layered genre novel

Y. B. Cambray

The Angel Hair Conspiracy

Pro It Out Publishing

PO Box 50021 Sarasota, FL 34232

Email: info@proitout.com www.ProItOut.com

Edition 1.0 2024

Cover Designer: Nasire Bey

Formatter: M.A. Kilpatrick

All the characters in this novel are considered to be fictitious. Reference to historic leaders is in respect, and only intended to enhance the timeline of the book. The information used is purely fictional.

Library of Congress Control Number: TXU001971019

ISBN 13: 978-0-578-96783-7 Papercover

Printed in the United States of America.

Acknowledgments

This novel is dedicated to my wonderful sister Barbara Kokoszka and my best friend Lanny Losure, may they rest in peace.

A special thank you to

Mahsa Zolghadr
Marcia Conley
Laura Kresl
Lauri Massoth
Dawn Amstutz
Molly Fink

For their support and assistance.

Author's Overview

The Angel Hair Conspiracy, is a mixed genre, multi-layered novel, of collusion between Nazi Germany, and an advanced stereotypic race of fair skin, light hair people, living in Norway.

This novel is not a story of military battles, but of a story of personal battles, following a time-line that coincides with the Second World War.

1940, World War Two. Norway, carefully selected and invaded, would provide Germany more than a military advantage, it could help advance Hitler's desire for a new race; The genetics were abundant.

Dr. Albrecht Brandt, a strict SS officer and organizing member of the Nazi's new eugenic program, quickly assembles a pre-selected medical team. Entrusted with secrets from the previous German ruler, Kaiser Wilhelm, Dr. Brandt initiates the Third Reich's nefarious eugenics project, in Oslo.

Norwegians, Elin and Olga Svensson, are unwittingly forced to serve in a select group constituting a secret labor force of intelligentsia. Elin, a medical doctor, is ordered to assist in a new Institute for Eugenic Research, located in an old hospital near Oslo. Olga, a renowned classical pianist, pregnant and frightened beyond belief, is pressured to promote cultural unity between Germans and Norwegians.

A brief trip to visit the Berlin Eugenic Institute allows Dr. Brandt and his colleagues the opportunity to observe technology beyond comprehension. They struggle to fully understand that the dark ethereal operation they are observing, is in fact the same program they are being trained for.

Leaving Berlin, and returning to their lodging deep in the mountains, Elin meets a mysterious stranger, behind the lodge, in the woods. He approaches Elin, and be-friends him.

As the war winds down, and Germany is losing its grip on Europe, Elin's strange friend returns, and warns him of the Nazi's intention to destroy the facilities, and eliminate all personnel in Oslo.

Dr. Brandt and Unk, his mysterious aide-de-camp, plan their escape. Elin, his frantic family, and friends, are quietly taken far North hoping to be rescued.

Yvonne Beck Cambray

Section One

Part One

A dusting of snow was falling on the streets of Oslo in the predawn hours of January, 1941. Olga Svensson, young, beautiful, and pregnant, stepped onto the balcony of her second-floor apartment. In the moonlit shadow of the doorway, she stood like a fine China doll. Her pale skin competed with the color of softly falling snow as she waited. Despairing blue eyes searched for movement in the eerily silent street. Fear captured her heartbeat, a fear shared with many since Hitler and the SS invaded Norway.

Exhausted, she stepped back inside and maintained vigil, face pressed to the window. A deluge of tears rolling over her cheeks quickly froze as they fell against the glass. Her laboring breath formed tiny crystal clusters that melted and froze again with the rhythm of her breathing. It was cold. She was tired. But most of all, she was worried. In anguish, she cried out, "Elin, where are you? Please come home."

As the opal-aura of dawn began to break over the horizon and filter through the snow, she forced herself from the window and collapsed on the sofa, momentarily escaping her anxiety in deep sleep. Normally, the opening of the apartment door would have awakened her, but today she didn't hear the creaking swing of oak on hinges.

Elin, entering the apartment in the grayness of morning, grasped at shadows until he found a lamp, turned it on, and felt his vision adjust.

Olga's body stirred; he moved towards her. Dropping an arm to the floor, she mumbled unintelligibly. He felt great relief. His beloved wife was safe, obviously tired, but safe. The heavy wool quilt had fallen, exposing her very pregnant body to the coldness of the Norwegian winter. Gently, he replaced it and walked to the bedroom.

Sitting on the bed to remove his shoes, he didn't feel the deep furrows that formed across his forehead. Worry about explaining his detainment to Olga was secondary. The bigger issue was the unyielding demands of his captors.

His head pounded as he relived the SS threats. Stress had become his enemy as well as the Nazis, and it had begun to take its toll. Reacting slowly but steadily, his body had become one tensely knotted muscle. Attempting to reach his shoelaces, his neck stiffened as intense pain plummeted down his back. Seeking relief in a welcoming bed of pristine white sheets and down pillows, his tired, twitching body soon surrendered to sleep, a welcomed reprieve. Hours passed, and the last splinter of sunlight had already grown faint when he awakened.

Olga, lying next to him, kissed him lightly on the ear. Her voice quivered. "I'm so glad your home. I've been physically sick with worry. Where have you been?"

Elin's voice was almost harsh. "I don't want to discuss it now. I need a shower and something to eat. Then we'll talk."

Patience was not Olga's virtue. She wanted to talk now, but the brevity and almost harshness in her husband's voice convinced her to respect his request.

"Hand me my robe," he demanded. She did. Still in his stockings, he hurled back the sheet and dropped his feet to the cold floor with the force of a hammer. He was out of control with frustration and anger. Olga watched in disbelief as he tightened his robe and stormed into the bathroom.

"I'm sorry you had a bad night and I'm sorry you're so angry. Why are you angry?" she pushed. Elin ignored the question, dropped his robe, and stepped into the shower. The steam rolled over his body like smoke hugging a cigarette. His silhouette twisted and turned beneath the water as lathered soap slid through the valley of his buttocks into the drain below. Olga, not one to be ignored, shouted as she turned to leave. "Remember you still have me, angry or not. I still love you. I'll be in the kitchen when you want to talk. Take your time."

Well into her second cup of tea when Elin sat down at the kitchen table, she said nothing. He too was silent, tilting and turning the teacup in such a way that little splashes spilled over the edge into the saucer.

"Are you nervous?" she questioned.

"Not nervous; scared. Scared beyond belief."

Sensing the seriousness of the situation, she cautiously pressed. "Is this something we can talk about?"

Elin hesitated. "I'm not sure. I don't want to upset you."

"Please, I want to know what's going on," Olga pleaded. "I need to know where you've been."

"All right," he warned, "but understand it's not a pretty picture, and it's going to become worse before it gets better."

Elin finished his tea, stood, and walked to the next room, returning seconds later with a stack of documents. He dropped them on the table and asked Olga to review them.

Examining each page carefully, she raised quizzical eyes to his face. "My God, where did you get these? All our medical records and university transcripts are here. Who gave you these?"

"My SS hosts," he replied in an irritated voice. "They gave them to me last night."

"But I don't understand. What do they want?" she questioned. "We know nothing of military or political matters."

"It seems Hitler, and more so Himmler, have interests other than conquest. It's reported that there is an obsession in Germany with blonde-haired, blue-eyed people. They're setting up a medical facility in Oslo to study a new science, eugenics, and since I am a doctor with the misfortune of a high scholastic ranking, they have ordered me to report to the hospital tomorrow morning for further evaluation and instruction."

Olga's eyes, no longer frozen in shock, filled with tears. Somehow, she knew their lives would soon be irreparably changed. All their hopes, aspirations and hard work would be for nothing. Biting her lip, she hoped to soften the woeful moan rolling from between her teeth. Unable to control the tears, she felt them roll down her face and gather under her chin before dropping onto her swollen stomach. "Does this mean you'll be taken away?"

His voice cracked. "I'm not sure, Olga. I pray they'll let me stay here with you. We'll know in the morning, after my interview. Try not to worry. We'll work through this. I'm sure as long as I'm useful, no harm will come to us."

Olga wrapped herself in his arms and wept.

The remainder of the evening was consumed with quiet reflections and thoughts of the future. They discussed the prospect of escape, but Olga's condition, so near her delivery date, prevented any further entertainment of that idea. Occasionally she would ask about the previous night, but Elin, often lost in thought, would briefly address the question and then change the subject, prompting Olga to worry even more about the obvious secrets he was harboring.

"Olga, I know it's cold, but how about a walk? Maybe visit mamma. Think you can make it? It'll do us good to get out for a while."

Encouraged by the uplifted tone of his voice, she squirmed to get out of the chair. "You know Elin, a walk is a wonderful idea, and if I can't make it, you can carry me," she laughed.

"Not a chance," he snapped back. "I'll put you in a cart and roll you there and maybe we'll have that baby tonight."

Olga smiled as he stretched and pulled at her coat, trying to button it.

"Okay snowman, tuck in your scarf and let's go," he teased.

Taking his hand, she carefully addressed the flight of stairs, several times squeezing his fingers, reassuring herself of his support.

The street was empty except for a few hardy souls walking dogs and mumbling through tight wool scarves. Elin commented that these neighbors had to be crazy to be out on a night like this.

"And what about us?" Olga giggled. "Are we crazy?"

"No," he objected, "desperate!"

The snow, now a light flurry, covered the scarf Elin had thrown over Olga's shoulders. "Let me shake this," he said. "I don't want my girl getting cold." Olga nestled against his chest while he removed the wrap. As he wound the scarf tightly around her again under the amber glowing streetlamp, Elin's eyes turned pleading. "Can we stand here for a minute? I feel like I'm in heaven, and this unspoiled beauty is covering the ugliness around us. Please, I want to remember this feeling." Again, he pulled her closer to the warmth of his body, and they stood as one under the safety of the light. Hearts beating in unison was the only sound.

"Better go," he said as their arms disentwined.

"I guess so," she reluctantly replied.

Magically, the stress of the day's events disappeared, and their steps lightened with anticipation of the warm fire and hospitality of Olga's mamma.

Turning the corner, they could see her house. White smoke from the chimney curled above the gables and mingled with the wind. The smell of burning wood perfumed the street and softened their hearts.

"Hurrah! I made it," Olga squealed as she rapped on the door.

Elin, nibbling at her ear, suggested that they not discuss their dilemma. "Let's not worry your mamma. We'll wait until we're certain before we tell her."

Olga turned, looking into his eyes. "You are so kind," she said.

Sonja opened the door, exposing the kissing couple on the step. "You know those passionate kisses sprout babies," she teased.

"Yes, we know," he laughed. "I think the last time we did this we sprouted a melon, not a baby."

The warm house was draped in soft, gentle light and shadowed images of a comfortable lifestyle. There were massive bookcases flanking the fireplace with a collection of books belonging to Olga's pappa. He had been dead almost three years, but the room was a living memorial to the great man.

"Hot chocolate?" Sonja asked.

"Tea would be better," Olga insisted. "I have to watch my weight – doctor's orders."

"May I help? I'm not pregnant, Elin chuckled."

"I can manage, just warm yourselves by the fire and I'll be back in a minute." Sonja left the room. Elin moved close to Olga, who was warming herself by the glowing embers.

"I love this room," she whispered. "See that chair? I spent hours sitting there listening to Pappa play the piano."

"Did he teach you in this room?" Elin quizzed.

"No, don't you remember? A tutor taught me after we left the country home. In the country, I had no one to teach me and would entertain myself playing with Pappa's piano. He hated me using his precious instrument."

He confessed that he had forgotten.

"I feel sad when I think about Pappa," she lamented. "As great a pianist as he was, he could never teach me. When he came home from the orchestra, he was always tired. He wasn't a very patient man either. Guess that's where my impatience comes from."

"Refresh my memory, what was the name of your teacher?" Elin inquired.

Olga hesitated, "Oh, when we moved here from the country so Pappa would be closer to his work, he hired the best teacher available. Mr. Alfred, I called him. He was as old as Methuselah with the patience of Job. After I became more accomplished, Pappa would play with me, but not teach me. When I decided to major in music at the university, he was extremely proud, telling everyone that he had produced a successor. Well, I guess he did, in a way. Do you remember how shocked I was when they offered me a position in the orchestra after his death?"

"You earned that appointment," Elin snapped. "The fact that your pappa held an important position has nothing to do with your talent. Don't deny your accomplishments."

Sonja returned with a tray of drinks and cookies. "I heard the statement, Elin, and I agree with you. Olga has always had a problem accepting the fact that she has an extraordinary gift. Cookies?" she inquired.

Olga, seemingly mesmerized by the dancing fire, ignored the comment. Some distant memory had her undivided attention, or perhaps the prospects of a bleak future had re-captured her thoughts.

"Elin," Sonja inquired, "how is your family? Is your mamma still nursing? And your sister, how is she?"

"They seem to be just fine," he said. "You know life in the north is different than here in the city. I don't worry as much; my family stockpiles food and supplies for the heavy snows. Yes, mamma is still nursing; she helps at the hospital. The war has created a large shortage of medical personnel. Pappa and Karla are still working at the bookstore. Oh, Karla's engaged to a man she met at school. They haven't set a date yet. I think they'll wait until things settle down a bit."

"Do you know him, Olga?" Sonja questioned, as she passed the cookies. Olga sat quietly, oblivious to the conversation, twisting her hands in a fretful manner. "What is it child, you seem so preoccupied. Is it the pregnancy? Talk to your mamma," she insisted.

Olga looked at Elin, hesitated, then explained that she was a little depressed. "Maybe it's the absence of Pappa, or possibly just the pregnancy," she mumbled.

Sonja shook her head. "This is not good."

Olga glared at her, unkind thoughts racing through her head.

Observing the strain, Elin suggested music. Sonja, in an effort to restore good graces, rose from the chair and scurried to uncover the grand piano which stood obscurely in the corner. "What a joy it would be to hear you play?" she pleaded her daughter. Olga acquiesced, lifted the lid on the storage bench and chose several favorite selections. Elin stoked the fire and settled nearby in a comfortable old chair as Sonja filled her hot chocolate cup and curled up under a blanket on the sofa.

The fire, now a raging inferno, cracked and hissed. Shadows from dancing flames climbed to the ceiling and performed to their own composition. Olga began slowly with Beethoven's Moonlight Sonata. The melody vibrated through the house. For Olga, the occasional "bravo" intensified memories of past recitals where concentration produced a oneness with the music. She recalled her Pappa's nervous instructions at her first recital. "Liberation; liberation from distraction is the most important thing to remember. The music is all you must hear, feel and breathe." But tonight, try as she might, her thoughts wandered. Memories flashed and tears fell.

Sonja, absorbed in her own retrospection, sobbed throughout the entire song. "I'm sorry," she sniffled when Olga looked up, hands hovering over the keys, the music ended. "You are such a beautiful pianist. Thank you for the remembrance."

Olga rose and glanced at Elgin. "Mamma seems a little tired and we have an early morning. Would you mind fueling the fire and getting my coat?"

Sonja stood, put her arms around Olga, and hugged her tightly. "Take care going home. Send for me if anything happens with the baby, and for heaven's sake, get some rest."

Elin tightened the scarf around Olga's collar, kissed Sonja goodnight and opened the door. "Good night; secure the lock," he said. "We'll see you soon." Sonja acknowledged his concern and waved goodbye.

Part Two

The streets were crowded the next morning as Elin forced his way to the bus station. Hordes of women and men were shouting, pushing, and shoving for positions nearest doors, all desperate to be first in line when bleary-eyed merchants opened their shops.

Thin-faced farmers were mobbed by pleading women as they unloaded their scant wares of meat and cheese. Food was in short supply. Panic had become the norm. Elin watched, though he wasn't sure why. In a matter of a few months, the Nazis had taken a prosperous, self-sufficient populous and turned them into frightened, desperate people. Even the threat of patrolling German troops seemed a secondary concern for the mass of hungry bodies pressed against boarded-up shop windows. "Hunger is a powerful weapon," he thought.

At the station, Elin positioned himself on a raised platform so he could see arriving buses. Recent gasoline shortages caused serious transportation problems, and if you failed to be among the first to board, you would wait hours. As he watched the assemblage of bodies, luggage and boxes, a voice called out over the noisy chatter.

"Elin, Elin Svensson! Here, over here." Searching the defensive eyes of a forlorn crowd, Elin located the familiar face. Olaf Knorr, friend and former medical colleague, stood in the refuge of a half-empty alleyway, waving his arms,. His tall, slender body stood above the crowd. There was an innocence in the way he smiled, and his eyes sparkled happiness as Elin parted the crowd with haste.

"Olaf, what are you doing here? I thought you were interning in Bergen."

Olaf extended his hand and pulled him close to the relative warmth of an old brick wall. "I'm so happy to see you," he said.

"I don't understand." Elin insisted. "Where is your family and why are you here?"

"I've been ordered back to Oslo by the Nazis to work on a new project," Olaf explained. "Christine and I came alone. The children are with family in Bergen until we get settled. We have a small apartment just around the corner. Why are you out so early this cold morning?"

Elin, lowering his voice to a whisper, said, "I have been instructed by the Nazis to report to the old hospital building on the hill. I'm going there now." Olaf looked quizzically at him. "I'm going there too," he said. "Could it be possible we'll be working together?"

"I don't know, "Elin replied. "It seems more than a coincidence that both of us are going in the same direction."

A screaming horn announced the arrival of the bus. Doors opened and people who were stuffed into every available space squirmed to escape the metal cocoon and scramble onto already overcrowded streets. Elin and Olaf, clutching each other's arms, pushed through the mass of bodies and into the already-filled bus. Thankful to have a ride, but unable to move or sit,

they stood surrounded by passengers who stared suspiciously at each other with soulful eyes. The tightly packed bodies made it almost impossible to breathe. Elin was uncomfortable, but at least he was near a window and could relieve his claustrophobic condition by peering into the street. He could no longer see Olaf, who had been pushed to the center, surrounded by a centipede of arms clinging to leather straps suspended from steel rods. Men in black leather coats surveyed the passengers, asking questions and staring intently at several. Elin wondered if they were SS. *Could they be watching me*, he thought? How easily paranoia took control.

The bus plowed out of the station on a snow-laden street. After about two blocks, the men in black got off. Elin was relieved that they were gone. Now he could focus his thoughts on the day ahead.

Rounding a bend in the road, the bus labored up a hill to the entrance of the hospital. Somehow, it didn't feel right. What had once been a place of healing and hope now appeared sinister. The cold, dark stone structure projected an image of institutional torture from the Middle Ages. Surprised that his thoughts were undertaking such a change for the grotesque, he assumed the war obviously was to blame by deeply affecting his own sense of security and purpose.

The bus slowed, then stopped. Loud hissing noises from the brakes echoed across the frozen ground and exhaust fumes bellowed, clouding the disembarking travelers. Elin, Olaf and a small band of obviously apprehensive strangers trudged up the driveway through massive iron gates proudly displaying the infamous Nazi-German flags. The interior grounds were patrolled by guards marching in precise robotic maneuvers. As they manipulated their perfected bodies, Elin felt compelled to stop and watch. They were proud, but most of all they were strikingly handsome, tall, blonde-haired, and blue eyed. Was this an example of Hitler's rumored great super race? It certainly was something to think about.

Elin and his companions proceeded virtually unnoticed until they approached the entrance door.

There, men dressed in black uniforms with swastika insignias printed on their armbands appeared, grabbing their arms and forcing them into the foyer. "Please, we're medical personnel reporting to the hospital for work," one of the strangers pleaded in a broken German accent. "This is no longer a hospital," a guard snapped. "If this is not a hospital, then what is it?" another questioned. "This is the Institute for Biological and Eugenic Research, organized by the Third Reich."

A deep, interrupting voice spoke from a darkened doorway. "You may call me Oscar; I am in charge of this facility. Please line up, state your name and occupation."

Oscar's shadowy figure moved into the light, revealing a man with strong features, dark eyes, a mustache and ruddy skin. His voice reflected confidence and his stature denoted authority. One by one, the men moved into formation. Each, without reluctance, stated their name and occupation. It was obvious they felt secure in who they were. Elin and Olaf were two of six physicians. The others declared themselves to be chemists, technicians and biologists.

Oscar opened a dark door behind him and escorted the men into a sterile, private room where he administered a written test. As Elin pondered a series of questions, an uneasy feeling began to settle. *How bizarre,* he thought. *What does sex with animals have to do with medicine? And why do they want to know how many times a week I engage in love-making?* Feeling very uncomfortable, he lifted his eyes and glanced around the table. Others, obviously embarrassed, projected glares of contempt. *Why are these questions important,* he wondered? Not only were they embarrassing, they were unnatural. His imagination ran wild. The idea they had been brought here to this malevolent place to participate in abnormal experiments worried him dreadfully.

Oscar checked his watch. "Take a break," he said. "You may smoke if you choose." Several detainees pulled out cigarettes and lit up.

Oscar observed as the men naturally shifted into small groups, revealing obvious friendships. Olaf motioned for Elin and another physician to join him. "What do you make of this?" Olaf questioned.

"I'm concerned," Elin said. "Those questions are unbelievable. Most of them were so personal and intrusive. I resent the invasion."

"Oh, I'm sorry," Olaf interrupted. "This is Dr. Helmut Keiser, pediatrician." Elin offered his hand and noted his pleasure at the acquaintance.

The small talk ended abruptly when a beautiful young woman in a neatly pressed lab coat entered the room. She was the first female the group had encountered since entering the building. As she migrated toward Oscar, all eyes focused on her. She placed her lips close to his ear and whispered. "Men," Oscar shouted, "I want you to split into six groups, each headed by a physician, and follow me." For the first time the men appeared nervous.

"Where are we going?" a young man asked.

"Don't ask questions," Oscar demanded.

The young woman led the way, swinging her hips back and forth in a suggestive gait obviously intended for Oscar. His lust was unmistakable.

A large door at the end of the hall appeared, and she stopped. Oscar instructed the group to be seated in chairs lining the corridor and to wait for them to return. It seemed like hours passed. The stress of not knowing what to expect began to manifest itself. Some men smoked, lifting their heads and blowing shaky smoke rings. Others bit their fingernails, and a few paced the floor looking pale, but none spoke.

Finally, Oscar returned, carrying a sheet of paper. "These men are free to go for now," he snapped. Then he read eight names from the list. Elin and Olaf were not among the dismissed.

A guard, who had followed Oscar into the room, gathered the small group of dismissed together and disappeared down the hall. "Those of you here," stated Oscar, "are worthy of working for the Third Reich. All of your needs will be attended to. Food, medicine, and clothing will be provided. Occasionally there will be special gifts, so your work will have its rewards. This will be your second home. You will work in shifts and in cooperation with each other. This is a high security facility, and no one will be permitted to come or go without clearance under the penalty of death. You must not reveal what transpires here. Believe me, we will know if you are discussing the projects. If you value your lives and the lives of your families, you will proudly serve the Reich to the best of your ability. We have one last test to conduct before you will be dismissed. I hope you find it pleasant." Oscar, turning to leave, parted his lips and ran his tongue over a smirking smile.

Surprised by the vulgar expression, the men stared in disbelief. "Oh, dear God," mumbled Olaf. "What in the world are they going to do to us now?" The young woman returned and reassured the nervous men that everything was going to be okay. "There's to be a physical examination," she stated. "Please, when your name is called, bring your coat and follow me." One by one each left the room. Suddenly, she called Elin's name. Blood gorged the veins in his neck as his face flushed. His fear became a mask. His heart pounded like a primeval drum as beads of perspiration formed on his brow. Slowly he stood, took a deep breath, and glanced at the remaining men. Olaf, sensing his fear, tipped his head in support.

The hallway, silent and threatening, darkened as Elin followed the young woman. She continued her silence as they left the building and proceeded across a large connecting corridor to an adjoining building.

Immediately Elin noticed familiar scents: alcohol, ether, chloroform, and sundry other medical smells. Just ahead, after passing, through heavy glass doors, Elin could see bright lights overflowing from a doorway, lighting the dark hall. The smells had intensified, and Elin knew they had reached their destination.

Entering the massive room, Elin's chart was handed to a nurse. She instructed him to follow her. The large room was sectioned with white curtains forming small cubicles. The nurse pointed Elin to one near the hall with number 17 stamped in large letters across the fabric top. She then asked him to please undress. Cautiously, he removed his clothing, using a sheet from the bed to cover his nakedness. As he sat in the corner of his fabric prison, he tried to comprehend what they could be doing. *Why so many cubicles?* It was almost like they were expecting a calamitous situation. *Maybe these are extra operating rooms, he told himself. I could be working here if there were a disaster in Oslo.* He tried to reassure himself that this was routine practice during times of war. Occasionally a door would open, and he would listen intently to the muffled voices. Unfortunately, the profound silence did not aid him in hearing what was being said.

Suddenly and without a sound to alert him, the fabric door flew back with a billowing gust. Elin, caught off guard, gulped the air and grasped his chest in fright. A robust little woman wiggled into the room. "I didn't mean to scare you," she laughed. It was the first sign of humor since being detained and it surprised him.

Taking another deep breath, he mused, "I hope you're not going to take my blood pressure. It's probably at an all-time high after that fright."

"We'll save it for last," she smiled. "My name is Elisa, and I'll be working at this facility with you and the others. Stick out your arm. I need blood." Gently, she extracted her sample, carefully marked it and placed it in a metal box with Elin's name on the side.

"Are you a nurse?" he asked.

"Yes," she answered in a strong German accent – and a damn good one too."

"What part of Germany is your home?" he continued, trying to be friendly.

"Berlin, all my life until now," she answered in a somewhat lonesome voice.

"Why are you here?"

"I go where they tell me, just like you," she snapped. "Until this operation is fully staffed, I will be helping in different areas. When it's 100% functional, I'll be working in my specialty."

"Which is?" he pushed.

"Children," she said proudly. "I work with infants."

"Children—what children?" he asked in a confused voice.

"You'll see for yourself," she answered. Elisa then directed her attention to the rest of the physical, asking pertinent medical questions and recording them on his chart. "The Third Reich wants only healthy staff members," she said. "So far, you look to be picture perfect. One more specimen please," Elisa requested, handing him a bottle with his name on the side. "I think you know what to do with this. Try to get as much sperm inside as you do outside, okay?"

Picking up his chart and blood samples, she informed him she would be back shortly to see if he needed help. Elin squirmed; thankful the grandmotherly nurse was not to be present for his command performance. He lay back on the cold bed, trying to relax and clear his mind. He had done this several times since Olga's pregnancy with no problem. He was confident he could do it again. He caressed his penis, thinking of Olga as he stroked himself with frequent thrusts. Moving slowly at first and then almost violently, he could not produce the sperm needed. *I'm too tense. I must relax.* His thoughts scanned encounters he and Olga had enjoyed. He recalled the first time they had sex—how exciting it had been. Even his secret affair with a former classmate couldn't bring the results needed for ejaculation.

Nurse Elisa returned, checked the bottle, and shook her head. "Don't feel bad," she said, "It happens to the best of men. But unfortunately, we don't have all day. I'm sending in help." Elin's face flushed with embarrassment as she left the room.

Shortly, the fabric door opened, and a tall slender body backed into the cubicle. The white lab coat had a familiar swish as the phantom of a figure fumbled to secure the aperture. "There," she said, turning to face Elin. "We now have privacy." Elin was mortified, it was the beautiful young woman he had encountered earlier. A thousand questions flooded his mind as she moved to the side of the bed. "Don't be afraid, I'm here to help. Please lie on your stomach," she instructed. Apprehension stiffened his body.

Reluctantly, he rolled over, positioning himself in the center of the bed. Her hands were touching him, gently caressing his tense shoulders. Warm oil dripped from her fingers and rolled into the folds of skin wrinkled around his neck. Like silk, her hands glided in and out of the creases. He couldn't help himself; even though his body fought the invasion of personal pleasure, he still twitched softly into relaxation.

"Feel good?" she asked.

He could only answer with a guilty moan. Anxieties melted and his fantasy grew with the movement of her body against his.

"It's warm in here," she said, dropping her coat to the floor. Her hands, slick with oil, moved cautiously under the sheet, massaging the crevice of his buttocks. As she reached for the most sensual spot, her naked breast floated across his back. His head flew up in surprise; his masseuse was leaning over him totally nude. "Is there a problem?" Her voice was butter. Not knowing what to say, he lay back down, and she continued.

A few minutes later, Elisa returned. The young woman smiled and handed her a full bottle.

Turning to Elin, she said, "I must go with Elisa, but before I leave, I want you to know my name is Anna. We'll be seeing each other again."

She paused, memorizing his face. Her kind eyes expressed a softness that sharply contrasted with the impatient glares of her colleague, Elisa. As she buttoned the last button on her coat she whispered, "Oscar is waiting. Goodbye for now."

Elin watched in silence. All he could manage was a faint wave as she left the room. He dressed quickly, gathered his belongings, and walked to the hall. Oscar arrived a few minutes later, poked his elbow into Elin's arm, and laughed knowingly. "I told you there would be pleasant rewards, didn't I?"

Sick with confusion and guilt, Elin nodded, exposing his embarrassment, and asked if he were free to go.

"Yes," Oscar replied. "We've made arrangements for you. Come, I'll walk out with you. You did very well today. I think you'll have a great future in the Third Reich. Please plan to return in two days at 9:00AM to begin your assignment."

Oscar parted the large, double entrance doors with one swift push, held his hand high, and summoned a green military bus to the front of the building. A young soldier jumped from the driver's seat and saluted with an extended arm. "Heil Hitler," he shouted, clicking his heels together. "Take this most important man home," Oscar instructed.

The soldier graciously escorted Elin to the bus and assisted him as he slid into a nearby seat.

"Heil Hitler, Heil Hitler," Oscar shouted as they drove away.

Part Three

As the bus lumbered toward town, the young German asked for directions. Elin carefully directed him toward a route that would be the least noticed by his friends and family. After all, it would be hard to explain his personal Nazi chauffeur without disclosing restricted information.

Approaching the outskirts of town, streetlights flickered under the snow-filled sky. It was late afternoon, but it seemed like midnight. The streets were empty. Harsh, chilling temperatures and threat of snow had forced most inside. Elin was relieved. Because of the weather, only a few curious onlookers noticed the threatening bus meandering the winding streets near his home.

"Stop here," Elin shouted. "I'll get out now. Thank you." He jumped from the slow-moving bus onto the sidewalk. The young soldier, unable to assist him, watched in surprise as Elin ran toward the corner, still about three blocks from home.

Stepping into the doorway of a small pub, Elin waited for the bus to pass. "Elin," a voice barked, "close the door. What for God's sake brings you out this cold evening?"

"Just a beer," he choked. "I just need a beer."

The ruddy faced old man filled the glass, deft from habit, topping it off with just the right amount of foam. "Beautiful, isn't it?" he smiled. "Don't know how much longer we'll be able to get this, sure is a shame."

Straddling a tall stool and resting his arms on the bar, Elin searched for something to say. "Where is everyone?"

"If you didn't have to, would you come out on a day like this?" the old man laughed. "Besides, people are scared. There's not much to celebrate unless you're a Nazi."

Realizing what had just been said, Elin looked nervously around the room. Of the three people sitting in the pub, two were from the neighborhood and the third, sitting in a corner by himself, was a stranger. Uneasiness squeezed his gut as he turned back to his beer.

The stranger approached the bar, stepped between the stools, and asked for his check. As he placed coins on the bar he commented, "Old man, treasonous words are better unsaid," then turned and walked out.

Elin was shaken. "Who was that?"

The bartender shrugged his shoulders and said he didn't know. For the first time, Elin had to face the inevitable. Spies were everywhere. He was no longer a free man; no longer could he voice a negative opinion or refuse service to the Nazis. The thought of being a prisoner under constant surveillance by the Third Reich repulsed him. Unable to finish his drink, he paid his check and slipped out the back door into the alley.

With penetrating eyes, he searched for the stranger in every doorway. Every shadow became his enemy. Every sound was a threat. Trusting no one, he cautiously left the alley for the street and hastened his pace. In his paranoia, he had lingered too long in the severe cold. He needed to get home. His feet were burning, indicating the early stage of frostbite. The wind slapped his face as he turned the last corner toward home, causing his eyes to pool with tears and his cheeks to redden with windburn. Puffs of snow peppering the darkened sky made it difficult to see the faint amber light of his apartment house. His lungs burned with every breath. He needed shelter. The amber beacon came closer. He took one long, painful gasp of cold air and ran as fast as he could to the warmth of home.

Once inside the dim foyer, he sat on the wide bottom step, catching his breath and rubbing his feet, thanking God that he could still feel them. He was exhausted. Using the steps as a prop, he leaned back, resting his legs and warming his hands. *I'll go up in a while,* he thought.

He lay there, looking up at the walls and chandelier, remnants of a once grand old home. How the years had taken its toll. The crystal light fixture above him now sported only two glowing bulbs. The other sockets were empty. The stair casing needed stain, and the wallpaper had lost its color in a streak from years of hands sliding along the railing. *What a miserable place.*

Mrs. Knutson, the downstairs neighbor, opened her door and jumped. "Elin, what are you doing?"

"I didn't mean to scare you. I needed to sit and get the snow off my shoes."

"Is Olga alright?"

"I'm on my way home now," he replied, "I'll let you know."

"Well, she seemed a bit troubled when I saw her leave earlier this morning," the neighbor continued, "I've been concerned."

"What do you mean? Isn't she home?" he shouted.

"There were noises in the foyer," Mrs. Knutson continued. "I opened the door and saw her leaving with a strange man. He was pulling her arm and she seemed reluctant to go. I closed the door before they saw me. I've listened all day for her, but unless she came back while I napped, I haven't heard her return."

Now in a state of panic, Elin scaled the stairs in seconds. The open door was not a welcome sight, but lights from the hallway washed the floors and the apartment appeared empty of intruders. "Oh, dear God" he cried. "Where are you, my love?" Overcome, he buried his hands in his face and sobbed.

"Elin, Elin is that you?" a muffled voice asked. "Elin, it's me, Olga. I'm in the pantry."

Like a blind man, in the overflowing dim lights he shuffled along the wall until he located the room. "Olga, are you okay?" he whispered.

"Yes," she said, "stand back so I can open the door."

Elin slid his hands along the door until he reached the edge. As the opening grew larger, Olga's arms searched the blackness for him. Reaching out for her, he took her arm and guided her fragile body into the room. "Are you alright?" he asked again, caressing her softly.

"Yes, I'm alright, but frightened. Is the door locked Elin? Please bolt the door," she begged.

"Don't move," he said. "I'll be right back." He secured the door and switched on the light.

Olga cried out. "Turn off the light, please, Elin! I don't want them to come back."

Elin took her in his arms once again, stroking her hair in a calming motion. "We're not prisoners Olga, and I'm no longer going to live like one. I think we should leave Oslo. We could go north and live with mamma and pappa. I don't think they could find us there. We could hide in the mountains."

"No, Elin, no. We can't leave," Olga cried. "Please promise me you won't talk of this again. There are things I need to tell you, important things. Let's go in the kitchen. I'll make tea and we can talk there."

Elin went ahead to light the stove. Olga checked the room once again and joined him in the compact kitchen.

Steam from the whistling kettle softened the clatter of China as Olga fumbled with the teacups in nervous anxiety. "You know they're watching us, Elin; someone is watching."

"I know," he whispered. "Try to control yourself, we're going to be alright. They need us for some reason. That's why we're under surveillance. I'm not sure what they want, but I do know they don't want us to disappear. Olga, please stop pacing and sit down. I need to know what happened today."

The two huddled around the cream-colored enameled table, hands joined. A single light bulb hanging from the tall ceiling softened threatening shadows lingering in the corners. Olga slipped her hand from his and caressed the warm cup. Elin patiently waited. "It was late morning, about 11:00," she said, taking a deep breath. "I was working on the baby's quilt when I heard voices in the hall. I didn't think much about it. When the noise became louder and someone ran down the stairs and out the front, I became curious. I opened the door to look out; that's when I saw them. There were standing there, just standing against the railing, staring at me. There was a frightening little old man and a younger man. I nearly fainted when they started toward me. In a panic, I slammed the door. I didn't know what to do. I was scared out of my wits. My hands were shaking so hard I couldn't turn the lock. I was trapped, and it terrified me.

"There was noise in the hall again: someone walking back and forth in front of the door. Then, for a second, it got quiet. The silence was paralyzing. I was afraid to breathe, afraid they could hear me. I held my hands over my mouth and worried about what they were doing. I braced my back against the door and prayed they would leave, but they didn't. Someone hit the door with a fist so hard it almost knocked me down. He pounded until the room trembled. He called out my name and pleaded with me to open the door. I knew there was no chance of escape, so I asked what he wanted. He said he was sent here by the authorities and needed to talk to me. Again, he asked me to open the door. There was nothing I could do, nothing. I opened the door, and they came in. He said their names were unimportant and that they were as shaken as I. The young man said he was there just to drive me to the authorities downtown as soon as possible and asked me to get my coat. I asked about the older man standing with him. He said he was there to assist me in anything I needed. I wanted to leave you a note, but he said we wouldn't be gone long, and I would be home before you were scheduled to return. I asked what they wanted, but they knew nothing. Somehow the old man's face softened, and I believed him. He helped with my coat, and we left. There was a black car waiting outside. He opened the back door, and I got in.

"We drove to a small brick building near the central district; the young driver dropped us off. We were directed to a lady sitting behind a desk. Several people were also there apparently waiting for something. I gave her my name, and we took a seat near the door. The old man said I would be alright and disappeared. It was so quiet--no one spoke. They all seemed frightened – I certainly was. It wasn't long until my name was called. 'Mrs. Svensson, come with me,' he said. I picked up my coat and followed him into a private office.

"A well-dressed man stood and addressed me, asking if I would like coffee or a drink. I said no thank you. He said his name was Helmut and he wouldn't take much of my time. He picked up a pencil and began to write while asking me questions about the family; where they were, who they were, what they did for a living, etc. He asked personal questions about us and our friends. Then he informed me that I would be required to take a physical and mental examination after the baby was born. He told me I was to be an important participant in the New Order and that I had already been approved. He said they were looking forward to working with both of us. I asked him what he meant: how would I be involved? He said I shouldn't worry about it and that I would be informed at a later date. He also said they expected full cooperation and immediate availability from both of us. His voice was pleasant as he said goodbye. He then called in the old man to drive me home. When we arrived home, the little man said he would be seeing me again, soon.

"Back inside the apartment, I had the feeling someone had been there. Well, anyway, I was too tired to even think about that, so I lay down on the sofa and dozed. It was getting dark when a noise woke me. Someone was turning the doorknob very slowly. It frightened me so much that I hid in the pantry. That's why I was hiding when you came home. I didn't hear anyone come in, so maybe they just had the wrong apartment."

Not wanting to frighten her further, Elgin decided not to mention the open door or his encounter at the pub. "Elin," Olga pleaded, "now do you understand why we will never be able to leave? They know everything about us. I know they wouldn't hesitate to kill us and mamma. Please, Elin, promise me you won't leave me. I couldn't bear the thought of losing you and our family."

"You're right," he said. "It's too late for escape, and I promise I'll never leave you. I love you and would die before letting them take me away without you and our baby."

His strong commitment was a great comfort to her. Relieved of at least that fear, she slowly relaxed.

"Is it agreed?" he questioned. "We will fully cooperate with the Nazis, even though we feel what they're doing is wrong."

"Yes," Olga snapped. "If we want to live, we have no choice, and I will support you every way I can."

Elin took one last sip of tea and gently put the cup on the saucer. Olga slid her hand along his arm and enticed him to bed with a persuasive tug.

Part Four

A cold wind moaned through the cracks in the window frame as the young couple curled their warm bodies together. Olga, too tried to rest, imagined the wind as an orchestra and listened intently to the fragmented melody. Elin, asleep but not resting, thrashed and turned.

Unable to comfort him, she wiggled her body away. As she struggled to roll over, a nauseated feeling came over her. The baby had become active, kicking and twisting with such force that it made her sick to her stomach. Hoping not to disturb Elin, she quietly got out of bed. As she stood, putting on her robe, a sharp pain ripped her back. She cried out but he didn't respond. Her stomach contracted and drops of water flowed down her legs, puddling on the floor. *This baby is crushing my bladder*, she thought as she headed to the bathroom. Every step produced a profusion of liquid. Every movement became uncomfortable. This wasn't just an issue of bladder control. *Oh, dear God*, she thought, *the waiting is over. I'm going to be a mamma.*

Now more excited than concerned, she closed the bathroom door, and in the privacy of the small room, asked God for a safe delivery and a healthy baby. The contractions became more intense. Dull aches rolled across her back. Subtle jabbing pains poked her ribs. The baby, held too long in confinement, stretched and contorted her stomach with elongated thrusts. Then, just as quickly as it began, the pain subsided. "It can't be over," she whispered to herself. Taking deep breaths, just as Elin had instructed, she waited. Nothing more than a dull ache lingered. She waited a little longer, removed her wet clothing and wrapped herself in a clean white sheet before returning to bed.

The massive old down mattress absorbed her body, curling great arms of protective feathers around her, shielding her from the cold and loneliness of night. Elin's steady breathing and soft snore became hypnotic, and Olga drifted off to sleep.

The thin veil of darkness had just started to lift when the pain returned. Olga clutched her stomach and moaned.

Elin rolled over. "What's wrong? Are you sick?" A sharp contraction caused a knotting of her fist and she cried out. Elin realized she was starting her labor. "Olga, have you passed any fluids?" he questioned.

In a frail voice she answered, "Yes, last night."

"You're in labor," he said. "I need to examine you. Straighten your legs." Olga reluctantly pulled back the quilt and relinquished the curled up position that felt like the only possible way to be comfortable. "Where is your gown?" he asked.

"I left it in the bathroom; it was wet,"

"I need to see it. I'll be right back." Elin rushed to the bathroom. The saturated gown was spotted with traces of blood. The slight hemorrhage appeared to be normal, and he returned to Olga's side. "We need to time the contractions," he said softly. "Tell me when you feel your stomach tighten and release."

"Now – now," she sputtered.

Elin looked at the clock. "I need to examine you; I'll be gentle."

Opening the top drawer of the dresser, he removed his medical bag. All that was needed had been stored for weeks. Medical supplies, diapers, blankets, and clothing were neatly stacked in their designated places. He uncurled the stethoscope and warmed the tip under his arm. In a whisper he asked Olga to try and be quiet. "I need to listen to the heartbeat."

She clamped her hands tightly to the bed post and held her breath for as long as she could. "Can you hear it?" she questioned.

"Oh yes," he replied. "Both are beating strong."

"Both?" she queried.

"Yes, yours and the baby."

"Good," she muttered. "I thought you meant twins." Elin continued with the routine physical, checking pulse and dilation. "Everything seems to be fine," he said. "All we can do now is wait until the little one decides to pop out.

"Olga, I need to layer the bed with towels. Can you move to the other side?" She held out her hands for help. Elin gently put his arms under her and slid her to the other side of the bed. As he positioned the pillow under her head, she flung her arms around him and kissed him passionately. Tears filled her eyes as she whispered how much she loved him. She spoke of the miracle they were experiencing.

"Olga," he instructed, "I need to move you back." She extended her arm and his hand locked tightly on her wrist. "Lift, lift," he persuaded.

As she awkwardly hiked her hips, another pain shot through her side. She dropped quickly onto the padded sheet and groaned.

"Another contraction?" he asked.

"It really hurts," she moaned.

"It's been a few minutes since the last; we're on our way. I am going to the kitchen and heat the water. Breathe deeply and yell if you need me."

It was impossible for Olga to get comfortable. The pressure in her back had become unbearable. There was no movement in the rock-hard, swollen stomach, only cramping and nauseating pain. Elin returned and took her hand. "The instruments are boiling, we're ready."

As the cramping became constant, Elin coached her. "Breathe deep, breathe deep, relax and bear down." Olga was wet with perspiration and becoming increasingly tired. "Bear down, my love. Push with the stomach muscles. It won't be long now."

She screamed in agony as he lifted her legs and folded her knees to a supporting position.

"Keep your legs apart," he reminded her. "I need to help you. Olga, breathe and push down as hard as you can. Now!"

She cried out, inhaling volumes of air between screams "It's coming, it's coming, I feel it moving."

Elin ran for the instruments, bringing with him the pan of boiling water. Olga, now straining with every ounce of strength, exhaled one last breath, and the baby's head broke through the birth canal. Tears streaming down his face, he washed Olga's legs with alcohol and saturated his hands before placing them on the tiny shoulders now squirming for freedom. As he pulled the small infant from darkness to the light, he whispered, "It's a girl, a beautiful little girl."

Olga raised her arms to receive her child. "Just a minute and you can hug her," he giggled. "I just need to check her." He lifted the little bundle of flesh, laid her on the sheet, and cut and tied the umbilical cord. Immediately, a smack on the buttocks produced her first breath and cry. Olga again raised her arms in anticipation of holding her. Elin wrapped their first-born in a towel and placed her on her mamma's chest. "I need to examine you again, then you can rest." Olga and the little one lay entwined together: mamma to daughter, daughter to mamma, as he completed the physical.

"Kirsten, Kirsten Svensson," she said softly. "How does that sound, little one? It's your name."

"Do you still prefer that name?" Elin asked.

"I love her name, don't you?" Olga snapped in a combative voice. "Would you prefer something else?"

Elin spoke quickly. "No, of course not; if you still want the name, then Kirsten it will be."

"Look!" Olga squealed. "She's holding my finger."

Elin moved to the edge of the bed and looked lovingly at his new daughter. Her little unwashed face had begun to contort from the drying body fluids. "She needs to be bathed," he said, taking her into his arms. "You look like a little prune. Pappa's going to wash and dress you then give you a million kisses," he teased in a silly, squeaky voice. "Then we're going to scrub your mamma."

Olga smiled, curled up on her side, and quickly fell asleep.

Elin hummed a soft lullaby as he sprinkled warm water over Kirsten's deeply creviced wrinkles. "You look like your mamma," he crooned as delicate blonde hair emerged from the froth and dried into a fuzzy ball. After he diapered her, Kirsten's little mouth pursed, and she searched for her fist. "Hungry?" Elin asked. "Let's go wake your mamma." Placing the little bundle next to Olga, Elin watched her little hand fumble against her face for only a brief moment before she fell asleep. Once again, he picked her up and placed her in a small bed. His family resting and exhausted, Elin lay down, kissed Olga on the forehead, and joined them in sleep.

Howling winds blasted the ice-clad windows as morning light danced through heavy lace curtains. Kirsten, unable to wake her parents with an occasional fuss, belted an earth-shattering scream. Both Elin and Olga woke up, looked at each other, and laughed. "There's nothing wrong with her lungs," they joked simultaneously. Kirsten's little hand moved in awkward jerks across her mouth. "Dinner time," Olga whispered. Elin placed the tiny bundle in her arms, and Kirsten awkwardly manipulated her breast.

"Elin, I think you should go for mamma before dark. She wants to be here. She really wants to help. Tomorrow you'll go back to the institute, and I'll be alone. I would feel safer if she were here with me."

"I understand," he said in a compassionate voice. "She should be here to share the joy of her granddaughter and be a companion for you. I'll go now and get her."

"You are a dear person," Olga murmured, entirely absorbed in the wiggling bundle struggling to nurse.

"Olga, listen to me," Elin cautioned, "I'm going now, and I want you to stay in bed. It's important. Do not attempt to get up while you're here alone. Do you understand?"

"Yes," she answered with a smile. "Please hurry and dress warmly; oh, don't forget to remind mother to wear her boots. You know how she hates them."

"I'll strongly insist," he teased. Elin tucked his curly blond hair tightly inside the stocking cap, wrapped his neck and mouth with a long wool scarf, and whispered, "We'll be back soon; stay warm."

The hallway was a flurry of activity when Elin and Sonja stamped the snow from their boots at the door. Kristen's crying had given away their secret, and neighbors were anxious to see her. Mrs. Knutson, standing at the top of the stairs, was first to approach them. She wanted to know about the delivery; was it a boy or a girl? Everyone had a question or an eager look. Elin invited them all to come over in the next few days— just not all at once, and not yet.

Sonja, not wanting to waste time with small talk, rushed inside. "Olga! It's mama, are you awake?" Sonja threw her heavy coat on the chair, kicked off the wet boots, and tiptoed into the bedroom. "Is she awake?" she whispered.

"Awake," Olga giggled, "and waiting for Grandmama."

Sonja, nervous and excited, kissed her daughter, then gently lifted the little bundle and hugged her tightly to her chest. "Oh, you're so beautiful!" she boasted, prancing around the bed. "And your Pappa thinks so too," she whispered confidentially as Elin disengaged himself from the eager neighbors and followed her inside.

Elin tried to engage the distracted women in plans for the admittance of the neighbors and moved deftly around the kitchen preparing refreshments and wine.

This was a time to be with family and friends, a private celebration far from the ugliness that that blustered and blasted in the frigid world outside.

Part Five

E lin checked his watch and briskly walked to the entrance of the
Institute: 8:50, right on time. A small crowd waiting to be escorted
to their prospective work stations gathered inside. In the middle of the
hallway stood two SS guards. Dark, threatening eyes glared suspiciously
at the early morning arrivals. Many faces were familiar. Some were not.
Olaf, standing near a side corridor, tipped his head and smiled as Elin's
scanning eyes spotted him. Quickly, Elin returned the greeting; it was not
an unfriendly gesture, but one calculated not to attract too much
attention.

"Nine o'clock," the guard announced. "Doctors, laboratory assistants,
nurses: follow me. Biologists, chemists, and remainders: follow my
comrade." The small group instinctively shifted into orderly columns and
followed the guards into the silent hallway.

Nearing a large, glass-enclosed corridor connecting two buildings, a
depressing hum vibrated the air. One of the guards raised his hand, and
everyone stopped. "Those of you assigned to my comrade will leave us
now. He will direct you to your positions located in this building. The
rest of you assigned to jobs in the West Medical Facility will follow me.
At the end of the day, reassemble here, and I will escort you back to the

entrance. Do not attempt to leave the building by yourself or feel that you can freely roam the premises. If you are not accompanied by an authorized representative of the Reich, you will be shot on the spot. Is that understood?" The guard paused, looked sternly at the group, then turned, clicked his heels, and motioned the medical group to follow.

As the heavy glass doors were unlocked, Elin noticed the linking corridor served several purposes. First, locked off, it secured the West Medical Facility from unauthorized entrance. Second, it helped to insulate smells and sounds. Third, no one passed through the glass clad linkage without being observed, making it impossible for personnel or patients to freely wander the fortified facility. In his first trip through the link, he had been preoccupied with the young woman, Anna, and hadn't noticed how secure and isolated the corridor was. Not until today did he realize that this was the doorway to his prison. The only way in, the only way out.

The humming increased in volume and developed a pattern of repetitive sounds varying in tones from high to low. Massive windows amplified the tormented vibrations as Elin and his fellow workers crossed the link, nearing the second set of doors. Never had he felt such a resonance. Apprehension mounted as the guard turned the key and gained entrance for the group. Years of training had prepared Elin for many things, but what he encountered when the massive doors were hinged back was the most heart rending sight he had ever experienced. The hallway was jammed with a mass of bodies of every size, shape, and age. The only thing they had in common was their fear. Families clung to each other as they sobbed. Mothers with small children cried out, fearful for their little ones. Men with glassy eyes tried to comfort women. Vibrations from their unified cry was nearly unbearable.

Elin pressed his hands to his ears, hoping to escape the terrifying sounds. But everywhere he looked, the pain persisted. Faces were etched like permanent tattoos, contorting as torrents of tears failed to wash away their fear. He and the others stood in shock, unable to move or speak. *Dear God,* he thought. *What is going on?*

The guard, unable to make himself heard over the noise, grabbed

Olaf and forced him through the crowd. Then he grabbed another from the group, then another, until all the medical team had been shoved inside a small waiting room. Unable to contain her emotions, one of the nurses began to choke. Her face flushed as an agitated guard moved toward her. Frantic to hide the tears, she turned toward the corner. With one swift slap on the back, he knocked her into the wall and then to the floor. Several of the men moved toward her, hoping to shield another blow.

The guard stepped back, removed his Luger pistol and issued a warning. "As members of the Third Reich, there is no place for sympathy. The people in the hall are here to serve, not receive. Any expression of concern for our enemy will result in your termination from the project and immediate imprisonment."

Dr. Keiser, standing near the shaken woman, cautiously extended his arm. In a grateful manner she squeezed his hand as he helped her to her feet. The guard, with his lips stern, looked one last time at the young nurse, then turned and left the room.

"What a horrible man," Dr. Keiser said. "I hope they're not all that insensitive. What is your name young lady?"

"I'm Johanna Paulson,"

"Are you Norwegian?"

"Yes, I live here in Oslo. I came from the Trondheim area to attend the former Royal Frederick University. I worked for a private clinic before the Nazis demanded that I join their project. What is the project?" she inquired.

Olaf, listening, replied: "No one knows; we've been kept in the dark. I have a sickening feeling though that those frightened, pathetic people in the hall are involved someway."

Elin turned his focus to the newcomers of the group. "I guess since we'll be working together, we should at least know each other. I'm Dr. Elin Svensson." Olaf introduced himself, as did Dr. Keiser. The remaining nine stated their names and professions. Johanna was a newcomer along with three other nurses: Joan, Margaret, and Christina. Dr. Johan Ashjorn, Dr. Alex Jonas, and Dr. Peter Sebastian were part of the original group. Christen Kailand and Knut Sigrid, laboratory technicians, were also new.

Dr. Keiser in his polite, caring way, expressed his pleasure in meeting everyone, and apologized for his German countrymen. "I do not agree with this war," he stated, "nor do I believe in forced labor, such as we have here."

Elin seized the opportunity to ask a personal question. "How is it that you, the only German doctor in the group, happen to be here now?"

"It's very sad" he said. "When Hitler came to power in Germany and his sadistic appetite for unnatural medical experiments began to emerge, I refused service to the Reich. The SS took me into custody, confiscated my personal belongings and imprisoned my wife. I have no choice: as long as I cooperate, my wife will remain alive, and they will not harm my children or their families. I am an old man. What is my life worth? Nothing! But my grandchildren have a lifetime ahead of them. I'm doing it for them, not the Nazis. Someday, if I survive, we'll be together again. That's why I'm here. That's why I'll do as they say."

Elin felt a sadness for the old man and gained considerable respect for his courage. It made him realize that any of the group could be faced with the same dilemma at any given time.

The old man's eyes filled with tears as he faced his colleagues. His thin gray hair and bushy eyebrows softened the redness of his face as tears ran over his puckered lips. "I need the comfort of your friendship," he pleaded. "I'm so lonely; I have no one. I have been away from my family for three months and have not been permitted even a letter. I haven't had a friendly conversation or a glass of beer in weeks. Please, don't withhold your friendship because I'm German."

Johanna pushed her way through the group to the front of the room where the old man was standing. "Dr. Keiser, I would be honored to be your friend." She put her arms around him and hugged him close. As the two embraced, the old man's emotions erupted in gasps.

Dr. Jonas approached the pair and expressed his support, but he pulled Johanna away, cautioning: "We cannot afford to be caught in these emotional embraces. I fear if one is reprimanded, we'll all be reprimanded. We have to be strong, if not for ourselves, then for each other. Is it agreed? Is it agreed?" he asked again in a forceful voice. His aggression surprised Elin. Before now he had been almost invisible, a small silent man with dark-rimmed glasses hiding behind a facade of calm. The affirmative nod from all was a relief, and the group immediately began to bond. Somehow, knowing they were no longer alone in an unknown experience mattered. Many expressions became softer, some even smiled.

A dark reminder forced its way into the already crowded room. The abrasive SS guard had returned, bringing with him Dr. Albrecht Brandt, a frightening looking man who glared with suspicion at his captive audience. Dark, soulless eyes appeared to portray a person void of compassion. He stood with his hands tightly clasped behind his back, silently observing, like a lion ready to pounce. It was difficult to predict what he was thinking or what he would do next. He said nothing, just stood and stared. Then he shoved his hands into his pockets and ordered the guard out of the room.

"No need to entertain an ignorant guard," he said with spite in his voice. "Now, let me see; which of you brilliant scientists are doctors? I certainly can't tell by the intelligent expressions on your faces."

Elin was offended by the lack of respect for his fellow physicians, but it was obvious this man was in a provoking mood. "Step forward, those of you that consider yourselves to be doctors. I want to see what kind of medical misfits I'm supposed to work with."

In an attempt to hasten the reluctant men, Dr. Brandt plunged his fist into the wall. "I said, move now." Elin and the rest of the physicians quickly moved to the front of the room.

"I am Dr Albrecht Brandt, Chief of Medical Procedures. Today you will be instructed in the various methods of sterilization used by the Third Reich. The reasons for and the methods used are of no concern to you. You are here to provide assistance. Furthermore, no one will leave the facility until all is accomplished. Listen carefully: I strongly suggest you refrain from personal involvements and focus on the assignment you have been given. Each doctor will be assigned two nurses. Come, let's get started, we have a long day ahead."

The auditorium was buzzing when Elin and the group entered. Most of the audience appeared to be German speaking, non-military personnel, engaged in idle conversation. Many wore white lab coats and several were in traditional surgical uniforms.

Dr. Brandt stepped to the rostrum. "Silence!" he shouted. Immediately, the room was void of sound. "That's better; now pay strict attention. You will be given only one opportunity to observe and learn. Those of you who do not succeed in mastering the process will be eliminated.

"The first order of business here at the institute is experimentation and sterilization of undesirables. All the patients have already been carefully selected. This includes retardates, alcoholics, ethnic and genetically diseased. You will follow the instructions of the evaluation committee without question. Each patient is different. Some will receive what you may consider unwarranted operations. Let me remind you again, those decisions are of no concern to you. You are to follow instructions explicitly, without alteration.

"Now let me explain the procedures that will be used. Women, for the most part, will be used for reproductive experimental purposes. Today, it's sterilization. The technique we use is to flush the womb with a chemical substance that will burn the lining of the uterus and damage the cervix. This can be accomplished with a routine gynecological examination. The Reich is very anxious to find a cost-effective means of mass sterilization, and we are hoping to refine this method so a multitude of sterilizations can be performed each day. On some rare occasions, women will be required to return and have their ovaries removed and sent to Berlin.

"The effectiveness of our procedure needs to be tested. Men will be subjected to several different methods. First, mass doses of radiation will be used to burn the testicles. Then, as with the women, several will return to have their testicles removed and sent to Berlin for a testicular dissection. Castration and vasectomies will be used in most cases. Now, if you will, comrades, line up for your assignments. Your name will appear along with your teammates and the location of your assigned medical cubicle. Be assured your work is for a worthy cause and is extremely important to the Third Reich. Now go meet your teammates: Heil Hitler!"

Elin merged with the crowd, waiting his turn at the registration desk. He watched as sober-faced men and women moved slowly through the waiting line and disappeared into the hall. Then it occurred to him. The medical cubicles Dr. Brandt referred to were in the strange room in which he received his examination. The room with all the white curtains. A large room for a large number of people. Elin separated from the crowd and proceeded down the hall with directions to the exact room he had visited earlier. The cubicles were as he remembered, except there were far more than he realized. Each row began with a large, printed number, and there were ten cubicles to the row. They seemed to go on forever.

Dr. Brandt, standing in front of the rows, gathered the small group of arriving physicians around him. Olaf called out to Elin as he walked toward the selected group. "Hurry, Dr. Brandt is going to demonstrate the sterilization procedure."

The patient, a young, severely handicapped woman desperately struggled against leather straps that pinned her arms and legs to a bed. Her cries were pathetic as she thrashed her head back and forth. Though she appeared slightly drugged, her eyes reflected undeniable fear. Dr. Brandt laughed as the table tilted, dropping the woman's head toward the floor. "This won't take long," he said as he threw open her gown and inserted a long, steel instrument into her vagina. Olaf clutched Elin's arm as a bottle containing chemicals was forced through the instrument into the womb of the patient. She screamed and passed out.

"See how easy that was?" Dr. Brandt boasted. "Wait a few minutes, then remove the instrument."

The smell of burning flesh was overpowering. Elin choked, covered his mouth, and vomited.

Dr. Brandt laughed. "You'll get accustomed to the procedure." A nurse rushed to clean the patient and wheel her away. "Next patient, quickly," the doctor demanded. He completed ten more sterilizations while waiting for the rest of his personnel to arrive.

Elin and the others left the demonstration in horror, directed to the center rows. "This is the halfway point," Dr. Brandt said. "Three of you will be assigned to the front half, rows ten to thirty. The other three will cover the back, rows forty to sixty. The remaining rows in each section are reserved for patients needing recovery time. Nurses will attend to them unless there is an emergency. Comrades, waste no time, we have massive amounts of work to do, and you are expected to become sterilization machines."

The room had come to life with arriving medical assistants. Dr. Brandt looked around approvingly, then continued. "Good, you're here; now find your assignments." Each row of cubicles had two nurses, just as promised. Other nurses gathered in the recovery areas. "Is everyone in place?" he inquired. "Splendid, you must use your time efficiently. Your staff is now complete and waiting for instructions. The operations will begin in one hour."

Elin opened the folded card given him; row thirty in bold letters was stamped across the middle. Olaf nudged his friend, "what number do you have?"

Elin flashed the number quickly then placed it in his pocket. "And you?" Elin quizzed.

"Sixty," he responded.

Nurse Johanna, assigned to the recovery area, smiled as Elin walked past. He briefly addressed her and continued toward his cubicle. He could see Dr. Ashjorn in the first set of cubicles and Dr. Jonas in the second.

Nurse Elisa, as well as a German nurse, Helga, were assigned to Elin. Entering the cubicle, Elin politely introduced himself and explained to the nurses the experimental procedure in which they were about to become involved. Both women gasped, shocked and appalled. Elin assured them the procedure would not kill anyone, but most likely would be extremely painful. "Prepare yourselves; we have no choice." Elin and his team had just finished their discussion when the first patient was ushered in, firmly held by two SS guards.

Part Six

The following months passed like a nightmare from which Elin couldn't awake. Patients changed, but everything else remained the same. "No alterations," Dr. Brandt would reiterate. Even the pleading, tormented cries of the victims never seemed to change. Elin soon found himself a prisoner to their pain, unable to escape the images he carried in his own soul. His nights became a terror of haunting dreams that dominated even his waking sub-conscious thoughts.

More and more, he desperately wanted out. Often, he would awaken with thoughts of escape, but he knew there was no escape from Hell. They would and could find him wherever he went. He hated the Nazis, he hated Dr. Brandt, he hated and was repulsed by the staff using young victims to satisfy their deviant sexual appetites, constantly raping them in the small, dark rooms of the labyrinthine hallways. He hated the brutality and lack of empathy. *Dear God,* he would pray, *save us from this nightmare.*

By the end of the following winter, Kirsten had grown into a strong, healthy baby. She was a beautiful child with eyes that danced like pools of shimmering blue water. Her fuzzy blonde hair had fallen out, and tiny ringlets of silky gold had replaced it. Deep dimples were ever-present.

She was a happy baby. During the day, Olga would lavish her with attention, spending most of her time attending to her needs, a luxury afforded to her by the Reich. But as evening approached, she focused her attention on caring for Elin. A warm bath was always prepared, and candlelight dinners usually followed. Perks of food and wine helped, but still she felt his stress and did everything in her power to make his homecoming pleasant. He was in terrible emotional pain, his face showed it, but he couldn't talk about his work or his worries. Many nights he held her so tightly that she could barely breathe. She worried constantly about his health, but most of all, she worried about his stability.

One morning, as the group assembled for the daily trek to the Medical Building, Olaf leaned close to Elin and whispered. "Meet me tonight at the wine bar on Ibsen Street: 7:00."

Elin returned a startled look.

"It's important," Olaf insisted.

Elin was reluctant to commit: the danger of being seen was ever-present. Still, Olaf insisted. There was desperation in his voice.

Elin's guilt overpowered him. "As your colleague, I would not advise it, but as your friend, I will come."

Olaf nodded, then thrust himself into the center of the waiting group.

All day, Olaf's words crept into Elin's thoughts. *What could possibly be so important? Maybe he just needs a break from everything, a friendly conversation. Yes, that's probably what it is, nothing more.* He tried to convince himself that nothing was wrong with socializing with friends. But Dr. Brandt's warning about personal involvement with their co-workers worried him. *Oh hell, everything will be okay if we don't discuss work,* he reassured himself.

Olga was frantic when Elin told her he was going out. "Why would you chance being seen? You know they're watching and I'm certain Olaf is also under surveillance. This is crazy, risking your life for a glass of wine."

Elin pressed his finger to her lips, "Enough, Olaf is my friend, and you'll have to believe me when I say it's important that I see him. I'm sorry my love, but there are things I cannot share with you. Tonight is one of those times. The SS has ways of extracting information, and if you were to be questioned, you would know nothing if I shared nothing, understand?" Tear-filled eyes are hard to leave, but he tightened his coat, kissed her, and told her not to worry.

Ibsen Street Wine Bar was a somewhat seedy neighborhood gathering spot, popular with less fortunate locals and not far from home. Elin knew the streets well and cautiously maneuvered in and around small clusters of people out for evening walks. The night air was still chilling, but as spring winds blew in warmer air, people swarmed the streets, escaping their long winter imprisonments. Nearing the wine bar, he stepped quickly into the shelter of a doorway and pretended to smoke, one last precaution before going in. He watched as couples strolled by. No one appeared to be following him.

Casually opening the bar door, Elin found the smoke-filled room alive with chattering couples. Young people were drinking and throwing darts, forgetting their problems in volumes of foaming beer. Several heavy old tables hosted young lovers sitting so close together that their heads appeared attached as they kissed in imagined privacy.

Olaf, already sitting at the end of the bar, waved. Elin made his way to his side and placed a hand on his friend's shoulder. "How are you, my friend?"

Olaf smiled, "I'm surviving. I chose to sit here so it would appear as if we were just enjoying a few beers instead of what I'm about to do."

Elin's smiling face quickly returned to its more habitual seriousness and concern. "And what, pray tell, are you about to do?"

Olaf looked straight into Elin's eyes. "I want to talk about the projects."

Elin's expression froze.

"No one will know," Olaf continued. "Look around, there are no SS here. Strange, new things are going on at the Institute that concern me and more than likely involve you as well. Elin, crawl out from that shell and pay attention. Observe and learn for your own sake. Please listen carefully to what I'm about to say."

Elin, angered that his friend had put him in such a seriously compromising situation, gripped his lip between his teeth and replied in a harsh whisper. "I do my job, not because I like it, but because I have to. I don't have to be involved in any other aspect of this horrible experience. Keep your secrets to yourself and keep your questions to yourself. I'm not interested in burdening myself with more guilt or anxiety."

"I understand," Olaf replied, "I feel the same, but at some point, you cannot close your eyes. Learn in order to survive."

Elin raised the glass of beer to his lips, slowly sipping the froth, buying time, thinking deep thoughts, trying to compose himself. Olaf as well sank into deep meditation. Setting the stein down with a thud, Elin turned to Olaf. "I do apologize. It's just that we're all under such stress."

"I know," Olaf comforted him. "But we need to be prepared for the unexpected. Elin, I just want to inform you so you'll be able to endure. You're my friend, and I want you to survive. I want us to be ready; no surprises."

Elin took a long sip of his beer. "Fine; tell me all the explicit details of the perverted, sadistic things taking place at our glorious institute."

Olaf's face grimaced, and he snapped. "Until you begin to take what I'm going to say seriously, I have nothing to share with you. I didn't come here to be scoffed at."

Serious again, Elin assured him.

Olaf clasped his beer glass between his fingers and focused his eyes directly on the foam. Then, in a searching voice asked, "Have you ever heard of Project Angel Hair?"

Elin leaned his head closer to Olaf and repeated the name, "Angel Hair; what is Angel Hair? No, to answer your question, I've never heard of such a project." Elin waited for a response, but Olaf just sat there looking into his glass. "For God's sake!" Elin scolded, "What the hell is it?" Olaf whispered, "Can I trust you with this secret, my friend?"

Elin hesitated; his interest had now been piqued; his mind was at full attention. "You've got my loyalty, and I would never betray the trust we share."

Olaf leaned forward and rested his arms on the bar in a posture of feigned relaxation. Elin followed suit. "I don't have all of the particulars yet," Olaf apologized, "but I have enough information for the two of us to begin to find out exactly what is going on.

"Johanna, one of the nurses, evidently has been involved in the Project Angel Hair for quite a while. She told me what she knows, but for some reason or another, there's a portion she can't remember. She's a beautiful, intelligent young woman, and, like us, is part of the forced labor group. She said they're holding her family in an undisclosed place until they finish with the project. Poor girl's frightened beyond belief but has started to confide in me as often as she can. She's terrified of the German assistants. If they even suspected we're discussing the project, we both would be killed, just as you and I would be eliminated for what we're doing now."

Elin's eyes danced with a mysterious gleam as Olaf talked of the unseen dangers. He knew all that, of course. What was new was that, for the first time, he was choosing not to care. He was here, wasn't he? With the adrenaline of defiance pumping through his veins, he felt almost fearless. "Tell me about the Project," he insisted.

The men scanned the room one more time. Everything seemed the same; no new faces had appeared at Ibsen's since they sat down.

In a whisper, Olaf began. "Over the last couple of months I've noticed strange activity in the area behind my row of cubicles. You probably haven't had the opportunity to observe the rooms on the back fringe since you're confined to the front section. All three of these rooms have large, frosted glass windows and bright lights. They remind me of operating rooms. There is only one door on this side, and it is always guarded. Every once in a while, I see Dr. Brandt going in or coming out, always alone. The strange thing is, I can see shadows, and it's confusing. There appear to be people on the other side, wearing tall hats or hoods and they cluster in the center around a table or cart. Of course, I can't approach the area because of the guard, and I never hear noises: not a cry or scream, only silence. It's really eerie.

"One day I saw Dr. Brandt come for Johanna. She was reluctant, but he grabbed her arm and pushed her in front of him. She looked back at me, scared, then disappeared behind the door. I was near the back, so I could see her shadow behind the glass. One of the hooded figures approached her. I could see a long pole touch her head before she disappeared. I think she fainted. After I watched the encounter, she started confiding in me. I think she needs to release the stress for her own sanity. I've been able to understand enough to know something truly bizarre is happening.

"Angel Hair is a high security project, and even the participants aren't aware of the experiments they're being subjected to. Johanna thinks the robes protect either the identity of the wearers or prevent exposure to x-rays. She said there have also been times when she has seen Russian and German doctors together in the room behind the door. She knows they're Russian because she recognized the language. I think this is a joint project." Olaf paused. He took a long drink of beer.

"Elin, what do you think of this tiny bombshell?"

Elin studied his hands. "I think it all seems so strange. Why would the Russians be involved here in Oslo; why would they care about the Nazi's nonsense?"

Olaf raised his eyebrows in a brief expression of bewilderment. "Last week, I noticed Johanna looked distraught. She said not to worry; I, of course, pushed for an explanation. She looked so drained. I hugged her—I didn't know what to do—and she told me she was pregnant and didn't know how it happened."

"That caught me off guard. So, I got snide and laughed, 'Come on, we all know how babies are made.' She started to cry, and I felt bad. She then explained that she hadn't been with a man for a long time. Dr. Brandt was the one who told her she was pregnant. He told her this was part of Project Angel Hair, and that the pregnancy would be short term. She asked why they chose her, and he told her she met all the requirements, as did most of the staff at the institute. He told her the pregnancy was experimental, using a new technology, and the father was you, Elin. When I say I felt embarrassed to hear that—well, she said she was embarrassed too. Dr. Brandt just explained it all away to her by saying that this was an ideal way to birth a baby, I guess. She had no say in this matter. She said she didn't even know when or where it happened. She only has flashes of nightmares of strange shadows—I thought of that room I told you about—and she knows nothing. She asked me to promise not to tell anyone. I told her I would never do anything to put her in danger. Now you know why I had to tell you."

Elin was speechless. His eyes squinted at his hands, and he turned them over, inspecting them as if they were some strange specimen. When he found his voice, it was stern. "I don't believe this; it's some kind of Nazi propaganda. It's impossible to have a pregnancy without sexual contact. You of all people know that. What kind of sick joke is this? I don't know why Johanna is telling this lie, but I tell you, I have never been with her sexually. Do you have any idea how much pain this lie would cause my family? I want you, as my friend, to ask her to give up this fabrication, this game, before someone gets hurt." Elin was visibly shaken. He rambled on and on about his fidelity and how much his family meant to him.

Olaf began to worry. His friend was no longer rational. What if he confronted Johanna? She would panic, and they would never know the dark secret of Project Angel Hair. Olaf grabbed his friend's arm and squeezed firmly. "Elin, Elin! No one has said you were with her sexually; she just said Dr. Brandt told her that you were the father. Remember she said they have a new technology. She never said you screwed her. This is why we must find out what the hell is going on. How can they just impregnate people without them knowing it's happening? We must find out, and Johanna is our only hope. Are you with me on this?"

"Let me ask you this," Elin quizzed, "Do you believe her, and can you trust her?"

"Yes, I do believe her; she has no reason to lie, nothing to gain. If you could see her pain, you would understand. I trust her as she trusts me. I am her friend and fellow countryman."

"Okay," Elin mumbled, "I'm with you. God help us both if this is a trap. What do we do next?"

"Just try and act normal; when I find out more, I'll get in touch. I am convinced there is a sinister project being conducted here, and I want to know what it is. Take note of strangers at the institute, and listen for any information not relevant to our day-to-day activities." Elin nodded his head, gulped down the rest of his beer, and informed Olaf he was heading home. Olaf stood, gathered him in his arms and whispered, "We'll get through this. We've survived so far, haven't we? Get some sleep, and I'll see you tomorrow."

The apartment was darkened when Elin arrived home. Faint mellow light glowed from the bedroom. Quietly, he unlocked the door, praying that Olga was asleep. He was in no mood to discuss feelings tonight. Stepping through the slightly opened bedroom door, he saw Kristen stir. Her little head bobbed, and soft light danced across her golden hair like a summer sunburst. Elin moved closer, smoothed out the wrinkles in her knotted blanket, and watched as she pulled her tiny arms under her body and resumed a peaceful sleep. Olga had fallen asleep with a half-opened book clinging to her chest. He gently removed it and slid into bed.

The next few weeks the institute were different. The horror was an unchanged reality, but Elin's mind had begun to be liberated from that of a slave to that of a rebel. He became more aware of the surroundings, and not only his, but those on the so-called fringe. He took notice of people coming and going, making mental notes of visits from Nazi hierarchy. He was amazed at how often they came. Where had he been in the past, or why hadn't he noticed? Olaf was right: he had withdrawn into his own protective shell.

One terrible day finally over, Elin joined the group in the hallway for their daily escorted departure. The guard, who was always there, was not in attendance. "Where is the guard?" Olaf questioned. No one answered. Olaf coughed ostentatiously. Elin looked over and visually connected. Olaf moved closer. "Wine tonight?" he mumbled. Elin cautiously looked around and tipped his head. The group, distracted by the unexplained absence of the guard, showed no notice of this casual encounter.

Johanna, standing off by herself, appeared lifeless. Her eyes were dull: depression was obvious. Elin understood Olaf's concern. The guard, out of breath and irritated, rushed into the hallway. "We're late, we must go. Dr. Keiser will not be joining us tonight. He has a late appointment." After a head count, confusion blanketed the group even more. Fueled by paranoia and Dr. Keiser's disappearance, Elin questioned whether he should go out tonight. *Maybe they're watching; maybe they know.* He considered giving Olaf the "no" sign, but the opportunity to make contact wasn't presented again. *Oh hell,* he thought, *I'll just have to be careful. I promised myself I wouldn't become a prisoner of these monsters, and I won't.* He lifted his head, threw back his shoulders, and walked like a man with renewed confidence.

The ever-present green bus and its cargo of military and scientific personnel sat waiting at the entrance. A peppering of soldiers going home for the evening conveniently discouraged normal conversations. No one dared speak for fear their comments might be overheard. Silence dominated. Elin's stop was one of the last on the bus route. Olaf had already departed, but before he stepped off the bus, he gave Elin one last look, silently confirming their appointment.

The sun had begun to set, and only a scattering of lights were illuminated when Elin approached his apartment building. Somehow, it seemed darker than usual. More lights in the old hall chandelier had burned out and no one had money available to replace them. The increasing shadows made it difficult to see exactly what might be lurking in the corners. A few small children sat quietly on the steps, and he briefly teased them with a scary gesture. Giggling playfully, they seemed to enjoy the attention.

Olga was busy in the kitchen when he entered the apartment. Humming softly to herself, she hadn't heard him. Slowly, he ran his arms around her waist and kissed her on the back of her neck. Olga jumped. "Elin! You scared me. Hurry, get your bath. I have something to tell you."

"Tell me now," he insisted.

"No, you impetuous creature, I'll tell you at dinner. Now hurry, hurry." Elin's curiosity had been piqued. Why was she in such a good mood? He hadn't seen her like this in months. He rushed through his shower and joined her at the table.

She didn't even wait to sit down before beginning her story, "I had the most wonderful day today. I was beginning to think I had lost the ability to enjoy myself. Of course, I'm speaking socially, but today I realized joy is still there; hidden under fear and anxiety."

"What happened? Tell me." Elin pushed.

"Do you remember the frightening little man that took me for my interview?"

"How could I forget that?" Elin stated squarely.

"He came to the apartment this morning, and was very friendly. He asked me to call him Unk. He also asked if Kirsten and I would like to have lunch with families involved in the new order. At first it concerned me, but just as you, what choice did I have? Unk came back at 11 o'clock in a black car and drove us to the Claus Hotel. You know, the one on Polson Street. A lovely woman met us at the door and escorted us to a dining room near the side street.

"The sun was shining through the windows and fresh flowers were everywhere. The room was beautiful! Tables were set with crystal and china and three of my friends from the orchestra were playing music. I felt like I was in heaven. Christina was there and I joined her and two other women. It was unbelievable. We all had so much in common."

"Wait a minute," Elin interrupted. "Where was Kristen?"

"Oh, everything was attended to. A very nice German nurse named Elisa took her to a nursery in an adjoining room. You should have seen her crawling around on the big white quilts, playing with other babies her age. She was so cute! Her very first party."

"Oh, my dear God," Elin whispered. "What did this nurse look like?"

"Rather normal. German, I would say, middle aged, short and slightly overweight. Short brown hair and a sense of humor." Elin was taken aback by the description. Could this be the same Elisa he knew?

"Do you know her?" Olga questioned.

"I don't think so, but was anyone else there, or was she alone with the children?"

"Why are you asking all these questions? I know you well enough to know there must be a reason."

"I just need to know that our child was in safe hands, that's all."

Olga looked uncomfortable. "There was an older man, a grandfather type, sitting on a chair in the room. I think he was helping."

"Do you know his name?" he asked, his voice forcedly calm.

"No, he didn't say anything, just sat there and watched the babies. He seemed safe enough."

On the inside, Elin was churning, afraid of he knew not what, trying to make sense of the whole confusing matter. On the outside, for Olga's sake, he tried to appear calm. "Then what did you do?" He asked with a reassuring smile.

"They brought lunch. It was absolutely delicious: chicken pot pie with vegetables, salad and bread. We were also offered wine. I had a small glass—it seemed appropriate. Then we had coffee and dessert. I was stuffed. The children from a local school sang, and soft music was played while we visited. The two ladies sitting with us were married to doctors, maybe you know them: Dr. Jonas and Dr. Ashjorn." Elin wasn't sure how to answer her question and he certainly didn't want to encourage a discussion about the Institute. "I think they may work in the same building as I do, but I really can't say that I know them." *Good*, he thought. *That sounds good.*

She then said something that knotted his stomach and shortened his breath. "A really nice man addressed the group before we left. He said we were important to the success of the New Order in Oslo and that he appreciated our support and understanding in these troubled times. He said important research was being conducted at the Institute, research that could benefit the entire world and that would eliminate human suffering. Isn't that wonderful, and just think, you're involved in that very research."

Elin snapped. "Don't be so quick to believe everything you hear, Olga. Nazis are shrewd politicians, masters of propaganda. Who was this speaker?"

Olga's enthusiasm began to wane as Elin's remarks forced her to realize she had become caught up in the glitter of the moment. He was right, how could she forget? They were at war. The Nazis wanted something. They were not interested in the welfare of Norwegian families, nor did they really need their support. It just made it easier if all was well at home. *What a fool I've been,* she thought.

"His name was Dr. Brand, no, that's not it, sort of sounds something like that, I'm not sure."

Elin's voice shook with something between anger and terror. "Dr. Brandt; was it Dr. Brandt?"

"Yes, that's it. Do you know him?"

"Yes, I do. He's the most sadistic man I know. I can't go into detail. Stay as far away from him as you can. He is nothing more than a devil. I'm sure they're preparing you for future involvement. Just remember who you're dealing with, and stay one step ahead of them. Play their game because you have to, but be aware of the danger. Be your wonderful, pleasant self, but watch your back. No one is your friend, for God's sake, remember that. Confide in no one but me, understand?"

Olga was surprised at his remarks; not that he said these things, but at the way he expressed himself. He spoke like a man in control, a man that knew how to play the game, a man determined to survive. She was impressed.

"You're right, you're absolutely right. I will be careful and not be so naïve. You just have to remember I haven't had enough exposure to the Nazis to know how to act. This is all new to me. But with your help, I'll learn."

Elin had been so preoccupied with Olga's story he had failed to notice the lateness of the hour. Suddenly, food unfinished, he jumped. "What time is it? Six-forty-five? I have to go; I'm sorry, but I promised Olaf I'd meet him. Don't worry, I'll be careful and try to be back soon. Lock the door. I love you."

Part Seven

The streets were empty, and a light rain had just started to mist the old stone sidewalks, causing streetlights to bounce fragmented beams through the mist like shiny metallic balls. It was quiet, and Elin relished every moment. It wasn't often he had time totally alone.

His head dipped toward the street. Tiny drops of rain rolled from his curly hair and washed his cheeks. It was a gentle rain, the kind you remember as a child, the kind you dance and twirl in. It brought back many fond memories. As he turned the corner on Ibsen Street, a voice called out from the darkness. "Halt!"

Elin froze.

A young German soldier stepped in front of him. "Where are you going?"

Elin resolved to remain calm. "I'm going there, just there to the wine bar. I need a beer."

"I could use one myself," the young soldier replied.

"Come, I'll buy you one, Elin offered."

"Thank you, but I'm on duty. Some other time."

A soft wind began to blow, and raindrops slapped Elin's face. The soldier smiled, "You're getting wet, better go." Elin raised his hand, then briskly walked across the street to the bar. The atmosphere was not quite as electrified as it had been the last time he was there. A few couples sat quietly while a cluster of singles laughed in the back. Elin sat in the same spot at the bar that he had occupied earlier.

"What's your pleasure?" the bartender asked.

"Beer; sort of quiet tonight," Elin answered.

"It's the rain. No one likes to get wet. What brings you out?" the bartender inquired.

Elin thought about his answer: trust no one, he reminded himself. "I have a good friend that lives in the neighborhood, and we like to relax once in a while over a glass of your fine beer."

The bartender looked at him. "I remember seeing you in here. It's nice to have you back. Do you live far?"

"No, not really, just a nice walk away." There, he thought. I answered his question without revealing my address. That's the way you play this game; I'm sure it is.

Olaf was late. Elin didn't like it. It made him nervous. The bartender brought over a bowl of crackers and set them down. "Looks like your friend stood you up," he joked.

Olaf rushed through the door just as Elin lifted the beer glass to his lips, draining the last drop. "I'm sorry, I had to help Christina. The children are all home now. Give me just a moment, please. I ran all the way and need to catch my breath."

Elin ordered another beer. The bartender nodded to Olaf. "We're glad you made it, friend; what will you have?"

"Beer, no wait, I'll have white wine. Elin, I'm really sorry. How long have you been here?"

"I've been here a while and was starting to get a little worried, especially after Dr. Keiser's disappearance this afternoon."

Olaf quickly sipped his wine and cleared his throat. "Elin, did Olga tell you about this afternoon? Did she tell you who was there? I think the old man was Dr. Keiser. What do you think he was doing there? And Elisa, do you think it was the Elisa we know from the Institute? One thing we know for sure is Dr. Brandt was there in all his charming glory. Why do you think this is happening?"

Elin grimaced. "Easy, my friend; let's take one thing at a time. Yes, Olga told me about her day. She said it was wonderful. That scares me. I hadn't thought about Dr. Keiser, but you're right, it probably was him. He wasn't at the Institute because he was there. Olga said he just sat and observed the children. That's his specialty, you know: pediatrics. It could have been a non-intrusive way of observing our babies. He could tell if they were suffering from any genetic abnormalities. That's what the Reich wants, only pure, perfect specimens of the human race. I think this could be the first step: observe and eliminate those with visible imperfections.

"I remember when Elisa escorted me to the examination room the day of our first interview. She informed me her specialty was children. I questioned that statement and she said I would soon see for myself. I don't know what her role is, but I do feel she's part of something nefarious. I don't think Dr. Keiser is involved in the project as a volunteer. I think he is being forced. Elisa is not, and Dr. Brandt is definitely in charge. Whatever is happening is under his direction. I wonder if this project goes all the way to Berlin, or it's just a local thing. Anyway, Olga fell into the trap. She thought getting together was a great idea, and Dr. Brandt was certainly charming. I had a serious talk with her. I think now she better understands that they have an agenda. Have you warned Christina? Have you explained the dangers of being too eager to please? Also, that she should not trust anyone but you. Olaf, I think you really need to talk to her when you get home. Have you seen Johanna?"

"That's why I wanted to see you tonight. She's not pregnant anymore. Yesterday near lunch break she seemed very stressed and asked me if I would examine her. I told her to wait until my nurse left for lunch and I would give her a quick check. She said she was hemorrhaging and was worried. When I checked, she was bleeding heavily. The cervix was dilated, but there was no pregnancy. I asked if she had a miscarriage and she said no. She told me someone took the baby. She felt sure Dr. Brandt was involved. The thing that scares her the most is that, once again, she only has partial memories of that night. She feels like she's losing her mind."

Elin stared out into the room. It was obvious he was dissecting the new information. "Are you sure she was pregnant?" he ventured. "No one validated her claim except Dr. Brandt. Maybe he's playing games with her."

Olaf interrupted, "but her uterus was enlarged. It had appeared to be about three to four months term, and this is what is really weird. She said Dr. Brandt gave her pills to take at bedtime, something to relax her. The next morning, she remembered that sometime during the night someone came into her bedroom. She was frightened but couldn't call out. It was like she was paralyzed. Vague memories of a cold instrument inserted into her vagina, and mists and shadows moving around a bright light are all that she can remember. Dr. Brandt surprised her by coming by early the next morning to check on her and drive her to the Institute. He said he wanted to be sure his little angel was feeling okay. She questioned him about the last nights' event, and he told her not to ask questions and nothing would happen. He said this was part of the Angel Hair Project and her pregnancy had been terminated. He said she would be called on again in the near future to repeat the experiment. She said she was thankful to be alive and said nothing more. Elin, I can't get a grip on what's going on. Do you have any ideas?"

"No, not really. It's a very strange situation. I'll have to think about it. Let's gather more information, and in the meantime, keep an eye on Elisa and Dr. Keiser."

"Listen," Elin urged, "I had better get home. I don't want to create suspicion among neighbors, and Olga will be worried. You know the key to this weird situation is Johanna; if she could remember more, we would know more. Try to keep her talking."

Part Eight

The next few weeks at the Institute were again terribly routine. Elin would see Olaf, but no attempt was made at contact. Maybe Olaf was being cautious, but more likely he had nothing to report. Elin began to miss the danger of the spy game, the intrigue and the 7:00 pm late night rendezvous. One morning, as the group met at the entrance, Dr. Keiser re-appeared. Everyone seemed pleased at his return. The majority of the group had assumed he had either been taken back to Berlin or killed. Elin's mind exploded with excitement. It felt like he had awakened from a long sleep. A titillating feeling and sense of adventure crept over him. He wondered if Olaf was feeling the same.

Dr. Keiser appeared to be in good health and smiled at his colleagues. Elin felt an overwhelming urge to talk to the doctor. Knowing odds of doing so were against him, he stepped back and waited, confident that what he lacked in advantage, he gained in desire.

The hallway was standing room only today. All the patients were Norwegians, most of them young—fifteen to twenty years old he guessed. There were both males and females, but the females seemed unusually fit and healthy. What could possibly be going on with this select group? As he walked past the sober, frightened faces, he couldn't help notice how much they all looked alike. Height and weight differed, but overall, their appearances were uncannily similar. Everyone had blue eyes, light skin, and light hair.

Dr. Brandt addressed the group just inside the double doors. "Dr. Knor, you are to move to cubicle numbered fifty. Dr. Keiser, I want you in the last active row, number sixty. Elisa, today you will assist Dr. Keiser. The rest of you will be giving physical examinations to the young people in the hallway. They will receive the same examination you received when you were being considered for service to the Reich. Because we expect a thorough and complete examination, you will not be rushed. We've split the group. Females will use rows ten to thirty and males forty to sixty. When the exam is finished, send them to the table at the back of the room. Are there any questions? Fine, let's get started."

Elin's first patient was a beautiful 16-year-old girl who was shivering uncontrollably with fright. She postured defensively.

"I'm not going to hurt you," he assured her.

"Why are you doing this?" she sobbed. "What do you want from me?"

Elin responded in a gentle voice, "I am only here because I've been ordered to do so, the same as you. I can't answer your questions. We are not privileged to information regarding the purpose of these examinations. So why don't you calm down, this is not going to hurt."

Tears streamed down her face as she slipped out of her clothing. She tightly wrapped a sheet around her firm young body before climbing onto the table. Elin watched as nurses took her blood pressure and extracted blood, all the time, thinking to himself, someday this might be Kirsten. The thought of putting his child through this experience repulsed him. "We're ready Doctor," a nurse called out.

Elin approached the table. The embarrassed girl wound the sheet tightly around her chest as he instructed her how to bend her knees. Reluctantly she raised her legs. Speaking softly, he said. "I'm going to examine your vaginal area. The instrument will feel a little cold, so don't be alarmed. If you relax, it will help." A frightened whimper drew the nurse to her side. Slowly, she pulled the clenched fist from the girl's mouth and held her hand firmly in hers. With the patient's legs opened, he inserted the instrument. Everything appeared normal. Healthy tissue, strong muscle tone, and a virgin. "There, that wasn't so bad," he commented, and slid the instrument from inside her.

"I'm going to check your stomach so relax your legs and lay straight." As she did, he noticed a darkened area on the skin high inside her upper thigh.

"Wait," he said. "What's going on with your leg?" He quickly adjusted the light and focused it on the girl. "What is this?" he asked.

"I don't know, it's been there about two weeks. I can't get it off. I've scrubbed and scratched, but it's still there."

"Who did this to you?"

"I do"t know. I just woke up one morning and it was there." Elin raised his voice. "You mean someone came in, placed a permanent tattoo on the most tender part of your leg and you do"t remember?" His sudden irritability startled the girl.

"I'm telling you the truth," she sobbed. "I don't know."

Elin questioned his nurse. "What should we put in the report?"

"Put the truth: tattoo on the inner right leg, that's simple enough."

"Should we say what it is?"

"Well, I suppose we should," she said, and began to describe the strange mark. "It's a circle around the letter 'H' and has an 'A' in the center of it. It appears to be about a half inch in diameter and is black in color. Do you think that's descriptive enough?"

"Yes," he replied. "That should do it."

Making a notation on the report, she commented, "I want to make sure we're not accused of being negligent. To omit something as obvious as that would surely subject us to criticism."

The two nurses, now satisfied, left to escort the next patient to the cubicle, giving Elin a chance to be alone with the young woman. As he checked her eyes and ears, he asked in a conversational way, "You know, that tattoo fascinates me. I wish you could remember more about how you received it."

"The only thing I can tell you is that in the morning when I awakened, my night shirt was inside out and the buttons in the wrong holes. I felt disoriented and extremely tired."

"Did you tell your parents?"

"Yes, I showed them the mark. They were shocked. My father didn't believe me when I told him it just appeared. They were as puzzled as I was. We just can't figure out how it happened. Mamma said the only strange thing she remembered was a bright light that lit up the front windows, she thought perhaps from a car passing by. It was late, and she was afraid to peek out. Finally, it went away, and she went back to sleep."

Elin pressed for more information. "Do you think it could have been the SS?"

"I don't know. How could they come into the house without anyone hearing them?"

Elin hesitated, "I don't know, but someone put that tattoo on you, and I would like to know who it was."

The nurse returned to the cubicle, "I'll finish, get ready for the next patient." Elin picked up his bag and stepped outside. He looked at the long lines of young Nordic women, beautiful women. *Why*, he wondered. *This is going to drive me mad.* By late afternoon, the line had diminished to a handful. Elin was exhausted. The nurses were also exhausted and eager to finish with the remaining few.

Olaf, finished for the day, stopped at Elin's cubicle. "Need help?" He smiled widely.

The nurse answered. "I think we're almost ready to join you. Shouldn't be too long, right, Dr. Svensson?"

"That's right," he replied. "It's been a long day. Can't wait to get home and have a glass of beer."

Olaf looked directly at Elin and tipped his head slightly. This had become their new code to meet. Elin discreetly acknowledged the signal and joined the waiting group in the hall.

Olga wasn't home when Elin arrived. A note lay folded on the kitchen table. "My love," she wrote, "Kristen and I are going to see mamma. She's lonely and needs our attention. I'll miss the warmth of your arms tonight but tomorrow I'll be home and we'll make up for time lost. Your food is warming on the stove. Be safe my darling. I love you."

Normally Elin would bathe before dinner, but tonight, he deferred the simple routine. Sitting quietly at the table, he felt loneliness creep over him. Tonight, he needed his family. He needed to hold his child, to feel her safe in his arms. Their absence caused him to realize how much he needed the stability of home. A place where things were as they should be. A place of peace and truth.

The silence was shattered by a knock on the door. Elin approached with caution. "Who is it?"

"Mrs. Knutson," a small voice answered. "I have a letter for Olga."

Elin opened the door and invited her in.

"I can't stay, but thanks," she replied. "Where is Olga?"

"She and Kirsten are visiting her mother. What is this letter you have?"

"A messenger brought it this afternoon. Olga wasn't home so he left it at my apartment. He instructed me to deliver it as soon as possible. When I heard you come in, I assumed Olga was with you. Is it okay if I leave it with you?"

Elin accepted it and bid Mrs. Knutson an intentionally calm good night. He examined the letter, curious about its contents, wondering who sent it. There was no return address. Temptation to open it nudged at him, but better judgment prevailed. He had to respect the privacy of his wife's mail. He had to trust she would share the contents with him. Reluctantly, he laid it on the table, put on his coat, and left for the bar.

Elin strolled slowly along the dimly lit streets. He wasn't in a hurry, he had plenty of time. Olaf wasn't expected to arrive for at least fifteen minutes. He watched as children played, running and hiding, taking advantage of the dark. Their innocent laughter, undaunted by dangers of war, gave him courage. It made him feel more confident as the crisp air of spring invigorated him. He breathed deeply, relishing the smells. The children, laughing and giggling, gathered in a small courtyard. The dim post light revealed young happy faces. It was a welcome sight.

A little boy called out to him, "Mister, come look."

"What is it?" he questioned.

The little boy pointed to the ground. "Look mister, the flowers are blooming. Aren't they beautiful?"

Touched by the sincerity of the small child, he realized that simple things could never be tainted by war or the Nazis. The unspoiled spirit of a child and the beauty of the Earth could endure the most horrible of threats. The encounter had been short, because like all children with limited attention spans, they quickly scattered into the gray fringe of the gardens. Tiny, cheerful voices called out, "Good bye, good bye!" Elin couldn't help but smile.

Part Nine

The wine bar was bulging with people. Someone had brought a guitar and the crowd was singing and swaying to the rhythmic sounds. His usual seat was taken, but he found a table near the back of the long narrow room. Pushing past tightly packed bodies, he searched for Olaf. He wasn't there. Strategically, he seated himself so he could watch the door and waited as the young, drunken crowd became rowdy. He was amazed. How was it possible that these people could so easily forget that they were prisoners? How could they dance and sing when so many of their countrymen were forced into slavery by the invading Germans? He wondered why the Nazis permitted such gatherings. Where were the patrolling guards, the SS?

Preoccupied with his own bitter judgment, he hadn't noticed a young waiter approaching his table. "Something to eat?"

"No, just beer."

"Do you like the music?"

"Of course, I like the music," Elin snapped. "But I don't understand how everyone can be so happy, given the fact that our country is at war."

The young waiter just stood and stared. "These people can do nothing about the war, just as you cannot. I think it's wonderful that they're finally emerging, leaving the darkened prisons of their homes, and seeking old friendships. We need each other now more than ever. Don't you realize that?" he scolded. "For God's sake—we're young and it's spring!"

Elin had to agree with the young man. His conscience overwhelmed him. Who was he to judge? What happened to the man he thought he was? Had bitterness and suspicion finally surfaced and exposed his inner-most self? Had he become sour? Where was his compassion? *This is not me*, he thought. *It just can't be.*

The waiter returned with his beer and slid it across the table. Elin raised a finger, catching his gaze. "I was out of place with my rude remarks. Please forgive me."

The young waiter smiled. "Don't worry. I'm sure you had your reasons."

Olaf's head bobbed above the crowd. Elin signalled him, and Olaf forced his way to the back and sat down. "What's the celebration?"

"Spring," Elin answered. "I think it is just spring." The young waiter worked his way back through the crowd and again approached the table. He took Olaf's order and turned, running into a man who had just walked up behind him. "I'm sorry" the waiter apologized.

"It's okay," a deep voice whispered, "I'll be joining this table. Bring me a glass of white house wine."

The waiter stepped aside and allowed the man to sit down. "Good evening."

Elin didn't speak.

Olaf stood and extended his hand. "Good evening, Dr. Keiser. We have just arrived. I'm glad you could join us." Elin was shocked and his expression showed it. Olaf explained that since Dr. Keiser had been moved next to him at the Institute, it had made it possible for them to speak, discreetly of course. "Elin," Olaf continued, "Dr. Keiser is just as curious as we are about what's going on at the Institute. He feels some-thing unhealthy is happening and wants to find out what it is. Is that okay with you?"

"Oh, my dear God," Elin choked. "Do you realize how dangerous this is? What if you were followed? We'll all be killed. I think we should leave now, before we get caught."

Dr. Keiser looked around, "It appears there are no SS here tonight, and I was extremely cautious when I left my apartment. My neighbor drove me in his truck, and I changed my coat and hat, see?" Dr. Keiser pulled an old knit hat from his pocket and waved it in the air. "I can't stay long; my driver will be back to pick me up in about an hour. He's gone to gather fuel and I'm supposed to be helping. Quickly share with me what you know, and I'll try to fill in the holes."

Dr. Keiser was not aware of Johanna's involvement but had heard the term "Angel Hair" in Berlin. He knew about the pregnancy experiments and plans for a nursery. He had been told that he and Elisa would be the attending medical staff for new infants. Elin listened intently, then asked if either of them knew anything about the strange marks on female patients they had examined at the institute.

Olaf interrupted, excited. "All the males had a strange mark on their left thighs. It was a triangle with the letter H inside."

Elin put his hand on Olaf's arm. "Wait, are you sure about the mark? All the females had a circle with an 'H' and an 'A' inside on the right leg."

"Yes, I'm sure," Olaf responded. "It was a triangle, and it did have the letter 'H' and now that you mention it, the letter 'A'. But the 'A' was a smaller letter. Is that right?"

"Yes," Elin confirmed. "What is the purpose of these tattoos, do you know?"

Dr. Keiser buried his head in his hands and ran his fingers through his thinning hair.

"What is it?" Olaf asked.

"Dr. Keiser, do you know anything about this and today's patients?" Elin questioned. "Did you participate in the examinations?"

"No," commented Dr. Keiser "They involved me in something else."

Elin looked at the old man, read nothing on his tired face, and commented that there wasn't anything special about the females. "They didn't have six toes or anything like that." The strange thing is they all had certain things in common, like.... they all were virgins. All of them had the tattoo on the inside of the thigh and were blonde, blue eyed, beautiful young women. The other thing is none of them could explain the tattoo. They simply didn't know how they received it. This is the most perplexing thing of all. "

Dr. Keiser looked straight at Elin. "Were they all healthy and started menses?"

"Yes," Elin confirmed. "Ok, that's important?"

"If what I think is happening, then yes it's very important."

"Olaf, tell me about your young men," Dr. Keiser again inquired.

"It's the same as Elin's story. All young healthy men with blonde hair and blue eyes. They carried the tattoo on the left leg. It was a triangle instead of a circle. And like the women, they couldn't remember how they got it. The one thing most of them could remember was a bright light of some kind. They remembered the bright light and nothing more."

"Very interesting," Dr. Keiser commented. "Did you extract sperm from these patients?"

"Yes, yes we did," replied Olaf.

"I suspect this is a continuation of the project started in Berlin," Dr. Keiser whispered. "If this is so, then your young patients are what they call breeding stock. When I was in Berlin, Soviet and German scientists were perfecting technologically advanced instruments. These were to be used to accomplish a short-term pregnancy. They needed a way to replace the thousands of genetic and ethnic rejections they destroyed every day. And if human growth could be accelerated, they could re-populate with a pure super race in a few short years."

"That's insane," Elin said. "It's not humanly possible. It violates all the laws of nature. What they'll create is some sort of monstrosity."

"Those are my thoughts exactly." Olaf interjected. "That's why it's important we find out all we can before this project is totally launched.

"What's Johanna's involvement in this experiment?" Dr. Keiser questioned.

Olaf explained, "Whatever it is that they are doing, they are able to do it without the knowledge of their victims. Like the young people today they remember only a bright light. We need to know what these lights mean. The other thing that upsets both Elin and I was her comment that the baby was Dr. Svensson's. She said Dr. Brandt told her she had been seeded. Do you know what this means?"

"Does she carry the tattoo?" Dr. Keiser asked. "Not that I know of, but I'll ask her to check." Olaf answered.

"It appears to me Johanna has been selected to be a guinea pig in this project," Dr. Keiser replied. "We must keep an eye on her. She must not suffer in any way. It is our responsibility to our colleagues."

"Dr. Keiser," Elin asked, "where have you been these last few weeks? We've been worried."

"I thank you for your concern. The Nazis sent me home to Berlin, and I have just recently returned. My wife is suffering from severe depression, and they were concerned she might commit suicide. If that should happen, they would lose their power over me. They know I'm the best in the field and they don't want to lose me. I'm positive they need me for this project. The short visit certainly was a delight and tremendously helpful. I pray it gives her the strength to endure. I pray I can endure as well."

"One other thing," Elin asked. "Were you at a luncheon a few weeks ago? Olga, my wife, said a man of your description was in the nursery observing the children."

"Yes, I was, with Elisa. We were instructed to observe and report any physical defects in the children. I'm happy to report there were none."

"Tell me, Dr. Keiser," Olaf interrupted, "what exactly where you doing in Berlin before you came to Oslo?"

Dr. Keiser paused, looked at the two men and said in a whisper, "I will tell you what I know but we'll have to find out the rest here in Oslo. When they first took me to the Helmut Clinic in Berlin, they were extracting sperm from young men, fair-haired types. Of course, there was a shortage of suitable specimens. There are not as many blonde and blue-eyed men in Germany as here in Oslo".

"So, you're telling me these men were held as virtual prisoners." Olaf rubbed his eyebrow, pulling out hairs.

"Yes, and worse," Dr. Keiser continued. "They were housed in a dormitory near the clinic. Every few days, they were milked. You know, forced ejaculation. The specimens were taken to a high security section of the clinic and stored in a freezer. One day, they took me to examine what they said was a young child. I was horrified. It was the most pathetic human mass I had ever seen. The tiny creature appeared human in many ways but in other ways was totally inhuman. A group of Soviet and German eugenicists had surrounded me and when I gasped at the sight of the little creature, they were not happy."

"Oh my God!" Elin uttered, "What did it look like?"

"Like nothing I've ever seen. The skin had a funny color, sort of a chalky white, like a dead body. It also felt strange. There was a strange texture to the skin. They told me he was five months old but was in the developmental stage of a fifteen-month-old. His head was larger, carrying an oversized brain. The heartbeat was slow and the lungs enlarged. I told them I could only guess at the health of this child because I had nothing to compare him to. They told me to examine him as I would any other child: watch, listen and observe his breathing, listen to his heart, and test his reflexes. I tell you now, I was confused and terrified. I asked them what caused the strange appearance of the little child. They said the only thing I needed to know was that it was the product of eugenic experimentation."

"I was informed that they would have have a large number of these children in different growth stages, and that I would attend them. When I refused, they sent me here. I think they're preparing to repeat the experiments here in Oslo. They're probably intentionally introducing us to the project slowly. They know we are in no position to refuse, and they intend to take advantage of all of us."

Olaf continued questioning the old man. "Tell us more about this child. How many were there?"

"I wasn't told how many. The only one I saw was in the examination room. I got the feeling though there were several. The little creature I saw was fully developed. His body was small but firm, not soft like a baby's body. The thing that startled me most was its face. He had larger eyes that had apparently been circumcised, meaning the eye lids were removed. And the ears were mere slits in the side of his head. This part of his anatomy appeared under-developed, probably from its premature birth. I also think the child was mute. He never made a sound. Not a cry or whimper, and that's quite unusual under the circumstances. After I refused my service, they took the child and his file away. I don't know anything about his blood type or internal make up. I hate to alarm you, my friends, but I think we could be involved in the continuation of the Berlin project. Everything fits: the sperm extractions, the physical appearance of the patients, and Johanna's short pregnancy."

Elin and Olaf remained quiet, unable to respond.

Then Dr. Keiser cautioned, "You must be prepared. Prepare yourselves mentally and physically. It's going to shock you professionally and make you question your rational thinking."

"This is crazy," Olaf mumbled. "Are we to understand they are developing an accelerated-growth human?" Dr. Keiser replied, "I believe that's what I saw. Think about it. With the development of advanced medical instruments and unlimited supplies of humans on which to experiment, the chances of success in this project are definitely possible. The Nazis are storing huge amounts of sperm in frozen vaults. They must have the means of implanting select sperm into chosen females. This is what Johanna was referring to when she said she was seeded. Don't you see? This has to be part of the Berlin project."

"Then, --then," Elin stuttered, "you're telling me it's possible Johanna really was carrying my child."

"Have you given them a sperm sample?" Dr. Keiser questioned.

"Yes," he answered. "They demanded I give them a sample. This is so bizarre. Anna was the nurse that assisted me when I was unable to comply."

Olaf dropped his head and moaned.

"What is it?" Elin asked.

"Anna also assisted me," he confessed. "I've never told anyone about that day. It was so humiliating. I just wanted to forget."

Dr. Keiser interjected, "Then it's possible they're using your sperm as well."

"Dr. Keiser, did they require your sperm?" Olaf questioned.

"No, no they didn't. I don't fit the requirements; don't you see. First, I'm too old, and second, I don't have the desired physical appearance and genetic traits. They're serious about this project and will not settle for anything less than their concept of perfection. I'm sure the two of you are very desirable, both mentally and physically. I wouldn't be surprised if someday you'll meet one or more of your own technologically produced off-spring."

"What a horrible thought," Elin muttered.

The crowd in the bar had dwindled to a few drunken men. Dr. Keiser looked around and then at his watch. "My ride hasn't come back," he said in a panic. "I live too far to walk, and at this hour, I'm sure I would attract attention."

The bartender yawned as he began to turn off the lights.

"I think it's time to go," Elin remarked. "Why don't you come home with me, Doctor? Olga and the baby are gone, and you can sleep on the couch. It won't be a problem."

"Thank you, my friend" he replied. "I think that's the best and only offer I'll get tonight."

"Listen," Olaf interrupted in a whisper. "I think we should find a new place to meet. We've been seen here quite a few times in the last months and there are now three of us. Shouldn't we meet somewhere more discrete?"

"You're right," Elin responded. I'll try and find a new place. Olaf, why don't you leave now. Dr. Keiser and I'll follow." The three mingled with the other exiting bar patrons and spread out onto the silhouetted street.

Olaf maintained silence as he strolled away in the opposite direction. "This way," Elin instructed. "I live north of here."

"Dr. Keiser, Dr. Keiser," a voice quietly called out. "Over here by the building."

Dr. Keiser jerked around, surprised to see his neighbor standing in the darkness. "I'm sorry if I startled you, but I couldn't risk being seen going into the bar. I had a run-in with the Nazis earlier at the railroad tracks. They didn't believe I was looking for fuel. I finally convinced them, and they let me go. I went straight home because they were following me. They waited awhile outside and then left. I came as soon as possible. Come, we must hurry. It's late and the patrols will be out. Do you want us to drop you off, sir?" He said, glancing furtively at Elin.

"No thanks; it would be safer if I walked."

Dr. Kaiser raised his hand in benediction. "Good night, and be careful."

Part Ten

Elin awakened early the next morning. He was accustomed to rising at daylight to care for Kirsten. Weekends were no exception. Sunlight broke into the room and slithered across the floor as he opened the balcony door. He watched hungry birds hopping along the ledge consuming seeds left over from last season's flowering pots. Their exuberant songs and ravenous appetites affirmed that it truly was spring.

Merchants began to stir on the quiet streets. It wasn't business as usual, but business war style.

The crisp, damp air gave him a chill. He shivered, tightened his robe, and walked to the kitchen. Still lying on the table was Olga's letter from the day before. Curiosity nudged and he picked it up. The temptation was overwhelming. He studied the handwriting, smelled the paper and tugged at the fragile flap glued to the back. Then as suddenly as he had picked it up, he put it down and walked away.

A slight breeze blew through the open balcony door, delivering a wonderful aroma. Klaus, the neighborhood baker, was also up early preparing for an onslaught of customers. The scent of fresh bread permeated the air and diverted his temptation from the letter to a different seduction: food. As he showered and dressed for the day, his thoughts were on his family. He was lonely, hungry, and curious. He paced the floor, unable to find pleasure in being alone. *Why am I tormenting myself,* he questioned. *I'll go to Olga, with fresh bread, take the letter, and spend the day with my family. That's what I want to do. That's what I'm going to do.*

Elin rapped softly at Sonja's door. It was early and possible that Olga and Kirsten were still asleep. Again, he rapped. Slowly the door opened, and Olga peeked outside. Elin quickly pushed her back inside and held her lustfully tight. "Couldn't wait any longer," he whispered. His lips met hers with a hungry passion. He needed her, he wanted her, and in a darkened corner of the centuries old house, he took her.

"My, my," she sighed. "What did I ever do to deserve this wonderful visit?"

He smiled and kissed her again. "I wanted to show you how much I missed you last night. You know I can't live without you," he teased. "Why else would I get up so early and bring an offering of fresh bread? I'm hooked. You don't mind, do you?"

"Don't be silly," Olga giggled. "I've been expecting you since last night. What took you so long?"

"You know me well, you wicked woman," he laughed. "Is Kirsten awake?"

"No, she and mamma are still sleeping. Let's just enjoy this time alone and together." Olga knotted the long satin sash around her robe and took his hand, kissing it tenderly as she tugged him toward the kitchen. "Tell me about your night," she pressed.

Hanging his jacket on the back of the chair, he sat down. Deliberately ignoring the question, he shifted to a conversation about Olaf. Then he remembered the letter. "Olga, I have a letter for you. It was delivered yesterday. Mrs. Knutson asked that I give it to you."

"A letter for me? Who would be sending me a letter?"

"I don't know, open it. I'm dying of curiosity."

Olga examined the tiny envelope. It appeared to be an invitation. Her name was written in beautiful penmanship, and the fine linen paper was most impressive. Excitement mounted as she carefully slid a knife through the folded top. Her long slender fingers gingerly removed the hand-written note and her eyes danced quickly through the message. "Oh, oh!" she cried. "It's a miracle. I can't believe it—pinch me. I want to be sure I'm not asleep. I can't believe it, I can't believe it," she repeated again and again. Holding the paper close to her heart and taking to the center of the floor, she twirled and turned like a child in a rain shower.

"Olga," he demanded, "what is it? Tell me what it is."

Olga waltzed over to him and placed the note in his hand. She folded her arms around his neck as he read the contents. "Isn't it wonderful? They're going to reassemble the orchestra and they're going to send a driver for me. Elin, I thought my music was a thing of the past, lost in the ashes of war. I'm so happy. I can barely stand it. Just think, Tuesday I'll be back at rehearsal, back with my friends, back with my music. Wait here my love; I'm going to wake mother. I can't wait to tell her the good news."

Elin sat quietly, a thousand questions bombarding his thoughts. A strange uneasiness bothered him. Olga, politically pure and innocent, could see only good in reuniting the orchestra. He, on the other hand, could see the Nazis taking advantage of another member of his family. *What is their game?* He was sure there was a reason for this generous gesture. Olga and Sonja returned to the kitchen in high spirits, prancing like a couple of tipsy ballerinas. Elin attempted to smile, but haunting fears spoiled his effort.

After breakfast, Olga dressed and bathed herself, then opened the piano. Kirsten, refusing to separate from her mamma, pounded the keys with a passion. Olga's patience grew thin. She was eager to practice, eager to feel the keys glide under her fingers. Sonja attempted to entertain Kirsten, but the child would have none of it. Her constant interruptions drove Olga to distraction and frustration. Elin frolicked with his daughter, but that too was to no avail. Finally, in desperation, he wrapped Kirsten in warm clothing, and he and Sonja excused themselves and left for the park.

It was spring 1942. Kirsten was a little over a year old and attempting to walk. She took great delight in holding her father's hand as she shuffled through the still-not-quite-green grass. Often, she would drop to the ground and crawl, laughing as her pappa scurried after her. Sonja, the typical grandmother, would fuss over soiled knees and desperately wipe dirt from her little fingers.

The park was crowded. Small children rolled on the tender grass under the early spring sun. Families sat breaking bread as homemade boats bobbed on the sparkling lake. Parks are a special place, a private space where Norwegians felt some freedom. Germans seldom patrolled here during the day and if they did, they simply walked through, bothering no one.

Elin, tired of chasing Kirsten, hoisted her to his shoulders. She locked her fingers tightly in his curly blonde hair, evoking a cry of pain from her pappa. Eventually, she was coaxed to move her hand to the security of his firm fingers and giggled as they ran and jumped through the less-crowded pathways. Sonja, unable to keep up with the playful duo, seated herself on an old cement bench near the heart of the once magnificent gardens. Elin soon joined her, out of breath. It was then that he noticed the old greenhouse, draped in years of ivy. Birds fluttered in the gables and stalks of dead roses, brown as wheat ready-for-harvest, a testament to abandonment, an unfortunate victim of the war. Old wooden doors stood open, exposing a rummaged interior, overflowing with gardening clutter. Sonja was hesitant, but he led the little group to investigate.

Picking their way through all sorts of debris, they noted the doors, windows and other openings. Still miraculously intact was a section at the rear of the building, likely old offices, conveniently opening into the park. *This would be perfect*, he thought. *A perfect place to meet Olaf and Dr. Keiser. If anyone should enter the building, we could escape through the back into the dark. It's worth consideration*, he convinced himself. *I'll present it as an alternative.* Sonja, long since bored with his preoccupation, waited outside. Surveying the structure once more, he imprinted it in his mind, then hastened to join Sonja.

Kirsten had become restless. It was nap time, and the fresh air had accelerated her sleepiness. They agreed to turn for home. Sonja chattered constantly as they strolled the winding streets. He heard only parts of the conversation, choosing instead to drift in his own thoughts of intrigue. He was beginning to like the greenhouse more and more. The seclusion of the park appealed to him. The isolation of the building and the absence of German patrols also made him feel safe. *Yes,* he thought, *this feels right.*

Olga had finished her practice and met the family at the door. "Wait here," she instructed. "I'm ready to go home." Putting on her coat, she reminded mamma that she would be back Tuesday. "Rehearsal should only be a few hours. Are you sure you don't mind looking after Kirsten?"

"I'm certain. I look forward to it. Now go, enjoy the rest of the day."

Part Eleven

The following Monday morning, a flurry of activity in the street surprised Elin when he stepped outside. He leaned against the apartment building as a convoy of German trucks filled with soldiers rushed by. He hadn't seen this type of military activity since the beginning of the occupation. There were so many troops; it worried him. As he waited, his bus rounded the corner, unaware of the convoy, and time stood still as it collided with an approaching military truck.

Elin jumped to safety as the bus driver attempted to control the skidding vehicle. Tires screamed as breaks froze. Soldiers, caught off guard, were thrown to the floor, and several tumbled from the open back. Elin watched, powerless.

The bus doors flew open. Elin rushed inside, hoping to be of assistance. Fortunately, most of the passengers had been thrown to the opposite side when the bus veered and were spared direct impact. A few had small cuts on their heads and were shaken. Other than that, everyone appeared to have been spared serious injury.

Elin and several others approached the truck. These occupants were not as lucky. The head-on collision left the German driver with a serious concussion and two of the young men who had been thrown to the street displayed obviously broken limbs. The remainder were bruised or cut—not badly.

The convoy stopped. Several mid-level officers approached to survey the damage and ordered the uninjured soldiers to push the disabled vehicle to the curb. A medical truck, part of the convoy, pulled over the curb, loaded the injured onto the back, and quickly disappeared through the traffic jam. The entire affair seemed oddly unremarkable to the Nazis.

In less than ten minutes, the street had been cleared and only the caved-in, old, green bus remained. Olaf, who had been thrown into the side window, complained of head pain. It appeared he had suffered nothing more than a slight contusion above the right eye. Taking advantage of the confusion, Elin whispered, "I've found a new place. Can you meet me at the old greenhouse in the park gardens tonight at 7:00? I'll be at the back." Olaf nodded, stood, stretched his arms, bent his legs and breathed deeply. "Nothing broken, guess we're all lucky today."

The driver attempted to restart the stalled engine. Metal scraped metal, and the old bus rocked and groaned before the engine fired. Elin seated himself as the wheels reluctantly started to turn, propelling the disfigured vehicle up the street.

Questions dominated conversations. The passengers, all of whom now knew each other on a first name basis, were not shy in their complaints. "Quiet!" shouted the driver. "I can't hear myself think. What is it that concerns you so much?" Hans, a young chemist, spoke first. "What concerns me is that large group of military personnel rushing wherever. Do you know anything about what's going on?" Several other passengers echoed similar thoughts.

The driver hung onto the steering wheel as he brought the wounded vehicle to a bumpy stop at a red light, and chimed in. "I probably shouldn't tell you, but this morning when I arrived to pick up the bus, there were masses of soldiers at the transportation terminal. It seems the SS discovered the headquarters of a large partisan group. All available troops have been called in to storm the facility. Just a couple of days ago, partisans blew up the pier in Bergen, and on Friday, a bomb was found in

Director Schmidt's office. I'm sure the rise in the resistance movement has caused unrest among the SS hierarchy, and those troops were going to assist in the rounding up of your foolish countrymen." Another question rang from the back, but the driver, now aware of just how much he had divulged, simply said, "no more questions."

The small amount of information the passengers just received shot through them like a bullet. Many raised their fists high in the air and smiled. This was a powerful sign of nationalist pride---a reason for rejoicing and renewed hope.

A strong sense of patriotism filled Elin's heart. Consumed with his own plan to spy out what the Nazis were doing in the name of science, he had forgotten the partisans—the brave men and women fighting to liberate his beloved Norway. The news of continued resistance affected him like an adrenalin injection. Raising his fist high, he turned and visually connected with Olaf. Both men defiantly waved their arms in renewed determination and profound patriotism as the crippled bus lumbered toward the Institute.

The old building came into view as the bus struggled to climb the hill, more than an hour late. Oscar looked frantic, pacing at the gate.

The narrow road leading into the Institute was completely blocked with a multitude of military trucks. Oscar signaled the bus driver to the edge of the road and ordered him to park. The driver opened the door, trying to explain the delay. Oscar simply shouted profanities at the soldier.

Ignoring the shouting, Elin took special notice of the activity at the entrance of the Institute. He saw what appeared to be bodies being carried by soldiers wearing protective clothing. One by one, the cadavers were stacked in the back of an open truck, covered with canvas, and driven away. The second truck had already moved into place when Oscar ordered the men off the bus and to the building entrance. Suspicions were validated. Black blankets were covering the dead, who were crudely tagged and secured only with string.

The strong smell of chemicals was nauseating. Elin and others pressed hands across their mouth as they passed. Several choked, gagged and vomited. Elin half ran to the door, gasping less-tainted air as he forced his way inside.

With the group reassembled, Oscar shouted, "It is unfortunate that you had to experience this unpleasant tragedy. You would have been spared had there not been a delay in your arrival. I recommend you put this behind you immediately and proceed as if you saw nothing." With that, he turned over the group to the guide inside the medical facility and disappeared.

Lingering stench in the main hallway remained worrisome. It was obvious there had been contamination, and the heavy smell of chemicals confirmed it. But what kind?

Today appeared to be a day for surprises. Waiting inside, along the main entrance hall, was a group of nervous, blonde, blue-eyed youths. Elin glanced over at one of the younger Norwegians. As the men passed by, her eyes tightened with unforgettable terror. As a prisoner himself, he felt over-whelming sympathy for her, but an acknowledgement would put her in serious danger. He made no move.

Elin entered his cubicle as usual. Immediately they brought in a 17-year-old boy. The nurse chuckled, "Guess we're doing extractions; low on sperm."

The young man frowned "What does she mean?" he questioned.

"This is a regular examination, don't worry." Elin answered.

"Don't worry?" the young man retorted. "You probably didn't see all the dead bodies they hauled out of here this morning. Am I going to be one of them?" Elin dropped his head and said simply, "I hope not."

Part Twelve

Olga's driver arrived early to take her to the rehearsal hall. She hoped for a little time to practice before her fellow musicians assembled. But to her dismay, many were already there, waiting, chattering, and fondling their instruments. Two of her closer associates sitting near the back of the room clapped in celebration as she walked into the great hall. Olga was surprised. She turned and smiled a blushingly before strolling toward the majestic piano.

As she stood admiring the instrument, a shadow entered her peripheral vision. Startled by the approach, she stepped back and turned to face her visitor. "Don't be frightened," the deep-voiced SS officer said. "Do you remember me? I'm Dr. Brandt. We met at a luncheon I hosted for wives of the research team. Surely you remember the afternoon at the Claus Hotel." Olga's heart stopped for a second as flashes of Elin's warning raced through her thoughts. Dr. Brandt extended his hand and led her to a chair. "You look a little pale; please sit down. I'll get you a glass of water." Olga peered around the great hall. Everyone sat in frozen silence, terrified by the presence of the SS officer.

Dr. Brandt returned with what appeared to be a cool glass of water.

"Here my dear, drink this." Olga's throat tightened as the SS officer moved closer. Dr. Brandt lifted the glass and tilted it toward her lips. "Let me help you," he said in a gentle voice.

Olga choked as the water rushed into her mouth and ran onto her chin. "Thank you," she blushed, pushing the glass away. "I'll be fine now. I'm so embarrassed. I guess I'm more excited than I thought." Hoping to explain away her fear, she lightened the conversation. "Thank you again for the opportunity to meet with the orchestra!"

Dr. Brandt smiled, "I understand."

Do you remember?" he asked again. "Oh yes," she responded. "It was one of the most memorable luncheons I have ever attended. And such a delight to meet other wives of the research team. We are all so proud of our husbands and their contributions to the cause. And you are to be commended as well on your most important work."

Olga continued her flowery dialogue, feeling it was important to flatter the egotistical doctor. Dr. Brandt's face glowed as he looked into her eyes. "I'm told you're as talented as you are beautiful. I have always said talent should not be wasted. That's why I decided to re-assemble the orchestra. Germans as well as Norwegians need a diversion. We all want to relax and enjoy ourselves. Don't you agree?"

"Yes, yes I do," she responded, "and we all thank you for the opportunity to serve through what we do best: making beautiful music."

Dr. Brandt interrupted, "So, if you don't mind, I'd like to stay and listen in for a while. Now relax and enjoy your reunion." The doctor, conspicuous in his uniform, meandered through the rows and seated himself in the deep back of the hall.

Arriving musicians filtered in, unaware of the sinister observer, laughing and hugging as they re-connected with former colleagues. But Olga, knowing he was there in the dark, felt supremely uncomfortable. His unusual kindness also bothered her. The way he smiled—it was almost flirtatious. The entire encounter somehow seemed entirely too contrived.

The complete assembly was present except for Thor Niessen, the conductor. Concerned colleagues questioned whether or not he had been contacted. No one knew of his whereabouts. Not one of the musicians had seen him in the past year. Olga was disappointed and discouraged. How could they possibly play without a conductor? It wasn't impossible, but it certainly was not the most desirable situation for an orchestra. Then, the door opened.

Thor entered on the arm of a young SS officer. They stepped to the front of the group, and the officer unlocked the handcuffs on Thor's wrists. To say that the orchestra was surprised would be an understatement. Thor managed a smile and expressed pleasure at seeing his colleagues after so long a time. He thanked the SS for allowing him to be a part of the reunion. Saying nothing more, he gently picked up the baton and tapped the tall black music stand. Everyone postured, and a pathetically out-of-tune chord vibrated through the room.

"My, my, we need a little practice," the old man smiled.

The group laughed and started again. By the end of the first hour, the orchestra began to come together. Olga's face glowed. By the end of the second hour, the music flowed, and the pleasing performance brought a warmth to the deeply creased face of their conductor.

The young SS officer stirred and pointed to his watch. Thor acknowledged his signal and closed his book. "It's time to go," he announced. "I've been told we will be able to meet twice a week until otherwise notified. I look forward to seeing all of you day-after-tomorrow, same time, same place."

The lines deepened in his face as the officer approached with the cuffs. Thor's tall, slender body slumped, and strands of long gray hair fell, covering his eyes. Olga felt his embarrassment as he struggled to raise his cuffed hands and remove the hairy obstruction. The rest of the assembly sat respectfully and quiet, watching as he was escorted from the room.

With their conductor and his strange escort gone, Olga remembered her sinister admirer. Cautiously, she turned from the piano and peered into the volumes of seats crowding the great room. The back of the hall was empty. He had gone, and she was relieved. Small talk erupted among the lingering musicians, and Olga joined her friends in a brief period of friendly conversation before returning home.

Early evening stars had just appeared as Elin arrived home. It had been a long, grueling day. His mood was sober. Olga gathered up Kirsten and started preparing dinner. Unlike her husband, she was in an almost giddy state of mind. Her day had been wonderful, but her husband echoed none of her enthusiasm. Trying to avoid conversation, she whispered nonsense at length to Kirsten. Dinner was set, and Olga gently tried to awaken Elin, who had fallen soundly asleep in his comfortable old chair. He moaned in opposition before opening his eyes. "Oh," he said, "I was dreaming. I didn't hurt you, did I?"

"No," she smiled. "Dinner is ready."

Elin poked at his food; his thoughts were miles away. Olga wanted to share her day with him, but his appetite for conversation was no better than his desire for food. Finally, he excused himself and retired to the other room.

Kirsten fussed. She wanted attention from her father. Olga called out, "please come and get Kirsten. She needs to be with you before bedtime. She misses you, and so do I."

Elin returned, kissed Olga softly, and picked up Kirsten. He was accommodating but quiet. Standing in the kitchen door watching Olga clear the table, he said, "I need to go out tonight. I can't tell you why, but I know you'll understand."

Olga glared. "No, I don't understand; all these secrets, all these meetings. Is it worth our lives? I can't think of anything less important. Forget the Nazis, forget their agenda, concentrate on our agenda. That's far more important." She turned away, not wanting Elin to see the tears welling in her eyes. "I'm sorry," she said, "I'm frustrated and worried."

Elin sandwiched Kirsten between them and pulled Olga close. "There are terrible things going on in Oslo, things you can't imagine. I need to know as much as possible so I can protect you. I need to know the enemy."

Olga sobbed uncontrollably, and Elin walked out into the hallway.

The door had not yet closed when he immediately re-entered the apartment, shutting the door behind him. "Olga, please quiet Kirsten. There are Germans in the building. I hear them talking." Olga quickly took Kirsten to the kitchen, hoping a biscuit would pacify her. It did. But Elin didn't leave.

Part Thirteen

A loud knock vibrated the old door. Elin froze. Olga clung to him. The door vibrated again with the pounding of a firm fist. Elin motioned for Olga to move back as he attempted to peek out into the hallway. Without hesitation, a large figure forced open the door, widening the aperture for his comrade.

The SS officer pushed into the apartment, stared suspiciously at Elin, then said something in German to the other person waiting in the darkened hall. "Forgive the intrusion and lateness of our visit," he then said. The voice was familiar, as was the face. It was Dr. Brandt. "I have come with wonderful news," he smiled. Elin forced his muscles to relax and asked him to take a seat.

Olga offered tea, but Dr. Brandt declined. "I hope I'm not interrupting your evening; I see you have on your coat."

"No, no, not at all," Elin responded. "I was just going for a walk while Olga put Kirsten to bed. Sometimes it's easier when I'm not here; you know how children are about bedtime." Dr. Brandt nodded. "May I hold the child?" he asked.

Olga looked at her husband for approval, then placed Kirsten in Dr. Brandt's arms. At first, she pouted and wiggled, but Dr. Brandt held her firmly and dangled a gold watch chain to entertain her. Kirsten focused on the shining object and settled into his lap. Olga watched as the doctor hugged and teased her. She detested the phony display of affection. Why was he doing this? Did he think she couldn't see through his insincerity?

Elin sat in patient quietness, but his stomach was sick, and sinister motives were all he could think about.

Dr. Brandt suddenly stood and handed Kirsten back to Olga. "What a beautiful child; so alert. Thank you for letting me hold her."

What is this? Olga thought again. She couldn't understand. Dr. Brandt looked fondly at Olga as he released his grip on the little girl. Olga felt the flush on her face as she backed away, "And now for the good news," Dr. Brandt bellowed. "Because you are both important to our cause, and because we reward those that are loyal to the Reich, we are moving you to a new residence. It's a home with a garden and room for children. But the best and most exciting is... there is a piano." His smile bared two rows of white teeth. "A piano for you, Olga."

He was waiting for a response. Olga was speechless. A thousand thoughts crossed her mind all at once. She looked at Elin who looked little more than confused. Then she spoke. "Dr. Brandt, we are ever so thankful for your kind gesture, but we are not worthy of all of this attention. I'm sure there are many more deserving. What about our friends? We hate to leave them."

Dr. Brandt interrupted, "The house is not far from here. Your friends can visit. I'm sure they'll be happy for you. Look at this place. It's a pitiful existence. I want better for you. Take your personal belongings, and everything else will be provided. Any questions?" he asked.

Elin stood and looked into Dr. Brandt's eyes. "Yes, I have a question. What happened to the family that owned this house?"

Dr. Brandt snapped back, "The Reich owns everything, and everybody: every dog, every cat; do you understand? Everything. It doesn't matter about the other families; they were accommodated. Any more questions? Then it's settled. I'll personally supervise the move." With that, he moved to the door, clicked his heels and shouted "Heil Hitler."

Elin raised his arm and quickly closed the door. "What a day!" he moaned. "What else can happen?"

Olga tugged at his arm, "Let's go to bed. It's late and I am exhausted."

"Oh my God," he exclaimed, "I've missed my appointment."

"Don't worry about your appointment. It's dangerous. There is nothing you can do," Olga consoled. "Let's go to bed."

The grayness of the bedroom was not its usual sanctuary. Shadowed imagery danced across the half-lit mirror. Elin suspected he might be delirious from exhaustion. Olga too, was uncomfortable, fading in and out of consciousness. Too tired to be awake and too exhausted to sleep. He worried about her. He also fretted about not meeting his friend and co-conspirator. He wondered if he too was having trouble sleeping. Could he possibly be awake? He decided to find out, no matter how dangerous.

Slipping into dark clothing, he ventured into the hallway. He could travel under the safety of darkness. No one would see him. Stepping in and out of the shadows, he quickly made his way to Olaf's. The house was dark: not a sign of life there or on the streets around it. Beginning to think this was not such a good ideal, he stared at the old building, hoping to muster the courage to continue.

Suddenly, a faint light appeared in the window. Someone was up. Elin ran to the building and quietly rapped on the door. No one answered. He knocked again. Slowly the door opened. It was Olaf. "Come in, come in," he whispered. "Are you crazy, what are you doing here?"

Elin responded, "I couldn't sleep; I felt like I betrayed you. I needed to let you know what happened."

"I think I already know," Olaf whispered. "When you were not at the park, I walked by your apartment. I saw Dr. Brandt and another officer go in. I presumed they were there to see you and possibly would visit me next. So, I rushed home. I've stayed close just in case they came. They didn't. What did they want? I have been sick with worry."

"I can't figure Brandt out," Elin responded. "He came to tell us that they are moving us into a house nearby. Why, I don't know, but he was in no mood to be questioned. He is personally supervising the move. Can you believe it? You know what worries me most of all: I think he is enamored with Olga. You should see the way he looks at her. I could be wrong, but I think he is trying to please her. He's been so accommodating. The orchestra and such. She is such an innocent. I fear for her."

"I pray you're wrong!" Olaf said. "I do have to tell you the park is not the place to meet. SS officers were walking their dogs there tonight. They would have spotted us for sure. I suspected you had probably encountered the same. That's why I was going to your apartment to let you know I was okay and to talk about another place to meet. We have to be extremely careful from now on. Dr. Brandt could be lurking in the shadows watching you and Olga for whatever reason. Now, my friend, you better go before someone sees you."

"You're right about everything," Elin lamented. "We have to be extra cautious. Goodnight, my friend." The men embraced, and Elin departed for home.

Part Fourteen

At daylight, Elin awoke with a jerk. "Having bad dreams again?" Olga asked.

"I don't remember," he replied. "Maybe."

Thoughts were formulating in his lucid dreaming—mostly on ways to meet with his secret partners. Where would they be able to go now? Could he risk talking to them at the Institute? The *how, how, how* pounded in his head. He worried about leaving his family alone. He didn't trust Dr. Brandt nor his agenda. No wonder he couldn't rest—and what about the Institute—the dead bodies, the chemicals, and poor Johanna. *What of that? How will I find out?* There was no end to the questions. He kissed Olga and proceeded to leave the building.

Sitting at the curb was an ominous black car—waiting—watching. A chill rippled down his back as he walked over to the car. The window opened slightly, and a friendly "good morning" chirped from inside. "Is Olga awake?" the voice inquired. The old man Olga had described emerged, extended his hand and said, "Call me Unk. I've been sent to help Olga pack and prepare for the move to your new home." He hadn't expected this so soon and was a bit perplexed.

"Yes," he said. "The baby is not."

"We'll be quiet," the little man responded. "Such a lovely family!" and he smiled.

Elin wanted to go back to bed, to skip to some other less confusing day. "Are you part of the SS?"

"Oh no," the little man answered. "I am part of a special interest group—not involved in the political waring side of this conflict. She's safe with me," he reassured.

The brakes on the old bus hissed to a stop nearby and Elin reluctantly boarded for work, nervously watching as Unk entered the building.

Mrs. Knutson peered through a crack in her door to observe Unk as he ascended the staircase. A soft knock followed, and Olga opened the door. Taking a surprised step back, "Unk!" she exclaimed. "What is it? I'm sorry I haven't dressed yet."

"Don't be alarmed," he replied. "I'll wait on the stairs. I'm here to assist in packing for the move. Dr. Brandt is impatient; he seems very anxious to please you. He'll be joining us in a little bit to take you to see your new home. We must get started now."

Olga took extra time in dressing. She wanted to look nice to go out.

Soft noises began to echo in the hallway. The door opened, and a young soldier carried empty boxes into the apartment and placed them next to the door. Neighbors were peeking out, understandably confused. Olga hadn't had time to tell them or her mother of their pending move. This was all happening so fast—her head was spinning— yet there was a sense of excitement: a new home, a garden, a piano; oh glorious day!

The young soldier addressed Unk and said he would return to remove the boxes later, then disappeared down the stairs. Unk came in and sat down in an old chair. Suddenly, he didn't seem so foreign. His grandfatherly softness was working. Olga relaxed and offered him tea. Unk again reminded her to take only personal belongings: no furniture, dishes, and the like. Those things were to be provided in the new home. She reminded him they didn't have a lot; besides the baby's things, there was not much to pack. He looked around and, smiling, agreed. The packing went quickly, leaving Unk time to visit and become acquainted with Kirsten. It was strange; she bonded with him instantly, her warmth obviously giving him great pleasure.

The timing of the move was good. Spring had blossomed into summer, and sunshine replaced gray. Kirsten and Olga were healthy and happy. Even the situation in Oslo somehow seemed more promising, despite the ongoing German occupation.

Late morning brought back the young soldier and a helper. Unk instructed them to move the boxes to the address they had been given. He then informed Olga they were going to have lunch with Dr. Brandt.

Olga froze for a moment. "What about the baby?"

"She's to come as well. Doctor's orders; shall we go?" Unk gathered the things needed to accompany the baby and carried Kirsten to the car waiting at the curb.

They arrived at a small, outdoor cafe. Dr. Brandt was waiting. Unk tried to assure Olga that the doctor wasn't as bad as he seemed, that he must present a facade of strictness to please the SS hierarchy. Olga listened, but her thoughts were on Elin's warnings: trust no one, but play nice, even if you're frightened.

Dr. Brandt stood, acknowledged Olga, and shook hands with Unk, which was very odd: no Heil Hitler salutes were exchanged. Small talk followed, giving Olga a chance to ask Dr. Brandt a few questions. She asked if he had a family. He turned away for a moment, seeming to hide some emotion. He informed her that his wife had died a few years ago; they had no children. The SS moved him to Oslo, and he had no friends. She suspected he was not only lonely but homesick for Berlin as well.

Kirsten was pleasantly entertained by the two doting men, and lunch was quite enjoyable. Olga began to relax and looked forward to the next move: a visit to the new home Dr. Brandt had selected. Observing the two men together was perplexing. It was a strange relationship. There seemed to be a great deal of respect and fondness between the two. After the light lunch, Dr. Brandt asked Unk to meet him at the residence.

It was nice to be outside and riding in a beautiful car on a sunny day. It made her feel important and almost privileged. But relentless reality slapped her in the face: *why you?*

The car meandered through the streets back toward her neighborhood but stopped short by a beautiful park. A stately old townhouse appeared before them; one of two, connected by a common wall. The two houses faced the street with a shared gated garden entrance. It took her breath away. She never expected this.

Unk opened the door and picked up Kirsten. "What do you think?" He inquired "Could you live here?"

She was speechless.

Dr. Brandt joined them, taking out several keys as he walked to the door of the building.

"Most impressive house!" Olga managed. "Is this where we're going to live?"

"Yes," he answered. "If it meets your approval."

Olga managed a response. "This is so beautiful; I can't imagine not loving it." Dr. Brandt looked at Unk with a satisfied smile.

The heavy wooden doors opened, surprising Olga once again. Her personal belongings had arrived and lay in the foyer. She turned to Unk. "Well, I guess it's settled. Our things are here and so are we. This will be our home." Suddenly she realized the most important question hadn't been addressed. Turning to Dr. Brandt she asked, "How are we to pay for this?"

Unk interrupted, "Don't worry, it's already arranged. The contributions you and Elin make will more than cover the cost, so don't worry—enjoy!"

The house was fabulous. Compared to their apartment, this was a palace. A curved staircase and large reception room loomed in the front. But the best was yet to come. Dr. Brandt took Olga's hand and led her to the lounge where a beautiful piano stood. She gasped with excitement.

"Are you pleased?" he inquired.

"Beyond belief," she whispered. Her eyes filled with tears. "I hope I'm worthy of this." Dr. Brandt quickly rebutted, "You are, you truly are."

Unk appeared with Kirsten, and Dr. Brandt excused himself, saying he had to get back to the Institute. Olga and Unk explored and admired the beautiful furnishings—even Kirsten's room was immaculately furnished. *Well planned*, she thought. *They knew I'd love it.*

Unk suggested they take the opportunity to go back and say good-bye to the old neighbors, since the family would be spending the night in the new house. He also suggested visiting Sonja as well. Olga acquiesced as he handed her the house keys.

Everything was incredibly fast, and as much as she pondered, she couldn't figure how all of this could happen in just 24 hours. Elin was right: the Nazis were extremely well organized. They knew what they wanted, and they knew how to get it. They could be very charming and devious at the same time. She just needed to remember that they had an agenda and not to get caught up in the games they were trained to play. She wondered if this was what Elin called Psychological Warfare.

Unk stopped at the entrance of their old apartment building. Olga gathered up Kirsten and turned to Unk. He smiled and nodded her towards the door. "I'll wait in the car while you say your goodbyes."

Olga entered the building and knocked on Mrs. Knutson's apartment door. "Come in!" a voice called. Olga obeyed.

"I saw you get out of the car from my window. I hoped you were coming here. What in the world is going on? Why have they taken your things?" The good woman had a million questions.

Olga briefly explained the situation as well as she could and told her to come visit anytime. It was a sad farewell for the old lady, but Olga was still on a high, and anxious to see her mamma. None of the other neighbors were in. She excused herself and returned to the car.

Sonja, working in her small garden, looked up as the big black Mercedes slowed down and stopped in front of the house. Her eyes widened with a mixed look of surprise and shock. Unk opened the door, picked up Kirsten, and approached the house with Olga.

Wiping soil from her hands, Sonja asked if they would rather go inside. Kirsten, seeing her grandmamma, began to squirm.

"Yes," Olga answered. "Inside is better. Oh, by the way mamma, this is Unk. I'll tell you about him later."

Sonja unlocked the door, reluctant. Kirsten, freed at last, began scooting and toddling about. Unk entertained the active little girl while Sonja, seizing the opportunity, motioned Olga to the kitchen.

"Who is that man?" she scolded. "What are you doing with him?" Questions rained down on Olga like a thunderstorm.

"Mamma, mamma, calm yourself. It's okay," Olga whispered. "He has been asked by the authorities to assist us in certain things."

"The SS?" Sonja hissed.

"Yes mamma. Now listen; we've moved to a new home, and I've come to ask you to trust me. I'll fill you in later when we can talk longer in private. Now I have to go. Elin will be home soon. We'll come back as soon as possible; I promise. Love you, mamma. Don't worry."

Sonja, a strong woman in her own right, stood in disbelief, fearful of the evils she felt were ensnaring her wonderful family.

Olga kissed her goodbye, and the three departed.

Excitement returned as Unk dropped Olga and Kirsten at the curb of their stately new home. Pulling away, he leaned from the window. "I hope you have an enjoyable experience in your new environment, and I'll see you soon."

The long day was nearly over. Sunlight had become a faded pink as grayness clamored for its share. Olga heard the old bus brake in the street. Elin stepped off onto the sidewalk. Olga called out, and he rushed to her side.

"No one told me," he said. "I can't believe it; is this our home?"

"Yes," Olga replied. "Isn't it grand? Let's go in. I'll show you around."

Kirsten had already fallen asleep, Exhausted, excited and with a renewed enthusiasm for tomorrow, the young couple drifted into a peaceful sleep as well.

Part Fifteen

The next morning, Elin chose to withhold the information he wanted to share with Olga. With all the attention she was getting, an innocent comment about new war information could slip out and expose them to interrogation or worse. He chose instead to humor her, listen to her music, and enjoy the new home.

Things were extremely strange at the institute. Johanna was almost comatose, going through the motions of her job, never smiling or talking. Olaf was busy with a new project, and Dr. Keiser was practically a prisoner in the back of the room. Security had been reinforced, and spying eyes were everywhere. New people came and went. Strange men often gathered near Dr. Keiser's section, some outside the private rooms with frosted glass, some mere shadows on the inside of the windows. *Who were these people?* It was driving him crazy. Dr. Keiser would have better access to the secured area and more information. Their secret meeting had become an emergency.

Mid-morning, Dr. Brandt strolled unannounced into Elin's cubicle, giving the young doctor a start. "How do you like your new accommodations, Elin?" Standing respectfully, Elin acknowledged his superior. It was obvious, to him, that Dr. Brandt was searching for a compliment. "It is a wonderful place," he managed. "Thank you; our family is most appreciative."

"Well," Dr. Brandt continued, "In a few days I'll have another surprise for you." As he left, he raised his arm in the familiar salute and left. Elin couldn't imagine what else he would do. *Why doesn't he just leave us alone?* A loud bell clanged. Lunch break.

Elin hoped to see his friends and try to signal a meeting, but how? Olaf arrived minutes later and sat at the end of a long, narrow table. Unable to engage, surrounded by strangers and friends, he sat as the sign instructed. "Eat Not Talk."

Johanna came in searching for an empty seat. Unfortunately, none were available. He watched as her frail body glided through the rows of diners. She had lost weight, and dark circles disfigured her cheeks in ghostly contrast to her ivory skin. It was obvious she was distressed. Were they using her again, he wondered? Olaf also observed her and glanced at Elin, slightly shaking his head. Their eyes locked and he knew Olaf also wanted to talk. They just had to figure this out. Security was extremely tight.

After lunch, Dr. Brandt called the doctors to the front of the hall and informed them that their duties were going to be expanded. They were to care for injured SS soldiers as needed, but in a different part of the Institute. They would be randomly dispatched. The casualties of war were mounting, and local hospitals were overcrowded and under-staffed. Dr. Brandt kicked his heels together and flung his arm high. "Back to work," he barked.

Days passed, and Elin found reprieve from his boring routine by caring for young SS soldiers. He also had the opportunity to discretely question them about the war: where they were fighting, and the outcomes of engagements. He learned that the Resistance had crippled the Vemork heavy water facility where it was rumored that the Nazis were building a super bomb. *Where is all of this high technology coming from?* he wondered. German scientists were pumping out new bombs right and left.

Unable to safely approach Dr. Keiser or Olaf, Elin thought they would never be able to meet again. Then, out of nowhere, the unexpected happened. Dr. Brandt approached Elin and asked if he and a small group of the staff could come to his new home for a "get together." He explained that the group had worked so well together in the past, that it might be nice to socialize a little—to relax and enjoy an evening away from the stress of work and war.

"Besides, it'll give you and Olga a chance to share your new home with everyone. Of course, everyone will be surprised. I'll supply the food and drink," he continued.

Elin was shocked at this request and a little embarrassed. *What will my colleagues think? I'm sure none of them have the extra luxuries that Olga and I have been afforded.*

His hesitation was interrupted by Dr. Brandt. "Shall I presume it's, okay?"

"Yes, by all means."

"Wonderful," Dr. Brandt responded. "We'll talk. I'm thinking Sunday, in about a week. I'll make the arrangements. Give my best to your wife." With that he turned and walked away, leaving Elin in disbelief. *What game is he playing now? Is this a plan to see Olga and to be near her?* His jealousy burned hot. Then he remembered Dr. Brandt's promised surprise. *This must be it. He has planned this all along. What a fool I've been.* Dr. Brandt had always seemed one step ahead. *Bringing my colleagues to our home and flaunting a privileged lifestyle will certainly discredit me as a lowly doctor working against my will under my SS captors.* He couldn't figure how he'd ever be able to convince anyone but Olaf to trust him. Such distrust seemed capable of spoiling everything.

The long day was finally over.

Leaping from the bus, he stepped more lightly as the new front garden's brightly colored flowers' drooping heads yielded to his approach.

"In the kitchen!" Olga called when she heard him enter. The two women in his life had gathered around a table laden with wonderful things. Sonja had come to visit and had taken out the beautiful china and silver to admire.

Elin frowned. "A bit ostentatious, isn't it? Well, I guess it's just as it should be—according to Dr. Brandt. Only the best for the Svenssons."

Olga looked puzzled. "What are you talking about?"

"I have a theory. This is a game, and I don't like it. I think he is pitting me against my colleagues, hoping they'll distrust me and begin thinking I'm in cahoots with the Nazis."

"What?" Sonja interjected. "No one would ever believe that of you; you're a Norwegian patriot, now and forever. Let the Nazis think what they want. Your friends know the truth."

"Oh, by the way," he sputtered. "We're having a gathering here at our new home for Dr. Brandt and members of our staff. He thinks we deserve a break from work and is making all the arrangements. Plans are to have it on Sunday, in about a week. Think you can handle it?"

Part Sixteen

Norway had been occupied for several years now, and the population had adapted. The invasion had been swift, and for the most part, the Germans benefited enormously. Local politicians made it easier for Norwegians to survive by negotiating and cooperating with the occupying authorities.

Food was still a massive problem, along with other wartime shortages. Under the Nazis' rationing and confiscations, many people sought to survive by fishing and growing their own food.

Olga was grateful that Dr. Brandt had access to the essentials they would need for entertaining guests. She understood Elin's concern but simply couldn't appreciate his constant state of agitation. How could she, knowing nothing of the horrors surrounding him. She had been confined to a small community of uninformed companions.

Several days later, Elin was preparing to leave work for home when Dr. Brandt popped into his cubicle. "Everything ready for our gathering?" he asked enthusiastically. "I've made arrangements for members of the staff to be picked up at 5:00 PM and driven to your new residence. Everyone is looking forward to the opportunity to meet socially. I'll see to the delivery of the food and drink early Sunday afternoon and hopefully all will go well."

Elin inquired about the number of guests attending.

"Oh, just the immediate staff members," Dr. Brandt answered. "And maybe a couple of officers – it'll be just fine. Be assured my SS comrades will not be a threat nor spoil the mood. They're really quite pleasant men."

Elin stepped out of the fabric prison and followed Dr. Brandt toward the Institute gate where the others were already waiting for the clanking old bus.

Dr. Brandt signaled his driver, raised his arm, and departed. All the men's eyes had watched, making Elin feel insecure and a little paranoid. *What were they all thinking?* It did look odd: Dr. Brandt walking with him. He scanned the group for understanding expressions, but excepting Dr. Keiser and Olaf, he found none. Most were probably too preoccupied with their own personal struggles. Olaf tipped his head to acknowledge Elin's predicament and Dr. Keiser smiled faintly. With a tremendous sigh of relief, he settled into his seat for the ride home.

The long ride gave him time to wonder again why they been singled out for special treatment. There were other ways this social could be a trap—a way to observe the group in a more relaxed environment, perhaps. What would they talk about? Would wine and drinks loosen lips? Would secrets be conferred? Could he use this occasion to schedule the next meeting of co-conspirators? The prospect of getting together again excited him and he carefully crafted a plan.

In the following days, Elin explored the new neighborhood, watching the activities of the surrounding neighbors and merchants. He located a few pubs off the beaten path. He searched obsessively for a secure and isolated retreat for him and his confidantes. Late one night, he found it: an old church built in the late 1700's with a tiny courtyard enclosed behind a forbidding wall. It appeared to be almost completely deserted. *Perfect*, he thought. *This will work.*

Part Seventeen

The summer sun silhouetted Sonja's slim body as she walked toward the house, opened the door and greeted her daughter. It was orchestra practice again.

"Unk is waiting for me in the car," Olga said as she greeted her mother with a light kiss. "Elin and Kirsten are in the kitchen having breakfast. Please, mamma, join them."

It was her music day. *Music, music, music!* she whispered to herself as she shut the front door and crossed the sunny front garden. Unk greeted her with a smile. He, too, looked forward to this day. It gave him a chance to hear and watch his favorite charge.

Thor's guard had already removed the conductor's cuffs and taken a seat in the back. Olga was happy she didn't have to witness the embarrassing performance again. The rest of the orchestra wandered in one by one, and the music began. Olga was in heaven, even if it were only for a few hours. Thor was pleased with the smooth transition, and the orchestra was soon back to their original excellence. He wrapped up the rehearsal with a wave of his wand and thanked his friends for coming.

Unk approached Olga with a request to leave as soon as possible. It seemed he needed to stop by the SS headquarters to pick up supplies for the upcoming party. Olga rushed to say goodbye to her friends and followed in Unk's shadow.

The short trip to SS headquarters left no time for conversation with Unk, and she wondered what type of "supplies" he was referring to.

SS headquarters proved to as threatening as she might have imagined. Olga had never seen so many black-suited officers in one spot. Unk asked her to wait in the car while he went in. The parade of "Heil Hitler" salutes and methodical heel clicks became its own form of music with its own rhythms. It entertained her thoughts and enabled her to pass the short period of time in a more relaxed frame of mind.

Unk reappeared at the large, iron-hinged doors and proceeded toward the car followed by two soldiers whose arms were full of boxes. Unk opened the trunk, and the boxes were carefully placed inside. More soon filled the back seat.

"Are you surprised?" he laughed, seeing her wide eyes. "Dr. Brandt has been very generous."

"So I see," Olga responded. "What is in all these boxes?"

"I'm not sure. We'll see when you get home."

Just as the soldiers placed the last boxes in the car, Dr. Brandt appeared unexpectedly. Olga, a little surprised, greeted him cordially and thanked him in the same sentence. He almost blushed with pleasure and congratulated her on her concert performance earlier in the day.

Olga looked at him with a puzzled expression. *How did he know about her day?* she wondered. Dr. Brandt explained he had only stopped by for only a brief visit; she must not have seen him in the back of the hall. He had invited a few of her colleagues to the gathering on Sunday.

"What do you mean?" Olga questioned.

"Several of your friends are coming and plan to entertain us." Dr. Brandt explained. "I hope it meets with your approval."

Olga was both surprised and pleased. "Oh, I think it's wonderful! Will I be able to accompany them on the piano?" she questioned.

Dr. Brandt was quick to respond. "I was hoping you would volunteer, and I must say I am certainly looking forward to the evening."

Olga smiled; she couldn't help herself. She too was excited. "May I ask you a question?"

"By all means," he responded.

"How many guests will we have?" she questioned.

"I've arranged for about 20," he answered. "You certainly have the space for a party, and these boxes are full of wine and such. I've made arrangements for the food to be delivered on Sunday. All you'll have to do is place it on the table. Maybe your mamma could assist you. Is that a possibility?"

She quickly assured him all would be as it should be. Dr. Brandt turned to Unk, thanking him for taking care of things and being so solicitous of Olga. Once again, she pondered the relationship between the two men—so familiar, so casual—it seemed almost unnatural in these times.

Part Eighteen

Summer, winding down in colors of gold and reds with mild breezes struggling through the dropping leaves, made a perfect day. It was Friday. People were busy darting hither and thither, gathering what was needed for the weekend. Olga was eager as well. It was going to be a glorious weekend.

Kirsten and Sonja were busy in the courtyard when she arrived home. Kirsten, a typical toddler, squealed with delight when she spotted her mamma. She had become a wonderful child—full of joy. Sonja often commented on how happy she was, but always added that she expected no less from her only granddaughter. The child's little body bounced like a ball as she navigated the walkway toward her mother. Olga lifted her to her chest, and their light hair intertwined: perfect duplicates.

"Mamma," Olga said, "Dr. Brandt has asked me to invite you to the party on Sunday. Would you like to come?"

Sonja nodded assent. "Oh, it will be fun to get dressed up and meet your friends," she said. "What time shall I come?"

The three women and Unk joked and giggled like teenagers as they unloaded the plethora of boxes from the car and plotted the details of the party.

Elin's day had not been as pleasant. Unfortunately, his workload had increased. Young people were now giving blood, Norwegian blood, bags and bags of it, for the war effort. It insulted him beyond belief. He recognized several of the tattooed women, but a marked frailty had replaced the glow of health he had remembered in them. Unable to approach them, he just observed with concern.

SS security had increased again. It seemed to go in cycles. This time they were busy moving bags of blood to large steel carts and then to the back of the hall behind the frosted glass windows. The men in white lab coats had also multiplied, carefully supervising the operation. Elin couldn't help but wonder where all this blood was going—maybe to Berlin, he speculated.

The stress of constant activity was starting to take its toll on several of his colleagues. The doctors were tired, and their assistants were also showing signs of strain. Even the long walk the group made every day to the entrance was slower than usual.

Dr. Brandt joined the group today, and one by one, he invited the doctors to the gathering. "Elin, it's all arranged," he said. "We'll see you on Sunday. Heil Hitler."

Olaf and Dr. Keiser looked at Elin with puzzled expressions. He responded with his own silent gesture. He hadn't been able to tell either of the men about the move. He wondered how they would accept his new accommodations. Would they be judgmental or happy for him? All he could do was wait and see.

Sunday, soon upon them, had all the splendor of late summer weather. It was perfect: Flowers in pots were in glorious full-bloom and Elin himself was blossoming with smiles. Sonja's steps were lighter than usual as she fussed over the table arrangements, and Olga rushed around preparing the food that had just been delivered. Dr. Brandt had indeed supplied everything they needed. Preparations complete and the family together, they spent the rest of the afternoon in pleasant conversation, resting and enjoying the summer sun.

Promptly at five, Unk arrived to assist Olga. Dr. Brandt and three guests—none of whom were known to Elin or Olga—followed shortly after. Dr. Brandt looked especially happy and unusually handsome. He was dressed casually in a light-weight jacket and dress pants, a nice departure from his stark black uniform. Olga had never seen him without his uniform and was pleasantly surprised by his beautiful black hair. His dark eyes danced as he greeted her with a bouquet of fresh flowers. Olga blushed and invited them inside. "Elin," she called out, "please come to the foyer." Dr. Brandt extended his hand in friendship and introduced his guests. "This is Ivar, a lover of music and the Chairman of the Nazi Party in Oslo. And this is Arne, a central government official, and his lovely wife Ida. I'm sure Olga will find her pleasant company in the future.

The group entered the reception area and were introduced to Sonja and Unk.

"What a lovely home you have," commented Ida. "And is this your little daughter?"

Kirsten, who had been hiding behind her grandmamma, sheepishly stepped out and ran to her mother.

"Yes," Olga said. "This is our little love."

"You certainly couldn't deny her!" Ida laughed.

Unk, acting the part of a British butler, took control of the drinks. Sonja gathered up Kirsten and took her to bed. It wasn't long before the other guests arrived—all chauffeured in black, SS-plated Mercedes.

The musicians arrived, gathered in the lounge and set up stands near the piano. Olaf and Christina looked in astonishment at the beautiful furnishings, as did the other guests. It was terribly awkward for Elin. Dr. Brandt, sensing his discomfort, interrupted the scattered conversations to announce to the entire gathering that they too would have the same type of home as soon as places became available. To prove it, he pulled out a set of keys and handed them to Olaf. "You and your family, being such close friends with Elin and Olga, will be moving into the adjacent house. It is important to have quality companionship, especially for the children. Don't you agree?"

Olaf was speechless. Christina gasped, "You don't mean it!"

Dr. Brandt smiled. "As soon as you can pack, we'll be there to move you."

The envious mood of the group quickly changed, and the party began —first with cautious conversation and then with full-blown laughter. Dr. Brandt had succeeded. Hostility had subsided, replaced by cooperation and gratitude.

As the local Norwegian officials mingled with the guests, Elin tried to make plans with Olaf, but it was impossible. But now the need wasn't as pressing now. Olaf would be moving next door. They would be able to freely talk. They just had to figure out how to include Dr. Keiser. Drinks, laughter, food, and Olga on the piano, provided a perfect party.

Part Nineteen

As the sun rose on a bright Monday morning, Elin, still a little hung over from the night before, managed to climb aboard the bus. The mood felt different. There were more smiles and heads tipping in greeting.

With the Institute in sight, the driver pulled out a slip of paper and announced the following doctors: Dr. Keiser, Dr. Knorr, Dr. Svensson and Dr. Ashjorn were to remain seated. Heads turned quickly and inquiring eyes connected. The driver informed them that they were going to a different location. "This will be the most secure facility we've seen," he added. Olaf tried to question him further, but the young soldier simply told him he was just a driver and had no further information.

After what seemed like an eternity, the bus stopped at a guard station manned by several heavily armed soldiers. Promptly, they boarded and examined the papers of the group. Satisfied with what they had found, they shouted "Heil Hitler," and opened the iron gates.

The location was truly isolated. A narrow road twisted and turned for several miles behind thr gate through dense forest. After ascending a cluster of small mountains, they arrived at the entrance of what appeared

to be a cave-type opening. The men looked at each other with apprehension.

The driver instructed the men to wait. Several SS soldiers secured
the outside door of the bus, and the group waited. Unattended, the men
engaged in conversation.

"I've never heard of this place," Dr. Ashjorn stated.

"Nor have I," Olaf stuttered. "Where are we?"

The soldier soon returned, followed by a familiar silhouette. It was
Anna, the nurse from the Institute. She addressed the group with the
comment, "I told you we would meet again, didn't I? You're to come with
me. I'll try to explain this facility and the project you will be engaged in."

The heavily fortified entrance opened to a large, curved steel door.
Given its weight, several soldiers were required to open it. Again, eyes
met in disbelief. Once inside, the door was again closed and locked. Elin,
alarmed by the prospect that this place might be a prison, began to sweat.
As they walked deeper into the darkness of the structure, a cooler
atmosphere enveloped them. It was obvious they were now deep underground. But why? What were they hiding? No answers were immediately forthcoming. Anna remained silent as she led the group through
canopied tunnels into a pleasant, well-lit reception area.

The environment was sterile, but non-threatening. Tables and chairs
with empty cups attested to prior attendance. "Have a seat," Anna
instructed. "Help yourselves to coffee or tea. I'll be back shortly." And
with that, she left the group.

Dr. Keiser, speaking softly, said he had heard of such facilities while
in Berlin. He couldn't explain the purpose, but suspected that they were
built underground to be safe from bombing. "It must be important for
them with all this security." he continued.

Elin reminded the men to pay attention and to mentally record everything they heard and saw. "We must remember and share information,"
he pleaded.

Anna reappeared after a few minutes and brought Dr. Brandt
with her.

"This facility is under my jurisdiction, as you probably guessed," he began. "You have been selected to participate in this most important project. It is part of the lifeblood of Germany, and we must succeed in our efforts. The only other facility like this is in Berlin, headed by Hitler's inner-most circle. They are expecting us to help hasten the results of their project. Now, Anna will explain what your duties will be."

Anna stepped forward, secure in her position and knowledge. She presented the strict requirements: "You will remain on the bus every day after the stop at the Institute. You will then be picked up first to return home, stopping only to gather personnel at the Institute. And lastly, under the penalty of death, you must not reveal, discuss, or insinuate anything that might jeopardize this project. Understood?"

The men looked at each other and nodded in agreement. Continuing the instructions, she informed the group, "you will start at entry level and then move to higher levels. You will be given more knowledge after you have proven that you can serve the project with the excellence required. You cannot question the present personnel or wander through this containment area without permission. I think you know the danger in disobedience. So, if you would, keep your curiosity to yourselves. Follow me, please."

Side by side, the four men lined up and, like puppies, followed her into another tunneled corridor. "Your first assignment will be in the nursery," she said over her shoulder.

"Nursery?" Elin repeated.

"Yes," she reiterated. "Come along."

The corridor with a connection of doors ended in an artificially lit and extremely sterile room, smelling like nothing Elin had ever smelled before. "This is the annex," she proclaimed. "You must step into a cubicle, remove all of your clothing, and put on the garments hanging inside, including the face masks and gloves." Motioning them to begin, she sat down on a long metal bench to wait.

When the men were returned to the annex, Anna had been joined by an extremely tall man clad in a white uniform, his face totally protected behind a conical helmet with narrow slits. The only visible body parts were his piercing, intimidating, blue eyes. Anna introduced him as "Big Max," overseer of the nursery.

Dr. Brandt returned to explain the procedures, informing them that neither he nor Anna would be able to accompany them to the restricted area. "So, listen closely," he demanded. "Max is not a doctor, but he is aware of what is needed for this portion of the project. I suggest you not upset him. He will not engage in conversation with you nor interfere with your duties unless he is convinced that you're not performing to his satisfaction. He will then report you to the authorities and they will take the appropriate measures. There are other doctors and nurses on staff that will assist you if needed. Now, go meet the charge doctor. Heil Hitler."

Max did not respond to the gesture nor speak. He walked toward the security doors, turning only once to see if they were all following. Just inside the doors, Max held up his hand in a halt position, then walked away. The men stood close together, frozen in amazement. Eyes danced in all directions. The room was massive, partially in dim light while other spaces were lit in extreme brightness. The domed ceiling moved with color: blues, greens and yellows all produced a calming effect. Several white clad personnel paid no attention to the arriving strangers and continued to administer assistance to the rows and rows of small metal boxes with strange cages covering them.

Elin was at a loss to understand what he was seeing. Troubling questions flooded his mind. Several minutes passed before a small white clad figure approached them.

"Heil Hitler," a muffled voice called out from behind the mask. "Welcome. No introduction is necessary. I'm Elisa from the Institute; remember me?" she chuckled. "You must be very proud to have been chosen to participate in this most advanced project. This facility and one in Berlin are the only locations and both are extremely well guarded secrets. But I think you already know that."

None of the men spoke. She had their full attention.

"I'm to be a liaison between you and Dr. Brandt. So, if there is a problem, let me know. Come, meet the charge doctor and receive your instructions."

Elin took mental notes as they followed her around the perimeter. There appeared to be some type of offices followed by double doors into a room that looked like a surgical facility. Across the back were frosted-glass-windowed rooms that were similar to the Institute's. The space appeared to be extremely large, with the frosted-glass curving against the contour of the ceiling. To the left of the entrance was a lounge: comfortable, but as sterile as everything else. Several personnel were sitting there and appeared to be engaged in conversation. *Good*, Elin thought, *maybe it'll be less restrictive here.*

On the other side of the lounge was a room with full-length glass walls. It had the only color in the entire space. Upholstered chairs hugged the walls, and small service tables were placed near each seat. It was a strange configuration of rooms for a medical facility. The equipment was also strange, what little there was. He also marveled at the metal boxes with cage tops that so many of the personnel were busy with—opening and closing. *What could these be*, he wondered? *Could this be the nursery? Where are the children? Are these boxes coffins?* His mind raced, trying to bring some rational explanation to this bizarre experience. Elisa knocked lightly on one of the office doors, and they entered.

A tall, slender woman stood and acknowledged them. She was beautiful, a picture of perfection, and spoke with an unfamiliar accent. Elin couldn't help but stare at her. She somehow seemed familiar. No "Heil Hitlers" preceded her introduction.

"I'm Dr Niniva. Welcome to Angel Hair."

Dr. Keiser gasped and turned to face the other men. "Is there a problem?" Dr. Niniva inquired.

"No," Dr. Keiser replied. "I heard about this project while in Berlin."

She interrupted, "Now you all are a part of it. I look forward to working with you and your colleagues. Now, for your orientation." She motioned for the men to followed her to the boxes. Elin was eager to see what was inside and moved as close as possible. Elisa opened the hinged top and let it slide back. There it was: one tiny infant wired to a mechanical device that appeared to help the little one breathe.

"Is this really the nursery?" Olaf questioned.

"Yes, just one of many," Dr. Niniva replied. "Now back to your instructions. These infants are in incubation and need constant monitoring. These gauges will let you know of any stress the infant is experiencing. You four will replace four other doctors that will move with their crop to the next level."

Elin ventured another question about the age of the child in front of them. Elisa removed a calendar disk from the cage top and explained the infant was exactly five months term. Confusion masked his face. How is this possible? What kind of technology would allow this? In all his medical experiences, he had never heard of such a thing. A thousand questions interrupted his thoughts, but he chose silence.

Dr. Niniva, experienced with newcomers, commented, "You will be taught many new techniques, but for now Elisa will advise you regarding your training and immediate duties. This will be brief and exciting, an opportunity to discard old ideas and embrace new ones. Thank you for your commitment; we'll meet again." She walked back into her office and closed the door.

Elisa looked at her watch and acknowledged that it had been a long day. "Let's go," she ordered, and the men followed her back to the nursery entrance.

Anna was waiting for them in the annex. She complimented the men on how well they reacted to their new environment and asked that they remove the white suits so they could be sterilized for tomorrow. The men quickly dressed and headed toward the bus, eager for the opportunity to possibly discuss their day privately. But unfortunately, Dr. Brandt was waiting, sitting in the front seat as the men entered the bus.

"I must talk to you," he said when the men had taken their seats. "As a doctor myself, I know you must have questions. Just let me share this with you. If you want to talk among yourselves about this project, you have my permission. But if any of this leaks out, you will suffer the consequences. I am just an administrator with a medical background. I am not privileged to the entire scope of this project. I only know it is a thing of national security for Germany and is now under the guidance of Hitler's inner circle. In time, you will learn more. But now, for your own protection, let things unfold in a managed order. Now for a few questions."

Dr. Keiser was the first, asking if all of the boxes contained infants.

"Yes," Dr. Brandt answered. "These infants are all under-developed and your job will be to administer to them until they can function on their own—as they would at the completion of any full-term pregnancy—at which time they will be removed, and a new crop will replace them.

Elin asked about feeding them.

"Again," Dr. Brandt explained, "the machines automatically dispense food at regular intervals as well as vitamins and other nutrients. We have been working on this project for quite a while," he continued, "and it is quite well perfected. I must leave you now. Heil Hitler!" he shouted.

"Oh my God," Elin whispered. "Did you hear him? We're free to discuss this project." The four drew together into a tight group and speculated about the scope of the project until they arrived at the Institute to pick up other waiting personnel. The rest of the journey home, they were like deaf mutes.

Part Twenty

Olga greeted Elin with the most wonderful kiss. She was still on a high from the night before. She handed him a glass of leftover wine from the party, and they sat down. She was so happy, Kirsten was happy—he hadn't seen them like this for some time. He couldn't help himself; the contagious laughter of little Kirsten climbing on his knee seduced him into putting the wonders of the day behind him and engaging in pleasant conversation. He asked Olga about her day.

"Oh, Elin, it was just unbelievable. Christina and the children came over to see the adjoining house. We drank and ate leftovers all day. It was like old times, sharing stories and watching the children in the garden. They will be moving in just days. The house is very nice and comfortable, but no piano," she grinned. "I guess I lucked out there. Oh, do you remember Ida, the official's wife? She came by and invited me and mother to a meeting. They're trying to get a committee together to repair the gardens in the park. Isn't that wonderful?"

Elin was still worried about all the attention Olga was getting. He wanted to remind her again about the danger of associating with the Nazis, but not tonight. He just wanted to enjoy the moment.

"Olga," he inquired, "What do you know about your special companion, Unk? He doesn't appear to be German or Norwegian. Where does he come from?"

"Isn't he wonderful?" she interrupted. "He's just a lovely old man. Actually, I don't know much about him other than that he has a strange relationship with Dr. Brandt. They're very friendly, use no formalities, and Dr. Brandt seems to depend on him for a multitude of things, yet he seems to be always there for me—almost like a personal assistant."

Elin must have had an unusual expression on his face. Olga laughed. "I'll try to engage him in more conversation and let you know. Are you jealous?" she teased.

"Not at all," he continued. "I'm glad you have someone to protect you when I'm gone. Keeps you out of trouble." Not wanting to concern her, he laughed and finished his drink. "More wine!" he called out. They spent the evening snuggled on the sofa until Kirsten fell asleep.

Part Twenty-one

The war elsewhere in Europe was raging. Rumors of Allied defeats by Germany filled the propaganda media. Elin questioned how much of the information was really true. He had heard the opposite, even that Berlin had been attacked. Could this be possible? Monday morning came quickly, and he was excited. Today was the first day of his new assignment.

The excitement didn't last. After they boarded the bus, it was announced that Dr. Ashcrof had passed away from a massive heart attack. Elin's heart sank; silence was the respectful manner observed by his colleagues. Everyone seemed to be in shock. Dr. Ashcrof had appeared to be quite well the last time they were together. Could there be a more sinister explanation?

Regardless of the cause, Elin was saddened. His colleagues were also saddened, and the team had suffered an important loss. Dr. Ashcrof had been a brilliant person with a comforting soft side to his personality. His smiles of encouragement would be missed.

Dr. Brandt greeted the group before entering the facility with his condolences. He also informed them that Dr. Ashcrof would not be replaced on the team. He then encouraged them to forge ahead with the knowledge that Dr. Ashcrof would have wanted it that way. The men resented the pep talk, knowing that Dr. Ashcrof would not have wanted any of these insane, secret medical procedures performed on any person or animal. He was a man of faith, devoting his life to healing and helping others—what an insult.

Elisa, waiting outside the entrance of the nursery, also acknowledged Dr. Ashcroft's death, then asked the men to follow her. She explained that they would not be working in the nursery today, but instead would have an up close and personal experience. The men were escorted into an area that they suspected was a medical facility. There were several tables, eight to be exact, equipped with various medical instruments which were placed in large circles. In the center was a small, raised platform with a circular podium. It was strange—not quite like anything they had seen or read about. In several ways, it vaguely resembled a lab class in college.

Elisa directed the three men to separate tables. As the team accessed the three nearest tables, the door opened and several other people entered and placed themselves at the remaining tables, including a man at the center platform. The eight were then joined by eight others. Everyone was dressed in sterile white uniforms with masks, except for the man in the center cubicle. He was in a silver, one-piece, jumpsuit-type garment. His outfit included a mask that covered only half of his face. "Welcome. I am your director," he said in a voice that displayed the same accent Elin had heard from Dr. Niniva. He also was tall with blond hair and piercing blue eyes. As the director stood observing the group, the platform slowly revolved, providing a full view of all the white clad attendees. Elin also observantly noticed various height differences among the group. He couldn't see faces but guessed there were several females among them. No one spoke, so individual identities were not observable. As the platform slowed to a stop, the director spoke again. "Today we have several new doctors in attendance. This will be a training exercise. Will the assistants please accompany each of the eight new doctors?"

Quickly, the assistants stepped next to the awaiting doctors. Elin became anxious as he examined the small, white-clad figure standing extremely close to him. He didn't like surprises. *What is the training session?* he wondered. Dr. Inku then instructed the assistants to bring in the patients.

"Patients?" Elin questioned. *I thought this was supposed to be a text-book training, not with actual patients.* He hadn't prepared himself for this nor had he prepared himself for what was coming toward him: a young woman was being assisted onto his table. She had no expression: zombie-like in appearance, obviously drugged but functional.

Immediately, weird things started to happen. The table contorted into a folded configuration and a strange glass container emerged from underneath. Strands of cables with a mask and instruments dropped from the ceiling. He stepped back in surprise as did several other doctors. Dr. Inku assured the men that everything was normal. He lifted his arms and explained that he was controlling the procedure from the platform. He then continued, "You were told things would not be familiar. That's why you're here to learn. The technology is advanced, but basic for Project Angel Hair. This is one of the basic steps, and by far, the most important. So please relax and learn." Assistants readied the patients and Elin could only observe in awe. The young women, like the ones he examined earlier, were fair complexioned, blonde haired and blue eyed. Dr. Inku asked the doctors to carefully observe.

First, masks were placed over the mouths of the women. Their legs were elevated, spread and clamped in place, as the glass containers were raised to meet the lower portion of the torsos. Elin, watching intently, noticed his patient was stressing. Her eyelids fluttered and her chest quivered with uncontrolled twitches. The assistant, obviously trained to respond, noticed as well and without hesitation administered an injection into the semi-conscious patient before returning to the task.

Elin moved closer to observe the glass container. It was the size of a dinner plate with two sections. The top section had holes and covered the lower section, which was probably no more than 8-10 inches thick. Attached to the center top cover was a long, flexible tube with a strange attachment. Elin couldn't imagine what it was. Before his thoughts could dissipate, the assistant placed the tube into the vagina of the young woman, and with suction in the hose, removed bloody fluids. *Oh, dear God*, he thought, as he stepped back in shock. *What is this?* He couldn't take his eyes off it. Large blood clots and other visceral material rested in the upper glass container as screened fluids filtered through the holes into the lower section. Immediately, the assistant removed the entire container and disappeared through the side doors. He was totally confused. What had just happened? Dr. Inku raised his arms to manipulate the controls and a new glass container appeared along with another hose. The assistant returned and proceeded to flush out the woman's vaginal cavity with what appeared to be some sort of solution. The assistant then stepped back as the table flattened out and the dangling instruments disappeared into the ceiling. Dr. Inku stood and announced, "Congratulations doctors, you have just experienced an extraction. Next time, you will be responsible for the procedure. Assistants, prepare to remove the patients." As Elin stood silently watching the automatic release of the clamps and masks, his heart skipped a beat. On the inner thigh of his patient was the familiar AH tattoo.

After witnessing several more extractions, the day's work was finally finished. The bus ride back to town proved to be quite interesting. The bus was literally buzzing like a beehive, each doctor talking at once. The stress and confusion had been overwhelming. They vented their pent-up energy as they talked or rather gibbered at each other until Dr. Keiser insisted that they stop.

"I can't hear anything! Calm down. Let's try to figure this out rationally. Okay, Elin, what is your theory?"

"Well," he replied, "It almost seemed like an abortion, but with all that strange technology, it is more complicated. An abortion could be done much more simply. Oh, by the way, did any of you notice a tattoo on the inner thigh of your patient?"

"Yes, yes," Olaf interrupted. It was like the one I saw when we first started at the Institute. And I agree with you about the abortion. What is also interesting is the careful collection of all the fluids. Did you study the containers? They were totally sealed and marked with a strange geometric symbol and number. I just don't know. Tomorrow we'll have to perform the same procedures. Maybe we'll learn more. Keep your ears and eyes open."

Elin focused on Dr. Keiser, "Tell me, Dr. Keiser, what do you think?"

"Well," he answered, "I have heard of similar experiments being conducted in Berlin. I think it has to do with eugenics. Maybe these specimens are going to Berlin. After all, look at the patients: typical of Hitler's dream race." Suddenly the bus stopped, and the men were jolted back to reality. They were at the Institute, ready to pick up the rest of the passengers and return home.

Part Twenty-two

The bus was nearly empty when Olaf looked back, making eye contact with Elin. He had an unusual smile on his face. Elin gestured with his hand as if to say, 'why the smile?' Olaf responded with a nod. The bus rushed past Olaf's stop. Elin suspected he would be getting off with him. He was right. The two men disembarked into a mass of human bodies—big ones and little ones alike, jumping, hugging, and kissing. Their families. There was so much happiness. The trials of the day were momentarily obliterated and replaced with the joy of Olaf's new home. After a tour of the new home and a light dinner, the two families parted ways, settling in for the night. Elin was relieved to have Olaf and his family near him and Olga. In these uncertain and dangerous times, families needed support.

Fall was moving in gracefully with a slight chill in the air. Elin threw a few small logs on the fire, and he and Olga settled in for a quiet evening together.

"How are things going for you?" she inquired.

He paused, knowing he couldn't really talk about his work, and told her about Dr. Ashcrof.

"Oh no," she gasped. "Is there to be a funeral? What about his family? We must visit them."

Elin's saddened voice replied, "The family has returned to Bergen, and he will be buried there. So, it seems we'll just have memories, no final farewells."

Olga, now in tears, sobbed "It's just so sad for all of us."

Elin held her close for a few minutes. Then he changed the topic. "How is your friend, Unk? I haven't heard you talk about him lately."

"I'll see him tomorrow," she said. "The orchestra is giving a performance. Mamma has been invited to attend too. I think it's for some sort of reconstruction group. You know—keep us busy with civilian duties—less time for war worries. Christina has offered to watch Kirsten. I love that she is here. We can help each other a lot. My love, may I ask you a question?"

"Yes, of course," he replied. "What is it?"

"Do you think we're safe? Do I need to worry about being social with the wives of the Nazis?" Elin tried to convey a brave exterior, but inside he knew the answer. "Remember what I said, trust no one; they all have agendas, wives and husbands alike. Some of the wives are actually spies; please remember that. Now, about the question of being safe. I think that as long as we're useful, we're safe. I see no reason to worry; just try to relax and enjoy the privileges we've been awarded. I'll let you know when to worry."

Olga was up early the next morning, busy with domestic chores when Elin left for work. The day was hers, and she looked forward to it. Confident and relaxed since he had assured her that they were indeed safe, she dressed for her outing.

A firm knock at her door echoed down the long hallway and she sprang to answer the door, anticipating Unk. It was not Unk, and the large silhouette startled her. "Good morning," a deep voice called out.

It was Dr. Brandt. "Unk is away on business and asked that I escort you to the concert. Are you ready?" he questioned

"Yes," she stammered. "Let me get Christina."

"Wait," he said, "I have a gift of cakes for Kirsten and the other children." Eagerly, he handed her a little brown bag tied with yarn. "Made these myself," he laughed.

Olga smiled, easing the tension between the two. "They'll love these," she replied, "thank you. I'll be right back." With that, she slipped outside and next door to Christina's house.

A soft knock ensued, and Christina followed her back home. "Good morning, Dr. Brandt," Christina called out in a soft, respectful voice. "We love our new home. Thank you for everything."

"You're welcome," he replied. "Olga, we must go. I have other responsibilities this morning."

"Yes, of course," she responded, and rushed to the waiting car.

"Lovely lady, that Christina," Dr. Brandt commented. "I'm so happy you have a friend close by. Olga, does it bother you that Elin works so much and you're alone most of the time? I guess I'm asking if you get lonely."

Oh my, she thought. *Better think about this answer carefully. Trust no one.* "Why, Dr. Brandt," she smiled in a girlish way, "How could I get lonely? I have an active child, good friends, and my music. I know my husband has to be gone a lot and has many responsibilities. I accept that part of our life, and I try not to burden him. He has told me his work is top-secret and I shouldn't inquire as to the nature of it. I respect his request and I make our family life the focus when he comes home at night. It appears to be a good compromise."

Dr. Brandt listened, then said, "Good; very good."

As Olga arrived, several women dressed in fall hats were gathering for the concert. "Oh, there's mamma!" she cheerfully exclaimed. The car stopped and Dr. Brandt said Unk would be back to take them home. She thanked him again and rushed to the side of Sonja. Dr. Brandt watched for a moment as the two women embraced. From a distance, they looked more like friends, not mamma and daughter. Olga, fair and blonde, Sonja dark and small. *Strange resemblance*, he thought.

The large vacuous room, set with tables and chairs had the energy of a prison, cold and unfriendly. But as women flocked to be seated, the atmosphere changed to friendly chatter. Colorful hats of all description lightened the room like a bouquet of exotic flowers. A light refreshment was served, and the meeting was called by none other than Olga's former party guest, Arne. "Welcome, friends of Norway and Germany. I am Arne, one of the new central government officials. I stopped by today to introduce my wife, Ida. She is the new cultural liaison between Norway and Germany. She will fill you in on the purpose of this gathering. So please enjoy yourselves and the wonderful orchestra that will entertain us later. Enjoy your morning, ladies. And now, Ida."

Sonja nudged Olga, "Wasn't she at your party?"

"Yes." Olga whispered. "She also told me later that they were forming committees to help improve conditions around Oslo. This must be what she was talking about."

Sonja quickly responded with a frown. "Olga, we are Norwegians; we hate Germans. We can't be seen working or assisting them in any civil activities. Do you want to be ostracized by our own countrymen?"

Olga was speechless. She hadn't given much thought to the appearance of cooperation let alone collaboration with the Germans. "Oh mamma," she whispered. "What shall we do?"

"We'll just listen and try to keep a low profile. Don't volunteer for anything unless it's forced on you—understand?" Olga nodded just as Ida began her speech.

"Good morning, ladies. I suppose you're wondering what it means to be a cultural liaison. Let me explain. Norway and Germany are neighbors, but our cultures are distinctly different. I have been asked by the new government to help assimilate those cultures and ease tensions between the Germans and Norwegians here in Oslo. Everyone here today is Norwegian but living in an occupied country. Try as we may, we cannot change that. My hope is to bring some normalcy back to our city, and I need your help. You have been chosen because people recognize your families and respect them. I know some will call you traitors, but in the larger scheme of things, Oslo and Norway will be in a far better place.

Our hope is to improve the situation in Oslo, beginning with better access to food and supplies. In other words, a more comfortable existence. This can only be done if the two cultures learn to live together amicably. Some of the things that have been talked about are: improving the condition of our parks, making it safe for families with children to walk and play, Sunday afternoon concerts in summer, and ice-skating rinks in the winter. These are things we can accomplish with the help of the Germans. This is not to be a forced agenda, but a voluntary one. Please, after the concert, sign up for a committee. Thank you, ladies. Now, Thor Niessen, conductor of the Oslo Orchestra, has requested that you all be seated."

Olga and several other orchestra members in the audience stood and proceeded to the platform. Everyone seemed excited, and the enthusiasm lightened her steps. Time seemed to disappear as she lost her worrisome thoughts in the hypnotic rhythms of the orchestra. After what seemed like mere minutes, it was over. Women stood with smiles and enthusiastic applause as she took a small bow and entered the crowd searching for Sonja. Arm-in-arm, they negotiated around the group of women signing up for committees and exited to the street.

A group of angry people were standing outside, speaking under their breath in disgust as the women exited. For the first time, Olga felt intimidated, not by the Nazis, but by her own people. "Come mamma," she insisted. "Unk will take you home. I don't want you on the bus now. I don't think it's safe."

Sonja agreed, and they entered the ominous black car under the glaring eyes of the onlookers. Unk noticed the uneasiness of his passengers and asked about the problem. He then reassured the women things would calm down and, as long as he was there, they would be safe. He also advised them not to take sides even though they were loyal Norwegians.

"Just try and keep neutral for the sake of your family and friends. You are in a precarious position—you have something the Germans want, and you are an asset to the Norwegian people. It's a fine line you must walk.

Please, be careful," Unk pleaded. "You know," he continued, "I think it would help if I drove a car that wasn't black or German-made. People associate black cars with Germans. So next time I'll drive something else. Would that help ease your fears?"

"Oh," Sonja signed, "that would be wonderful, Unk. Thank you for your kindness."

Part Twenty-three

There was an unusual number of soldiers on the bus in the morning, and Elin could hear them chattering about the war. He deliberately focused his attention on the garbled sounds and was able to surmise that things were not going as planned. They talked of air raids by the Americans and British, as well as Jews wearing yellow stars that were being gathered up and deported. How Elin yearned for information delivered by his own government's news programs. Almost all radios had been confiscated, and newspapers were now all German propaganda. How could he know the truth?

The soldiers disembarked, and Elin moved back near his colleagues. "Were you able to hear news of the war? he questioned.

Olaf replied. "The men sitting near me had no problem speculating on the situation. I heard one of them talking about the resistance and the sabotaging of the Vemork hydro-plant. He also said the resistance had paid dearly for its foolish patriotism. Apparently, the Nazis have attacked Telavage as a reprisal for the continued resistance."

The men looked at each other in surprise—why hadn't they heard these things? Had they been deliberately isolated and protected from the truth? How could they have forgotten about the war and the brave people on the front lines of resistance? Guilt filled Elin's heart. Had he been so consumed with his own problems that he hadn't considered the sacrifices of his own countrymen?

Dr. Keiser whispered, "Listen, I didn't want to tell you, but I have a contact from the homeland who says things are very strange in Germany and throughout the occupied countries. He said there are rumors of thousands of people disappearing, almost daily, some on trains and others unknown. The term he used was the "unfits." He warned me that Hitler's inner circle has spies everywhere, and that I must be extremely careful. My friend has risked his life telling me these things, but he feels safe enough with his position in the SS that it should shield him from suspicion. He is like us: forced into service. I'll let you know more as I receive news. He also has someone keeping watch on my family in Germany and informs me of their well-being. I trust him like my own brother, but it's best if he doesn't know about you and vice versa. Please, for our sake, keep this information to yourselves and be on guard."

The men were now on edge as the bus wound its way through the forest. A feeling of concern replaced the anxiety of a new experience awaiting them.

Anna was waiting with a welcoming smile as the men entered the facility. "Good morning," she said in an almost musical voice. "I hear good things about you," she continued. "Dr. Brandt is most pleased with your cooperation and your willingness to experience new things."

No one responded as they quietly followed Anna to the nursery.

"For the next few weeks, you'll continue with techniques that you were taught yesterday and then we'll see what new adventures they'll present to you." She politely said her goodbyes and Elisa escorted them back to the medical site. Dr. Indu was waiting at the podium. Everyone else was in place except the three late arrivals. "Please begin," he ordered.

Elin and his colleagues looked around; where were the assistants? Dr. Indu quickly informed the three bewildered physicians that there would be no assistants today. They were to be totally responsible for the experiment themselves. "Now, follow the others and learn." Immediately, the men joined their colleagues and route to obtain their patients from nearby rooms. On the first attempt, the procedure proved to be awkward, and Dr. Indu on several occasions had to assist Elin and his colleagues with the instruments. But after a few failures, they met with success. The process became routine and efficient: in and out in just a few minutes. So many young women passed through the doors that count was eventually lost.

The day was almost over, and Elin secured his last patient, taking extra time to observe the surroundings. The patient's waiting room, previously full of semi-conscious women, had been emptied. Many of the women were now lying on tables. Assistants were busy dressing and attending to the needs of several that appeared ill. *Where were they taking these women*, he wondered, as he escorted his last extraction from the table.

Elin and his colleagues disrobed and headed toward the bus, escorted by Anna, as always. "Nice job today," she commented. "See you tomorrow."

Again, the men clustered on the bus hoping for insight into the bizarre happenings of the day. "What do you think?" quizzed Olaf. "Any ideas about what's going on?"

Dr. Keiser leaned into the group and speculated that it had to be part of the Berlin project. He was sure the material collected at the facility was being sent to Germany. "Did you notice," he continued, "the air strip running along the side of the road, beyond the trees? The only reason I know is because I briefly spotted a small plane landing this morning. I think they're possibly air-lifting personnel and specimens."

"Very interesting," Elin commented. "I totally missed the plane. I'll watch tomorrow. Maybe it's routine or scheduled. What I'm curious about the most is what the specimens are used for. They seem very protective of them. I was only permitted to hand the glass containers to a person standing outside the door to that annex. Did either of you get to see inside?" Both men nodded no. "I would love to know what's inside," lamented Elin.

"I'm sure in time we'll be told." Olaf interjected.

The bus suddenly stopped, and Dr. Keiser was thrown to the floor. "What now?" the driver called out as soldiers pounded on the doors.

"Heil Hitler!" they called out. Several entered the bus and began to search the empty rows, coming closer to the men clustered about two thirds of the way back. "Heil Hitler!" shouted a young SS officer. "Papers, please," he demanded.

Elin and the other quickly responded. The surly officer seriously examined each document, looking directly into the eyes of his detainees. "Where have you been?" he demanded. "What are you doing on this bus?" The three froze, not knowing how to answer. They made eye contact with each other searching for answers, but none came. As the young officer became more intimidating, a strong, deep voice commanded him to step aside. It was Dr. Brandt. The officer snapped his heels, raised his arm, and retreated. "Sorry," Dr. Brandt said. "The Institute has been attacked and the military is nervous. The resistance set off a bomb in the back, killing two guards. We had to increase security. We had also forgotten about the bus coming until someone expressed concern about the late arrival. I had a blockade in place; that's why you were stopped. We can't afford to be careless. No harm done—try to relax and enjoy the rest of the evening."

The men silently waited as the bus filled with personnel and a number of soldiers heading back to town. As it had been in the morning, the scene repeated itself, chatter everywhere. Elin was happy to finally arrive home, escaping the constant noise of German soldiers.

Part Twenty-four

Olga greeted her husband with loving arms, and little Kirsten, hungry for attention, clung to his leg. All was good. He was in his safe space. A crisp, fall wind softly blew into the open windows of the dining room as the couple finished dinner. Elin needed a reprieve from the constant mental strain and insisted they take a walk with Kirsten.

"Oh, please let's visit mamma?" Olga pleaded.

"Good idea," he responded, and the couple ventured onto the street. Arm-in-arm, they teased and laughed with each other, just as they had done in their younger days.

"Feels good," Olga sighed, "good to be together as a family, good to be alive and healthy. I'm so thankful, even if things are as they are. We're still together. I know many are suffering and I pray for them. I pray for the war to be over and for you to be strong. I love you so much. Stay strong."

Elin, touched by her loving comment, squeezed her arm and kissed her lightly on the cheek.

German patrols were visible everywhere, and Olga inquired about the reason. "Has something happened?" she quizzed.

He told her the resistance had been actively bombing sites and that the Germans had increased security in the area. He didn't tell her about the bombing at the Institute for fear she would worry while he was away. Then she shared with him how people were treating the women that gathered for meetings or lunch. How the glares and stares of their countrymen was so intimidating. "It has gotten so bad that Unk has agreed to drive a car that is neither German nor black so it won't draw attention to us. What should I do, Elin? I need to be able to go to rehearsals with the orchestra and other things expected of me. Tell me what I should do. Unk says to try and be neutral, keep a low profile and be cautious. Do you agree?"

"I do agree," he answered. "Your Unk seems to be a wise and protective. I'm sure he'll advise you correctly, but as I always say, trust no one."

Sonja's house appeared a few blocks away, and Kirsten reacted with a young child's gibberish. Elin sprinted with the carriage, and Kirsten laughed with such pleasure that he and Olga became intoxicated with their own laughter, the type of laughter that releases months of pent-up emotions. Feeling good, he vigorously knocked on Sonja's door.

Sonja was shocked to see her family standing there, laughing and teasing with Kirsten. "What is it?" she questioned. "What is going on? Come in and tell me."

The young couple, still on a high, hugged and cuddled Sonja until she begged for air. The mood was contagious, and Sonja became infected, prancing around with Kirsten and singing old Norwegian folk songs. Kirsten was delighted. Elin apologized for his long absence and inquired "How are things going for you?"

Sonja paused, "Well, I guess I've become a bit paranoid. It feels like someone's watching me, not all the time, but often. Do you think it's the SS?" she quizzed.

"Oh mamma," Olga sighed. "Why on earth would the SS spy on you? It must be your imagination."

"Well," she continued, "the neighbors have made comments and often ask about Unk and the special attention I seem to be enjoying. I don't know how to address the problem. They seem angry about it."

"Mamma, calm yourself. Remember, we didn't have a choice. Maybe this is protection for you as it is for us. I'm sure no harm will come to you. Now let's enjoy our little reunion. Things will be just fine." Sonja relaxed after Olga's comments and the three settled in for a cozy evening.

Part Twenty-five

The next month again became routine. Elin and his colleagues grew increasingly restless. The only excitement was an occasional word from Dr. Keiser's contact. Olga's life also settled into a habitual schedule. She and Sonja busied themselves with activities that didn't expose them to the watching eyes of the Germans or their neighbors. They volunteered to make bandages for the war and quietly lunched with ladies of the cultural society. Even Unk, with his now non-conspicuous car, seemed to have been absorbed into local culture.

The winter holidays were quickly approaching, and the Cultural Society had been put on notice. They would be responsible for entertaining the local government officials and visiting SS officers. It was hard for Olga to imagine enjoying the holidays with so many struggling just to survive. Food and supplies were becoming harder to get, just the opposite of what had been promised. News that the German populace was also experiencing shortages and newly felt hardships quickly spread through the Norwegian population, giving people hope that the war might sometime soon come to an end.

Unk arrived early to pick up Olga for the Tuesday morning rehearsal. It was just before Christmas, and the orchestra was practicing almost daily for a glorious event honoring the visiting German dignitaries and fellow Norwegians. The Cultural Society also had been busy extending invitations to important guests and securing increasingly hard-to-get wine and food. The Germans made it perfectly clear that the image was to be of a successful integration of two cultures. They were determined to keep the propaganda machine working to aid the occupation and squelch the resistance's reports of success.

"Here, this invitation is a security-clearance for the family," Unk announced. "Of course, you both were already cleared, but Sonja was not." He smiled, then handed Olga a stack of packages. "These are for your family." Olga stepped back in surprise. "Unk, where did you get these gifts? I can't accept them. It's not right with so many sufferings."

"Please, Olga," he pleaded. "Let me have a little pleasure. I'm an old man and I need to share these with you and your family. We've been together for several years and I love you like my own child. So please, humor me and accept this small token of my affection."

Olga softly kissed him on the cheek and placed the gifts under the tiny sparsely decorated tree near the fireplace.

Part Twenty-six

Even in inclement weather, the old bus lumbered up the street on schedule to take the men to work. Olaf and Elin had briefly speculated about the events of the day, then plunged head first into the mass of passengers already inside. Today, there were no soldiers to enlighten them, and the still-intimidated personnel from the Institute retained their code of silence throughout the brief ride. Elin was happy to see them exit and moved back to join his colleagues, Olaf and Dr. Keiser. At last, they were free to converse openly about their work.

Anna, usually at the Institute door, was not waiting for the men. Instead, Dr. Brandt stepped forward and asked the men to follow him into a private office. Elin, not thrilled with surprises, stepped behind Dr. Keiser and Olaf as they entered the room. Immediately, three black-clad figures stood, clicked heels, and saluted Dr. Brandt. "Sit down, comrades," he commanded, and all of the men seated themselves. Elin, now increasingly worried, wondered what the SS were up to. Were they here to eliminate him and his colleagues? *Why else*, he wondered, *would they come here?*

He must have appeared nervous, because Dr. Brandt looked at him and the other men and assured them things were in order and not to worry. "These men are here from Berlin to inspect this facility and increase your involvement in new experiments."

Elin felt a hard-lump form in his throat. Two words throbbed like a drum in his head: *increase, and experiment, what does that mean? Oh, dear God, how much more? What are they doing? We don't understand the procedures we've already participated in. Now we're to be involved in more accelerated and newer experiments. I just can't imagine the purpose of these programs.*

Elin's thoughts were suddenly interrupted when Dr. Niniva entered the room. Dr. Brandt introduced her to the three officers and asked if it would be possible for Elin and his colleagues to tour the facility with them. "Are you sure?" she questioned. "Are they ready to see the scope of this project?"

"I've been ordered to accommodate their exposure." he insisted. "The orders came from the highest authority. I'll take personal responsibility for their briefing."

Dr. Niniva glanced over at the awaiting SS officers and questioned whether they had been here before. The three, arrogantly confident in their authority, assured the doctor that they had been here on numerous occasions and were here now to see that everything was in order.

"They understand that you're new here," Dr. Brandt politely interrupted, "and they look forward to working with you and your staff, Dr. Niniva. Now please, colleagues, follow me to the lounge," Dr. Brandt insisted, "I'll brief you on our visitors and the projects here at the facility."

Dr. Keiser ventured the first question. "Who are these men? Are they medical doctors?"

"No, not exactly," Dr. Brandt replied. "They are scientists and medical specialists in research, mostly involved in eugenics and biochemistry. As a matter of fact, Dr. Karl's grandfather was the most famous biochemist of the late 1800's who pioneered cell dissection. The other two, Dr. Omsbaugh and Dr. Beck are noted authorities on eugenics. They have been involved in such work many years prior to the war. So, as you probably have guessed, Hitler's inner circle commandeered them into service as soon as possible.

"They are very critical to the success of Angel Hair. They wear SS uniforms only for the sake of protection. So, try not to be intimidated. I want to reiterate; the technology here is unlike any other you may have heard or dreamed of. It is very advanced, complicated, and counter-intuitive. The projects you have been involved with thus far are basic. The foundation stone, so to speak. I am not privileged to all aspects of the project, but I am authorized to share with you what I know. This is the process: first, young, healthy people are chosen. They must possess the desired traits in their appearance and genealogy: light hair, fair skin, and blue or green eyes. Second, (you will remember this from the Institute), they must undergo an exam to establish virginity and rule out a variety of health issues. Third, they will be artificially impregnated with select sperm from chosen males. They are brought here at their 3-month term for what you've experienced: the extraction. Forth, the material extracted is processed in the biochemical laboratory, which you will visit today. Fifth, the fertilized embryo is incubated for the next several months and then placed in the mechanized containers in the nursery. Sixth, the babies are incubated in the containers until term, at which time several things happen. Some are placed in German homes to be raised by loyal German families. These children possess special talents and are what Hitler calls his 'New Race.' But the majority are taken away to an undisclosed place, not known to me or to my colleagues. I know this is a lot to digest, but now you have a partial scope of Angel Hair. Any questions?"

Anxious to have answers, Elin asked about the tattoos and how they were able to discretely administer them without the knowledge of the patients. Dr. Brandt replied, "I've not been told explicitly, but it was hinted that they have been subjected to hypnotism, a practice Hitler is fond of, and at some point, a suggestion brings them to select locations where the tattoos are applied and other procedures are performed."

Dr. Keiser eagerly asked the next question. "What is the purpose of a new race and how can these children achieve this?"

"Oh, simple," Dr. Brandt replied. "As the children reproduce, they will pass the new genes planted in their cells to the next generation. They can only reproduce with compatible partners. It has been carefully planned and will be strictly controlled. The reason has not been disclosed to us. Now, colleagues, no more questions. We must join the others for the tour. Heil Hitler!"

The SS visitors were pleasantly involved in discussion with Dr. Niniva as Dr. Brandt entered the office with his colleagues. Sweet rolls and coffee sat temptingly on her desk.

"Colleagues, help yourselves to refreshments." Dr. Niniva said with a wave of her hand, "then we'll proceed with the tour."

Dr. Karl and Dr. Keiser exchanged a few pleasantries, recalling medical experiences in Berlin. Dr. Beck inquired if either Olaf or Elin had ever visited Berlin. Both shook their heads. Then Dr. Beck offered information regarding plans for the group to continue their involvement in the near future. Elin looked quizzically toward Dr. Brandt.

"Oh, yes," Dr. Brandt quickly responded, "We are in the planning stages now, and in the near future, we will visit the Center for Eugenic Study in Berlin. We'll advise you of the date. Now, comrades: the tour."

Dr. Niniva escorted the men to the nursery first, and several containers were opened to reveal beautiful, fair-skinned infants who were somewhere near term.

"Is the blood work monitored frequently?" Dr. Karl inquired.

"Yes, of course," Dr. Niniva responded. "It is an automated system with the utmost security. We have had no problems."

"Good." He looked satisfied.

Elin was surprised at the similar appearance of the babies: almost twin-like. From there, the men entered the colorful lounge adjacent to the nursery. Olaf and Elin both surprised, stopped and stared.

The room was filled with young women, some familiar, holding and touching many of the incubated infants, just as mothers would do on a regular basis. Dr. Brandt, realizing Elin was surprised, addressed him, "Are you okay?"

Elin remarked that he hadn't expected to see nurturing in this facility. "It's part of the program. We have come to recognize the bond between infants and their mammas to be an important part of a superior race. The stimulation creates a sense of security and connection. This is an important emotion; all intellectually superior individuals must experience this. These young women are the biological mammas and are required to return numerous times to maintain healthy relationships with their children. Of course, they will never be allowed to take the children, nor will they remember the experience." Elin felt a sadness for these captive Norwegians, captive in the same sense as soldiers, unable to escape service to the Nazis.

The entourage continued, viewing the medical facility as well as other areas of interest. Elin knew exactly what he wanted to see and became anxious as they entered the area behind the glass doors to the medical facility.

This was the hub, the heartbeat of Angel Hair: the laboratory. It was amazing and unexpected. Elin didn't know where to look first. His eyes danced like a bouncing ball, up and down, side to side in awe. The room was massive, white, and sterile with what seemed like hundreds of people working in sectioned off areas—open but contained. White lab coats and masks adorned everyone in sight. A few looked up but quickly returned to their projects.

"Impressive, isn't it?" Dr. Brandt commented. "Technology beyond belief. This is the womb of the Super-race. These scientists are splitting genetic materials into new cells and materials that even I don't understand. Look, comrades; this is the future."

Elin gasped. Row after row of glass containers held unbelievable specimens, some he could recognize, some he couldn't. He was stunned.

The men then entered a darkened room at the far end of the nursery. This too was completely unexpected; the air was different—very moist and thicker than normal air. The room held the same type of mechanical boxes as the nursery but administering to them were not white coated personnel, but hooded individuals slowly moving around the room, almost like birds watching their nests. Elin felt even more fearful. *Who are these people*, he wondered? Dr. Niniva approached one of the robed and hooded personnel and spoke in a language Elin had never heard before. She then moved to one of the boxes and the assistant opened it and removed a small entity. Dr. Keiser stepped back in disbelief as Dr.

Niniva approached holding the infant. "Look familiar, Dr. Keiser?" she questioned.

"Yes," he replied. "I saw the same thing in Berlin; it's human-like but not human in the sense we recognize."

"This entity is not yet fully developed, but is the same that you were asked to examine in Berlin," Dr. Niniva continued. Dr. Karl asked to hold the infant, but the assistant refused him. In the dim light Elin could see the assistant's large dark eyes and distorted cranial features. It startled him. Overwhelming relief was felt when the robed assistant replaced the infant into the box and Dr. Niniva advised the men they would not be required to participate in the experiments that resulted in the little creatures presented here. Other specialized doctors were required, but out of courtesy, she had wanted to inform them of the experiments so there would be no future inquiries.

Elin was eager to leave the dimly lit room as the robed personnel gathered behind him, closing and bolting the door. The men appeared shaken as the group returned to Dr. Niniva's office. Dr. Brandt both thanked and congratulated Dr. Niniva on the success of the project. He then briefly commented on the appearance of the entity. "When we get to Berlin," he continued, "you will see things nightmares are made of. This little entity is just one of many you will be exposed to. I'm not at liberty to explain just yet, but soon I hope to provide more information. I know a plane is waiting for our SS comrades, so I'll excuse the three of you. Colleagues, you may retire to the lounge and relax."

Dr. Niniva opened the door and motioned to Elisa to escort the officers away. Dr. Brandt and his colleagues exited the side door. The lounge was accommodating but void of warmth. The men sat quietly, obviously trying to digest what they had just seen. Olaf started to speak, but Elin gestured with his fingers to be silent. Olaf looked back with a questioning glare. He then understood and nodded his head. Dr. Keiser also acknowledged the gesture, and the men remained silent.

As Elin clutched a cup of tea between his hands, he stood to observe the activities in the open areas. Suddenly he bent over and whispered to Olaf, and Olaf stood. Dr. Keiser also rose and joined the two. There were numerous young women returning infants to their designated boxes. Elisa, closely watching the women, reminded them to kiss and hug their babies before returning them to their enclosures. They then lined up single-file as if they had been programmed. None of them smiled or talked. They went through the motions as if rehearsing for a play. Elin openly remarked about the total lack of emotion or expression. Both men agreed that it all seemed very odd, but what wasn't odd here at the facility? Elisa directed the women past the lounge with glass windows and the men, still standing, got a closer view of their cold, expressionless faces.

Not a woman turned to acknowledge their obviously interested onlookers. Olaf questioned where Elisa was taking them. Elin remarked that it was possible they were leaving the building since the front door was the direction they were headed. "Of course,", Olaf answered, "that would make sense; they are going home just like us."

Elisa returned shortly to escort the men and to entertain questions. Elin couldn't contain himself. "Where were those young women going, and why were they so expressionless"?

"Oh my," Elisa commented, "you are inquisitive. They are sedated for their own protection. They won't remember any of this; security, you know," she said with a know-it-all smile. "And as to where they're going, a bus takes them back to a campus where they go to school and live in dormitories. Their families enjoy the benefits of free education and housing. They don't have to feed them either," again expressing an arrogant smile. "I guess beauty does have advantages."

Dr. Keiser ventured forward with a question about the dark room and the hooded and robed individuals inside. Elisa's humor disappeared. "Don't ask me about that project. It's not something I've been cleared for, but I've seen the infants—a horrible manipulation of eugenics, I think, but what do I know?" Setting her sarcasm aside, her humor returned, and she laughed. "I suppose they're little green men from the moon. Let's go home."

Elin still had a million questions, but he'd have to wait for another day.

Part Twenty-seven

Olga and Kirsten were waiting outside when he arrived home. Happy to see his family, his mood elevated. Kirsten was at the age of excitability: funny and entertaining. He couldn't help but laugh at her. She loved her daddy, and his affection for her was obvious. Olga wrapped her arms around both of them and kissed Elin passionately. "Mamma has invited us to dinner tonight, and I accepted. Hope you don't mind. It's the holidays and a reason to be cheery. We all need a diversion, right? Olaf and Christina have also been invited—we'll all walk together. It'll be great fun."

Olaf had just entered his home, so Olga gave them a few more minutes before knocking on their door. Christina and the family came out, responding merrily as the two families assembled into a cheerful group of loving friends. Olga and Christina walked arm-in-arm, chattering about all sort of things. The children ran and skipped stones in the walkways, their little round cheeks red with expression. Elin and Olaf brought up the rear which gave them an occasion to discuss in private the events of the day. More questions arose than answers, but just being able to talk without fear of prying eyes and listening devices released pent-up emotions and stress.

Sonja's home was a welcome respite to the war-weary families. The front door was adorned with pine clippings and cones, dried red berries, and antique ribbons, in keeping with holiday tradition. The smell of firewood burning permeated the air, a reminder of older times. But this was not the good old times, as was soon made manifest in the shortage of sweets and cakes on Sonja's table.

Sonja rushed from the kitchen at the sound of the guests' entry and squealed with excitement. Her little family and friends had arrived. Well prepared, she had brought down old toys and books from the attic for the children to play with. Kirsten was happy to just have someone to chase and tease her. It was a happy time despite the hardships.

Sonja could only offer leftover wine, saved from the party earlier at Olga's new home. She had hidden it away in hopes of using it for the holidays. Now was the time. Olaf proposed a toast to the upcoming New Year and to the gift of libation. Cheers and laughter followed, hearts warmed by the glowing fire. After the few bottles were emptied, Olga opened the cover on her old piano. Holiday music, as loud as possible, echoed throughout the house. Everyone was singing and dancing. The children underfoot were jumping with joy and clinging to their parents' legs. Sonja beamed as she pranced around with little Kirsten.

After several invigorating songs, the exhausted group fell into the soft cushions of the sofa, and Sonja told stories of their families and of holidays past. In time, the children became restless. A simple dinner was shared, and a gift of a fruit was given to each person before their departure for home. "Hugs and kisses are free," Sonja insisted. "Let's all share those gifts," she giggled. The children, not wanting to engage, hid behind each other, dodging the grasping arms of the adults. Eventually they gave in and returned the affection expected.

When the young families found their doorsteps again, the bloated moon was beaming with enough light to expose a stack of packages placed in front of the doors of both families, bringing excitement to the children and anxiety to the parents. "Now what?" Elin questioned.

Olaf responded, "advantages, comrade; remember, rewards for our service." Quickly, the two families carried away the boxes and disappeared into the privacy of their homes. The Nazis were not celebrating a traditional Christmas, so Elin was a little confused about the gifts. For the Nazis, this season was more about pagan traditions like Winter Solstice, and families could only celebrate Christmas in the privacy of their own homes. No public displays were permitted.

Kirsten, already asleep in the arms of her father, was put to bed. Elin and Olga returned to examine the packages. They were beautifully wrapped and quite inviting. Among the many was one for Sonja, along with a sealed letter addressed to her. The couple questioned if they should read it, but Olga was uncomfortable without her mother's permission. Taped to their boxes was a simple note wishing all a happy Solstice season and expressing gratitude for their loyalty. "Please open your gifts upon arrival. Enjoy." Signed, Dr. Brandt.

The first box, labeled "Family," contained chocolates, a rare treat indeed. The next small box opened to loose tea and a jar of honey. But the box with Olga's name took her breath away. It was a long, flowing ball gown so beautiful that Olga's eyes filled with tears. Attached was a note. *Hope this is the appropriate size; I wish you would wear it to the Holiday Gala. Looking forward to seeing you in it. Affectionately, Dr. Brandt.*

Elin was enraged, "How personal!" he shouted. "Who does he think he is? Olga, have you in any way encouraged him or enticed him into thinking you might be available?" He paced the floor in a jealous rage, ranting all sorts of accusations.

"No!" she cried out. "Never have I had any type of personal relationship with him, only professional encounters. I'm sure there is a reason for these gifts—probably political," she continued. "After all, Olaf and Christina also received gifts. Have they enticed him?"

Elin, feeling foolish, calmed down and apologized. He had let his anger boil over and explode against the one he loved the most, his most trusted friend and companion.

Olga, an understanding person, accepted his apology and nudged a package toward him with his name on top. "Open it," she insisted, trying to contain her curiosity. Elin carefully unwrapped the box. Inside was a note, identical to Olga's and a wonderful suit of clothing for evening wear. His face flushed red. Realizing how badly he had reacted, he lowered his head in embarrassment.

"You see," Olga remarked. "Nothing personal."

A soft knock on the door startled Olga. "Elin, someone's at the door. Shall we open it?" she whispered.

"Yes, of course," he replied as he got up to respond to the soft knocks. Olaf softly apologized for the intrusion and asked if he and Christina could come in.

Olga rose, concerned that something had happened. "What is it?" she questioned. "Is everything okay?"

Christina moved closer. "Yes, everything is fine. The children are asleep, and we wanted to spend a little time with the two of you. It's rare that we are alone at the same time and the children asleep this early. These moments are truly gifts."

"Speaking of gifts, have you opened your boxes?" Olga inquired.

"Oh yes," Christina giggled. Can you believe it? I haven't had a dress like the one I received, ever! Did you also receive a dress?"

Olga rushed to a small side chair and lifted the gown to her body. "Yes, I did," she replied. "Is this the most beautiful gown you've ever seen?"

Christina examined the yards of fabric flowing around Olga's body and graciously suggested that Olga's dress was much prettier than hers. But she continued, "I am still so grateful for the gift, and it is unbelievably beautiful." Olga put the kettle on the stove and suggested they try the new batch of tea they had just received.

Their caution quickly gave way to a fully speculative conversation about the future. Elin openly asked questions he otherwise would have kept to himself, as did Olaf. Christina and Olga sat quietly, unaware of most of the information disclosed in the aggressive exchange of dialogue between their husbands. Olga now began to realize just how much she didn't know about the Nazis and their projects and why it was so dangerous for her and Christina to be listening to their conversation.

"Listen," she insisted. "The pot is boiling. Shall we continue this conversation at a later date and break for a hot cup of tea?" Christina stood and followed Olga into the kitchen. Olga warned Christina not to reveal any of the information she had just heard. "It's better if we know nothing of the Nazi projects. It's for the safety of our families. Do you understand?" she questioned.

"I do," Christina answered. "I don't know why they lost control of their emotions and exposed us to these secrets. What were they thinking? Now we'll have to be extra careful about what we say, especially around Dr. Brandt and Unk." The two women vowed never to discuss what they had heard and to be more cautious in their dealings with the Cultural Society and local officials.

The two men were silent in front of the fire as the women returned with tea. Elin looked up at Olga with concern. "I'm sorry." he said. "We were caught up in the moment and didn't consider the danger we've just put you in. We've said things tonight that should have been kept quiet. I am asking both you and Christina to keep these secrets for the sake of all of us. Do you think that's possible?"

"Yes, of course," Olga responded. "Christina and I now understand the strain the two of you have been under and what just happened is natural. We have vowed to each other to keep these secrets and we vow to you the same. Can we now enjoy the best of the evening and forget the bad?"

Part Twenty-eight

Elin and Olaf politely waved to Unk as they departed for the facility. Unk, waiting in the car, returned the gesture with a smile. He often came early and patiently waited for Olga. Everyday had become a practice day since the gala had been announced. Olga was late today. Unk had begun to be concerned and had started walking toward the house when she rushed out and handed Kirsten to him. "Please take her to Christina," Olga requested. "I'll be right back." Kirsten was passed over, and Unk returned to wait for Olga. She appeared shortly, shambled and flushed, carrying Sonja's gift.

"Are you ill?" Unk inquired. "I don't think so," Olga replied. "I'm just so tired. I don't sleep well. I have strange dreams and hear noises in the house. Sometimes I feel as if someone is watching me. Is that the definition of paranoia?"

Unk didn't respond verbally, merely shrugging his shoulders.

"Unk, may I ask you a question?"

He turned and briefly faced her.

She continued, "What kind of man is Dr Brandt? He doesn't quite fit the profile of a Nazi, at least from the stories I've heard. Do you know him well?"

159

"I've known him for a long time. We were friends long before the Nazis came to power. We met in Berlin where he was a well-respected physician. His wife was lovely and died early. He takes his orders but tries to live a life of mutual respect. He is like the rest of us, trying to survive in a bad situation. If he seems obsessed, it's because he's lonely. He truly respects you and Elin and wants to be a part of your happiness. Anything else?" he asked.

"No," Olga replied. "Thank you for an honest answer."

Today, the full orchestra gathered in a large civic auditorium with a grand stage towering over the main floor. It was just a week before the gala, and women from the Cultural Society were joined by many strangers, all busy setting up tables and chairs. Large garlands with glorious ropes of silk and satin were being hung from the ceiling, tied in the center of the hall with little lights that looked like a million stars dangling in the heavens. The dance floor had been sectioned off with columns of topiary tress forming a grand entrance onto the dance floor. Olga had never seen such a splendid room. The grand stage was also decorated with pine garland ropes and volumes of red ribbon. It truly looked like a fairy land.

Thor called the orchestra, and friends previously engaged in hugs and holiday greetings seated themselves. The music and arrangements were flawless.

The moment was magical, and Olga was extremely happy. Thor made an announcement to the musicians after the main performance: only those asked to remain on stage would be required to stay and perform. All others were excused. He explained they needed a dance band for the remainder of the program, and several would be asked to fulfill this request. "Those of you who are needed are posted on the podium. If there are questions, please see me after rehearsal."

Oh my, Olga thought. *What if my name is on the list? What shall I do?* But to her surprise, it was not. She approached Thor. "Who'll play the piano?"

He informed her that they had managed to bring other musicians to fill in. Many of them were members of popular bands and familiar with dance music. "Are you disappointed?" he questioned. Thor had not known that Olga and her family were invited guests, so Olga just smiled and replied with a gracious no.

"Olga!" a voice called out, "over here!" It was Sonja stepping from behind a large pine tree.

"Mamma!" she replied. "I didn't know you'd be here today." Sonja motioned for her to come over. The two hugged, and Olga proceeded to help her move trees into a pre-planned pattern.

"Why didn't you tell me you were coming today?" Olga questioned.

"I didn't know myself until the last minute. Ida came by and insisted I help today. What could I do? She picked me up. Oh, by the way, you were marvelous and the orchestra spectacular."

"Mamma, I miss you. It's so hard to get together these days. Time is so limited."

"I know," Sonja acknowledged. "Listen," she continued, in more of a whisper, "have you heard anything about the war? Has Unk said anything?"

"I've heard Russia is advancing and Germany is pulling back. I wish I could believe it! That would be the best holiday gift ever. Mamma, Unk never discusses political things, and I'm afraid to ask him anything about Germany or the Nazis. And you should be careful about who you listen and talk to. Spies are everywhere, you know. Come, Mamma, Unk will drive you home."

Sonja excused herself to say goodbye to Ida. Olga bid her farewells to Thor and others, still practicing dance music. Sonja soon caught up with Olga and proceeded toward the exit. In the distance Olga could see a dark figure leaning into Unk's car. As they approached, Dr. Brandt pulled his head from the window and extended greetings to both ladies.

"I hope you enjoyed the gifts," he politely remarked.

Olga immediately responded. "Dr. Brandt, we were so surprised; thank you for remembering us. I hope you'll be pleased when I wear the beautiful gown to the gala."

Sonja, unaware of the arrival of the gifts, watched both faces in confusion. Dr. Brandt turned to Sonja and asked about her gift. Olga interrupted, remarking that she had not yet had an opportunity to present her mother's gift. "It's in the car," she insisted. "Unk, please pass the box to mother. She can open it now and Dr. Brandt can see it."

Sonja's face glowed with excitement. "A gift for me?" she giggled.

"Yes," Dr. Brandt replied. "Open it."

Sonja slipped into the back seat with the gift as Dr. Brandt eagerly watched. Slowly, savoring each move, Sonja opened the box. Inside was another beautiful gown and a note that it was for the gala. Sonja squealed with joy.

Dr. Brandt smiled. "You'll be the most beautiful lady there," he complimented. "Be sure and save a dance for me. Now I must go. A pleasant day to all."

Sonja was overwhelmed and caressed the fabric in disbelief as Unk drove them home.

It was midday when Elin returned home early, surprising Olga and Kirsten. "Has something happened?" she questioned.

"No," he replied. "Dr. Brandt has given us a little vacation time until after the gala and New Year's celebration. It's only a few days and then back to work. I also must tell you he has made plans for Olaf and me along with Dr. Keiser to visit the facility in Berlin the first week of January. So, I think this time off is a Nazi perk. Still, let's not dwell on the negative, but enjoy the positive. Happy holidays, my love."

Time passed quickly in anticipation of the gala, Christmas and New Year. An abundance of activity dominated the short vacation, and the young family, together, enjoyed every moment, thankful to be alive.

The day of the Winter Gala had finally arrived. Olga flitted around like a hungry robin searching for worms. First this and then that, unsure of her hair or makeup. Christina was called in and out of Olga's home. She too was worried about her hair and all the last-minute details of the evening. Unk had already informed Olga of the travel plans. He would arrive early for her because she had to prepare for the concert. He would then return for Elin, Sonja, Olaf, and Christina.

The day was charged with excitement. Olga, exhausted from the constant demands on her time, finally insisted the young family take a break and relax. Elin and Kirsten were more than happy to oblige.

The twinkling of chimes awakened Olga from a sound sleep. It was the alarm of her vintage clock. *Time to get going,* she thought. Quietly, she showered and wrapped herself in a large towel. Elin stirred but did not wake. She didn't want to awaken him, not yet. She needed time for herself to prepare mentally for her grand performance tonight. She hadn't performed for this many people in a long time, and her nerves were on edge.

After applying her makeup and pulling her long blonde hair into a well-coiffed roll, she softly nudged Elin, hoping to wake him and not Kirsten. As he opened his eyes and looked at her, he smiled. "Is it time?"

"Yes," she said. "I must go. Unk will be here shortly, and the sitter will be by soon as well." Elin stood, taking Olga in his arms. "You are so beautiful. All eyes will be on you, but don't be nervous. Your family will be there to support you, and please try to enjoy the evening; heaven knows we deserve it."

Olga dropped the towel, revealing a perfectly tantalizing body. Elin found it hard to contain himself. "Later," she teased. "We'll celebrate."

The gorgeous dress hanging in the closet was finally retrieved. Olga slipped into it and pulled the strapless bodice to her chest. It was like a glove—a perfect fit.

Elin gasped. "You are breathtaking. Will you marry me?"

"Don't be silly," Olga giggled, feeling more confident now. "Zip me up."

He softly kissed her neck and whispered, "Good luck tonight, and I'll see you soon."

Olga stepped into her shoes and wrapped the long, satin shawl around her shoulders. All that was left was to pull the long evening gloves over her smooth hands and await the arrival of Unk.

The civic center was ablaze with lights. Volunteers were busy with final preparations and other members of the orchestra were entering the building. Adrenaline pumped through Olga's veins. She was charged.

Unk stopped the car at the entrance and hastened to open the door. As she stepped toward the sidewalk, he held out his hand to assist her. His smile was like that of a proud pappa.

"Good luck," he whispered. "You look like a fairy princess. You make me happy just looking at you. I'll see you later." He released her hand and disappeared back into the black limousine he had acquired for this special occasion.

With all the positive comments, Olga felt confident. Her steps lightened, and she joined her fellow musicians on the grand stage. All heads turned toward her as she gracefully moved toward the piano. She could feel their eyes. Several of the women approached her and inquired about the dress, stating it was the most beautiful dress they had ever seen. Olga didn't know what to say other than thank you. "Where did you get it?" one of her friends asked.

"Oh, it was left in a box at the house where we live."

The ladies became very quiet. What else could they say? Olga was relieved and no longer felt guilty. In fact, what she had told them was true.

The large auditorium was majestic. Pine trees in large pots laced with pine garlands attested to the fact that this was not a Christmas event, but a natural winter affair. Round tables with candles and pine branches adorned each numbered table. Crystal glasses and silverware were precisely placed on the tables. Stiffly starched napkins seemed to salute as they stood perfectly straight at attention. Waiters and servers were busy setting up the long tables with bar supplies and coat checks. Nothing had been spared. The Nazis and the Cultural Society had outdone themselves. Olga felt badly that the common Norwegian families could not enjoy this gala with her, but it was out of her control, and she had to focus on the job at hand. After all, this was her job: to entertain.

Thor, the conductor, arrived and instructed the stage crew to close the large velvet draperies, confining the orchestra behind a closed wall of fabric. He lightly tapped his baton, and the orchestra was seated. Olga surveyed her colleagues as they tuned up their instruments. A sense of pride came over her. *I am so honored to be a part of such a select and talented group*, she thought as she carefully organized her sheet music.

Suddenly, the velvet curtains slowly opened, and Thor tapped his wand. The orchestra immediately silenced. A well-dressed man approached the center of the stage and addressed Thor.

"I am Ivar, Nazi Party chairman in Oslo. Standing next to me are Arne and Ida, central government officials and cultural chairmen. We are in charge of this event."

Arne and Ida waved to the assembled musicians with approving smiles.

"We need to adjust the lighting and microphones. Are you about finished?"

Thor, confident in their preparation, dismissed the orchestra for a short break. "Remember," he ordered, "you may smoke or visit the bathrooms, but in 15 minutes, return here to the stage and be quiet. The guests are starting to arrive."

Ivar thanked the members and said he had been looking forward to this evening for months. The stage was cleared and the lighting programmed before the curtain closed again. Olga took the opportunity to stand in the side aisles and watch for her family. Already the large hall was starting to fill with early arrivals looking for their assigned tables. Several were seated and enjoying drinks and conversation. The room had become energized with laughter as smiling faces connected with each other.

Olga struggled to accept the laughter. Forcing out images of friends and old neighbors struggling to survive became a challenge. It wasn't easy. She couldn't remember when she had last heard laughter of people on the street. She yearned to hear them again. But tonight, she must change her focus with renewed hope. Indeed, a large portion of the laughing audience was, in fact, Norwegian.

The wait seemed like an eternity, and Olga was becoming restless, often peering through the side curtain to look for Elin. It was impossible to spot him. There were so many people, and they all looked the same—men in black evening attire and women in full length gowns filled the room. Waiters were busy serving drinks, and chatter dominated the air space. Olga had never seen anything so grand.

Tap, tap, tap. Thor's wand redirected her thoughts to the business at hand. "It's time." he said. "Be seated."

In front of the orchestra, just beyond the draperies, a voice sounded over the microphone.

"Honored guests, please find your seats and fill your glasses. You are in for what we hope will be a most wonderful evening. I'll give you a few minutes to find your tables."

The room soon became quiet, and the audience respectfully directed its attention to Ivar.

"I would like to welcome all our invited guests to the first Winter Gala. My name is Ivar, chairman of the Nazi Party in Oslo and co-host of this evening's event. The other hosts are Arne and Ida of the central government and Cultural Society. This event was planned for the sole purpose of bringing our two cultures together: German and Norwegian. Since music and food are international, what better way can there be to start the evening? The program for tonight is a short concert by the extremely talented Oslo orchestra, directed by Thor Niessen. It will be followed by dinner and dancing. We ask that you enjoy your drinks, but silently respect the music. Enjoy! Heil Hitler!"

The lights slowly dimmed, and the massive curtain parted to reveal a group of loyal, dedicated Norwegians ready to share an evening of holiday cheer with their fellow Norwegians. Like most of their country-men, they dismissed the Germans as part of their society and most often simply failed to acknowledge them at all. The music had been carefully selected: no traditional Christmas music had been included, only clas-sical German and Norwegian pieces. In a little over an hour, it was over. The audience stood with a thunderous ovation and shouts of "Bravo, Bravo!" Thor bowed in three directions as the cheers continued. The orchestra members rose, and the loud cheers set the flickering flames on the massive candles to dancing. Success was unmistakable, and the curtain closed the performance.

Waiters quickly cleared tables of glasses and cheese canape's, preparing to serve dinner. Olga and her fellow musicians exited the stage and joined the dinner party, eager to enjoy the remainder of the evening. Elin, waiting patiently for Olga to appear, rushed to meet her, took her hand, and lead her toward the reserved table they shared with Sonja, Christina and Olaf. As she passed, fellow Norwegians held their glasses high in a respectful toast. Tears rolled from her eyes in an emotional release as she smiled knowingly to her fellow countrymen. It was over now, and the family could focus on other issues.

The tables had all been cleared and bottles of French champagne had appeared: spoils of the French occupation, they were told. On the stage, a quartet provided soft background music. It softened the ambiance and provided a more friendly atmosphere. Olga relaxed, as did Elin. The holiday season had officially begun. Despite the war, the family had a wonderful evening. What more could they expect: wine, dinner, dancing, and champagne for toasting? All was well until they left the building.

Outside, hundreds of people filled the street in a quiet candlelight protest. German soldiers with guns at their sides stood in protective positions ready to retaliate if provoked. Olga had not expected this, but as she thought about it, she could not be surprised. What did the people have to lose? They had already lost the most important things in their lives: freedom and autonomy. Her fear changed to hope. The pride of Norway was still alive, and she wanted to vocalize her pride as well.

But her cards had already been played. She and her family were prisoners of war.

The protest held the mood in the car firmly in silence. Unk tried to comfort the group, but the reality was clear: facts were facts, and however innocent they were, they felt guilty by association.

"I'm glad it's over," Elin announced. "Let's try to put this behind us. We still have our children and our families. We have an obligation to survive and protect those things most precious. Someday maybe things will change and if we survive, our children will survive. We owe that to them. Do we all agree?"

A soft "yes" came from the group. Elin whispered in Olga's ear, "I'm sorry about the way tonight ended, but we'll be okay. Tomorrow is another day."

Unk stopped the limo in front of Sonja's house and politely escorted her to the front door.

"Good night, Mamma," Olga called out. Sonja blew a kiss and disappeared behind a closing door. The young families arrived home shortly and bid Unk a good night.

"Will I see you soon?" Olga inquired of him.

"Yes, my dear," he responded. "We'll be in touch. Now try to get some rest."

Kirsten was asleep next door with a sitter and Olaf's children. Christina insisted that Olga let her spend the night and promised things would look brighter in the morning.

It was rare that Olga and Elin had the luxury of sleeping late. Kirsten was an early riser, but today was a gift, and the young couple found time to enjoy the uninterrupted pleasure of lovemaking.

Refreshed and rejuvenated, Olga prepared a small breakfast, and they spent another rare moment together in uninterrupted conversation. After the protest at the Gala, both families decided to keep a low profile during Christmas, sharing time with each other and Sonja, having small, traditional meals together. It wasn't as grand as past holidays, but it was sufficient.

Christina was lucky enough to have found the almond in her porridge and acted as if she had won a grand prize. She strutted around the room teasing everyone with her treasure.

A few days prior to Christmas, a box was left at the door containing a few bottles of champagne, cheese and a simple note with no name, only the words, "Enjoy the Holidays." They all assumed it had come from Dr. Brandt, possibly leftovers from the Gala. Regardless of its origin, family and friends opened one bottle and each had a single glass. "Merry Christmas," they toasted.

Elin had slipped away and returned in a white beard and hat. The children giggled.

"Are there any good children here?" he asked in a gravelly voice. The children raised their hands and shouted, "I am!" He then passed a small box to each of them: gifts that were left at the front door earlier by Dr. Brandt.

Their little faces glowed as they patiently opened each small box. There were dolls for the girls and cars for the boys. "Merry Christmas," was the final word before bed.

Part Twenty-nine

The new year was fast approaching. Elin and Olaf obsessed about the upcoming trip. When would they leave for Berlin? How long would they be gone? Who would look after their families? "Maybe Unk," Elin commented. "Yes, I'm sure Unk will protect them. He'll stop by soon and I'll ask him. I know he loves the children, and I trust him with the women."

Feeling better about a possible solution, the men returned to the thing they did best: speculating about the future.

New Year's Eve ended on a quiet note and until late New Year's Day, it was as uneventful as they could hope.

Section Two

Part One

It was 8:00 P.M. on New Year's Day, and a sharp knock at the door startled Elin. Cautiously, he approached and opened the door. It was Olaf and Dr. Brandt.

"Come in," he insisted. "What's wrong?"

Olaf looked worried, shifting his weight side to side in a nervous dance.

"I've asked Olaf to join us in this conversation," Dr. Brandt explained. "It's easier to inform the both of you together, since you both are involved. By order of the German government, you are to arrive at the Institute of Eugenic Research in Berlin as soon as possible. We will leave early tomorrow morning. Bring only minimal amounts of clothing. All your needs will be attended to."

Elin and Olaf were speechless, words froze in their throats.

Dr. Brandt continued, "I've asked Unk to oversee the needs of your families so don't worry, things will be alright. I'm sorry for the short notice, but it seems there are heightened security concerns, and we have to protect our schedules from growing opposition. Norwegian spies, we've been told. So, go now, and inform your families. We'll be back early in the morning. I can't tell you exactly when, only that it will be before daylight. Good night. Heil Hitler." With that, Dr. Brandt disappeared.

Olga, listening from the doorway, panicked and began to cry hysterically. Olaf excused himself to get Christina. "We must talk about this together, family to family," he said.

Christina and Olaf, arm in arm, walked slowly into the house, her eyes red, tears streaming down her cheeks. The two women clutched hands and wailed as the men tried to reassure them of their safety. For more than an hour, the families discussed survival plans: what to do if the men didn't return, and how would they protect the children.

Elin reminded Olga and Christina that they had an ally in Unk and that he would know how to deal with any problem they encountered. "Have faith," he continued. "Just remember this is a project of great importance and nothing will happen to us, I am sure. So, let's leave it at that and not worry. We'll be back soon; I know it."

Olaf took Christian's hand and lead her toward the door. "See you soon," he said to Elin with a parting glance.

The dark sky had just started to clear when the dreaded knock vibrated throughout the house. Elin, unable to sleep, was awake and ready. Olga, asleep at his side, woke with a start.

"Are they here?" she whispered.

"Yes Olga, they are. Please be brave. I love you. Take care, and try not to worry."

Olga, sobbing uncontrollably, followed her love, her life, to the door, clinging to his arm for as long as possible. Pulling away, he joined Olaf and the SS officer in the grayness of early dawn.

There was an eerie silence hanging over the city, and today the black car appeared only as a shadow, gliding through the streets, discernable only by the sound of the tires rumbling over the pavement.

Elin tried to notice every landmark he could, hoping to determine where they were going. Suddenly he knew. It wasn't a visible sighting, but a pungent smell that alerted him. The two men looked at each other. Olaf also recognized the smell and raised his shoulders in the question they were both asking. Elin asked the driver if they were at the fishing docks but received no answer. He didn't ask again.

The mood was sober, almost surreal. Olaf bounced his knee in nervously. The car slowed and came to a stop at the end of the pier. "Wait here," the driver instructed.

Olaf uselessly asked Elin, "why the fishing pier?"

"I have no idea," he responded. "Maybe we're going by boat. If flying, we would go to Berlin in one of the planes parked behind the facility. I guess I was wrong. This is very strange. I'm not sure what to make of it."

The soldier soon returned and asked the men to step out of the car. He handed both of them stocking hats and heavy coats. They had just finished putting them on when a familiar voice greeted them. It was Dr. Brandt and Dr. Keiser approaching from the shadows.

"Sorry for the caution," Dr. Brandt commented, "but this mission has to be protected and kept secret. We've had to resort to extremes. Berlin notified us of advancing British and Allied planes in the area, and we couldn't risk exposing you to the danger of an air battle. So, colleagues, we will be crossing the water in a large fishing boat: Norwegian of course. Hopefully we won't be spotted or fired upon. Now tighten your coat and follow me; we'll be on our way."

Part Two

In the near distance, Elin managed to see the outline of a large boat, swaying and tilting in the cold water. A number of men were waiting, some German, some Norwegian. "Heil Hitler!" a voice rang out. "Heil Hitler," Dr. Brandt responded, and the four men climbed aboard. "Welcome," the captain greeted. By his accent, Elin could tell he was Norwegian, which was somewhat comforting. Stepping to his side, was another man dressed as a dock worker. He was German, and answered to the name Walt. He and Dr. Brandt briefly spoke as the captain prepared the boat for the journey.

"Go inside," Walt instructed, "and let the captain finish his job. It is much warmer in there." Elin was happy to do so.

It was freezing cold, and the four men were certainly not adapted to this type of exposure. The little cabin was as simple as one would expect for a working boat, and the four men settled around a small table, cramped, but comfortable.

Dr. Keiser began the conversation with concerns about the safety of the trip. Dr. Brandt only could respond with information given him, which usually meant nothing. He explained the boat would anchor in a small harbor controlled by the SS, a place so secret that most officers had never heard of it. It was primarily used for submarines. They would then be taken to a depot used for supply trains. This train was heavily guarded and was camouflaged to effectively blend into the forest and countryside. It had been built quickly and secretly. The laborers were Polish prisoners of war, so most Germans knew nothing of its existence.

Elin began to question the importance of this project. Why such precaution? Was there more to this than he could imagine? The steps to secure their safety were unbelievable. Why were they so important? Breaking his silence, he dared venture the question. "Dr. Brandt, why is this project so important that Germany would take a few simple doctors and provide them with the security I see all around us, both here and in Oslo?"

Dr. Brandt fired back, "I told you all in the beginning this project is vital for the German people. It ranks as high as bomb building and rocketry. That's all I can say now. When we get to Berlin you will see for yourselves and someone other than me will brief you. Understand?" he asked.

"Yes," Elin responded. He asked no more questions.

Dr. Keiser used the opportunity to ask about a visit to his wife.

"I'm sure it can be arranged," Dr. Brandt answered. "I'll see to it personally."

"Thank you," Dr. Keiser whispered.

"Now colleagues, relax, this trip will take some time." Dr. Brandt excused himself and went outside, returning with a box that he placed on the table. "Colleagues," he laughed, "help yourselves to a gift from France." Inside were rounds of cheese, several selections of wonderful baguettes, and bottles of expensive French wines. The men, who had not eaten, quickly consumed the food, toasting the French with filled glasses.

Dr. Brandt slowly slid down in his chair. The constant rocking of the boat, somewhat like a baby in a cradle, soon lulled him to sleep. Elin, exhausted, closed his eyes and joined the doctor in a much-needed rest. Hours passed, and not until a loud horn blasted its approach, did he awaken. Embarrassed, he sat up straight in his chair and glanced over at

Olaf, who smiled. Dr. Brandt immediately jumped to his feet and exited the cabin.

"Where are we?" Elin inquired. Dr. Keiser felt that they had arrived at the port and the captain was near enough to signal their arrival. "Makes sense," Elin said.

Dr. Brandt rushed back into the room and announced the boat was ready to drop anchor. "Please gather your belongings and follow me. Stay close by," he cautioned.

Dr. Brandt followed by his colleagues down the ladder. They were met by several SS officers. Elin and the other men stood behind, unsure of the reception they were about to receive.

"Papers," one of the officers demanded. Dr. Brandt opened a locked black briefcase and presented several documents to the inquisitor. "When I call your name, step forward," he ordered.

Each man took his turn. Questions were asked and photographs checked. Dr. Brandt, obviously irritated, stood by in a protective posture as each man was cleared to enter the port.

"Heil Hitler," the SS officer chanted.

"Heil Hitler," Dr. Brandt and his reluctant colleagues repeated. "Come, hurry," he pleaded. "We must be on that train in just a few minutes."

The men rushed by the armed guards to board a supply train going to Berlin. There were only a few passenger cars, and each was heavily guarded. Elin tried not to make eye contact with the soldiers as he boarded. Once inside, Dr. Brandt presented their papers again, and everyone was asked to take a seat. A cocky SS officer strutted down the aisle and stood in front of the men. "I want to look at the faces of such important people. Your papers are signed by Germany's highest authorities. What makes you so special?" he inquired. Dr. Brandt stepped forward and asked the officer if he would like to inquire personally before der Führer. The officer quickly stepped back and disappeared into the next car, not to be seen again. "Don't let these zealous officers intimidate you," Dr. Brandt warned. "They don't have enough to do here. I'm sure he was just looking to get a rise out of you."

Part Three

The sun's first light speared its rays through the thick forest creating a pattern of vertical lines on the windows of the train. Elin, eager to see the countryside, found it difficult to see anything clearly. The contrast between dark and light was hypnotic, and he had to withdraw from the window, resorting instead to talking about the winter Gala.

The trip seemed to be taking forever, and small talk was boring. Elin found himself once again falling into a fitful sleep. With no one to talk to, the other men also dozed off, probably relieved to retreat from the uncomfortable silence.

Several hours into the trip, Elin was jostled out of his seat when the train came to a sudden stop. No whistle sounded, and no conductor advised the men where they were. Instead, Dr. Brandt informed them that they would be getting off the train now.

"Are we in Berlin?" Olaf asked.

"We are nowhere," Dr. Brandt replied. "Gather your things and follow me."

Dr. Brandt was right—they were nowhere. There was no town or city, merely a sturdy platform with steps leading to a single road. Waiting there was a covered civilian truck.

"Please, get in," the driver instructed. He had the appearance of a farm worker, but Elin sensed SS. His thoughts were confirmed as Dr. Brandt approached and raised his arm high in the familiar salute. The back of the truck was opened, and the men with their luggage were promptly seated inside. Dr. Brandt and the driver closed the back door and drove away.

The small amount of light filtering into the back end of the truck created a sinister ambiance. Olaf whispered the question on all of their minds. "Where do you think we are, and where are we going?"

Dr. Keiser suggested they may be somewhere between Hamburg and Berlin. "I would guess we'll be kept in a private home, probably near Berlin, but not in the city. I think they want us to be as inconspicuous as possible..."

"That makes sense," Elin interrupted. "Out of sight, and no questions about the project from outsiders."

The monotonous sound of the tires on the road suddenly changed from a smooth, continuous hum to a jerky, crunching, disconnected vibration.

"Gravel road," Dr. Keiser suggested. "We've left the highway." Elin held tight to his seat as the truck swayed back and forth on the uneven surface. Uphill and down, they continued until there was no light at all. "Deep forest," Dr. Keiser again suggested. Then they stopped. Dr. Brandt flung open the back doors and announced their arrival.

Part Four

Elin was amazed. They were indeed deep in the forest. It was beautiful. The burbling of a small, swift creek was the only familiar sound. Ice crystals covered the rocks and light snow was on the ground, sheltered from the sun by towering pine trees. Before them was a hunting lodge built with massive logs and stone pillars. Elin had never had the opportunity to stay in a lodge, even though Norway had many such places. He was both surprised and concerned by the isolation.

"Well, colleagues, are you as pleased as I?" Dr. Brandt exclaimed, "I had no idea they would place us in such a personal and intimate facility with our own driver and house staff. I look forward to the privacy and getting to know all of you better. This is Josef, our driver," Dr. Brandt explained. "You can trust him."

Josef clicked his heels together and dipped a small bow before his new passengers. "I'll take good care of you," he said as he helped carry the luggage toward the house. "Heinrich and his wife Helen are going to take care of your daily needs. Helen is a wonderful cook, and Heinrich will keep us warm and safe. They are very pleasant people and have been custodians of this property for many years. Heinrich knows every inch of this forest. He and his family used to own it. The Reich permits Helen and Heinrich to live here as long as they maintain the property."

Elin felt a tinge of guilt. This was obviously their home, and he and his colleagues were certainly intruders. It must be very hard for Heinrich to accept someone else having control over his ancestral land. A middle aged, rosy cheeked man opened the door as the men ascended the steps to the porch. "Welcome," he greeted. "I am Heinrich, and this is my wife, Helen." The two stepped forward to help with the bags of their new guests Once inside, Dr Brandt introduced his colleagues and explained that the visit would be temporary. "They are doctors from Norway," he continued, "here to work on a special project in Berlin. They are not at liberty to discuss any aspect of this project, so don't question them. It's better for all of us. Do you understand?" Each of the three nodded their heads in affirmation. "Good. It's been a long journey; may we please retire to our rooms?"

Josef led the way to the second floor hall and a number of bedrooms. "Does it matter which room you take?" he asked Dr. Brandt.

"No," he replied. "I'm sure they're all more than sufficient. But I'll take this one. It's near the stairs."

Elin chose the next one, and Olaf and Dr. Keiser took the other two at the end of the hallway. "Unpack, rest for a while, and rejoin us downstairs in an hour," Dr. Brandt instructed. "Josef, tell your mamma we'll eat dinner at 7:00. Thank you for your assistance," he said, as he closed his door.

"Mamma," Elin thought. *Did I hear correctly? Helen is Josef's mamma? It must be so, why else would he call her that?* He was confused.

He had been sure Josef was SS, but it appeared that he was not. The whole family was obviously under the control of the SS, but not a part of it. He was convinced they were as he and his family: victims of war. Even though there was no love lost between the Norwegians and Germans, he felt a fair amount of compassion for his host family.

No longer needing to pretend to be a fisherman, he removed his borrowed clothing, folded it, and placed everything in a bag. He might need these later—best not to lose them.

It had been several days since he had laid down in a bed. He eagerly removed his shoes and indulged himself in a plumped-up feather bed so thick with down that he could barely turn over. It quickly consumed his exhausted body, much like quicksand. Rest didn't come easily. He was in and out of lucid dreams. Anticipation of his dinner appointment also kept him from deep sleep. When Olaf knocked gently at the door, Elin found himself in more of a drugged state than rested. "Who is it?" he called out.

"Are you awake?" Olaf questioned.

"Come in." Elin answered. "I'm awake."

Olaf and Dr. Keiser entered the room behind him.

"It's time to go downstairs. I'm starved. Are you ready for dinner?" Olaf whined.

"I think we're all hungry," Elin answered. "Wonder what's on the menu tonight. Probably French cheese and bread," he remarked sarcastically.

The men were pleasantly surprised when they entered the large sitting room. Heinrich had prepared a roaring fire, and Dr. Brandt quickly sat in a large, overstuffed chair. "Come sit," he called out. "Dinner is almost ready; I think you'll be impressed with Helen's cooking." Elin had to admit the smells were unbelievable; he could barely wait to eat.

After a few minutes of small talk, Helen called them to dinner. The table was set for all of them, which surprised Elin. He had expected that they would dine privately but was pleased that his host family would join them. It meant friendly conversation as opposed to talk of work and Nazi schemes. Josef poured each a glass of wine, compliments of the Reich, they were told. Helen and Heinrich approached the table each carrying a large platter with meat and vegetables. Elin was shocked: meat and vegetables! Where did they get this food? He hadn't seen so much meat in months.

Heinrich promptly answered his unspoken question. "The forest has been good to us," he boasted. "A fresh kill and stored root vegetables; couldn't ask for more."

Helen seated herself and passed the vegetables. Heinrich served the meat, and the men ate until the platter was empty, devouring every morsel. "We have more," Helen said. "Enough meat for a week." Dr. Brandt lifted his glass and proposed a toast to his hosts; his colleagues lifted their glasses and expressed their gratitude as well.

"Shall we retire to the warmth of the fire?" Dr. Brandt asked. All but Helen followed him. She excused herself to clean up. Dr. Brandt had yet another surprise up his sleeve. "A bottle of brandy to warm the heart," he said, producing the welcome enjoyment from a sack. A delightful end to an exhausting journey.

Part Five

E lin settled quickly into his new routine, but Olga was not adapting. Uncertain of her husband's whereabouts or safety, he was quickly becoming depressed and reclusive. Her security had been compromised with the loss of Elin. She bordered on paranoia. He was the love and protector of her life. Not knowing where or how he was brought darkness to her eyes and heart.

Kirsten also missed her father, asking for him so often Olga began taking her to bed with her just to console her. It was a difficult time for both Olga and Christina, but in the absence of the men, their friendship blossomed into a bond more like that of sisters than friends. Oftentimes, after the children had gone to bed, they sat together, talking of the future and what it would bring, trying to be optimistic and hopeful. But the reality was still war.

Frightening rumors were circulating. Sonja would often repeat stories she had heard from neighbors and friends. Olga had none of these: no neighbors, and few friends. She and Christina had been so isolated that they wondered if this had been planned. Olga's social life ceased to exist. No parties, no orchestra, no Cultural Society. It was as if without Dr. Brandt, no life remained. She had certainly underestimated his importance and his impact on her. Even Unk was not visiting much. He came every few days to bring what food he could and to check on the safety of the two families. Many times, Olga would try to engage him in conversation, but he couldn't stay. He seemed different without Dr. Brandt. Almost afraid, certainly more cautious.

Olga found herself more and more at Sonja's house. She couldn't bear the loneliness, and her imagination often took her to places she had never been before. She began hearing strange sounds at night, often feeling as if she were being watched. Some mornings she awakened exhausted but couldn't understand why. Kirsten as well was restless and irritable. More and more often they would stay at Sonja's house overnight where they could enjoy an uninterrupted sleep.

Days became weeks, and Olga became frantic to hear from Elin. She didn't know what to do. She knew no one except Unk, and she didn't know how to get in touch with him. She just had to be patient, wait, and hope he would call her soon. When he did, she planned to confront and pressure him for answers.

And she continued to be plagued with strange dreams, shadows, and sounds. One evening, while visiting with Christina, she confided in her, hoping she would understand and not judge her sanity. Christina listened respectfully and suggested it might be stress. Olga confessed that some things she couldn't remember but many were so real it frightened her. She worried for the safety of Kirsten. Christina encouraged Olga to share some of these dreams with her. Olga hesitated, but then said that most of the memories were the same: a blinding bright light would come into the room and dark shadows would surround her bed. She was so frightened that she couldn't move or speak. Then they would lift her up into the light. That's all she could remember. The same dream had repeated itself several times.

Christina was quiet.

"What is it?" Olga questioned.

"Sometimes, late at night when I get up with the children, I see bright lights in the courtyard. I never venture toward the windows because I feel it could be soldiers searching for someone with spotlights. Maybe that's what you're seeing as well."

Olga stared out into the room. "For some reason it doesn't feel like that; something strange is going on. I'm going to ask Unk if the Nazis are spying on me and if so, why. Please, Christina, next time you see lights, discretely look out the window."

"I will, my friend," she responded. "Now I must go home and check on my family. Try not to worry. I'm here for you."

Several days passed, and the dreams stopped. Olga started to feel better and as her confidence returned, she vowed to stay strong. She had a beautiful little girl to care for. Christina suggested it was just the stress.

Late one afternoon, Unk came to visit, bringing a few supplies and long-awaited news from Elin. Olga was so anxious that she could hardly wait for Unk to set aside the provisions and join her in the sitting room before pummeling him with questions. "Please, Unk, quickly tell me about my husband. Is he okay? Where is he?"

"Slow down," Unk asked, "I'll tell you all I know."

Olga folded her hands and sat in impatient silence.

"Dr. Brandt sent word to me yesterday explaining things were going well. He couldn't elaborate, but I was to tell you Elin would be coming home very soon along with Olaf. They have finished the training in Berlin and will continue the work at the facilities in Oslo. He seemed pleased and asked about you. That's about all he said." Olga's eyes filled with tears. In a muffled voice, she sighed, "Oh, thank God!"

Unk, realizing Olga may have thought Elin might be dead, patted her arm and told her that things would be over soon. Her family would be back together.

Seizing the opportunity, Olga asked Unk about the Nazis and the possibility that they were spying on her. "Why do you suspect they're spying on you?" he questioned.

Olga explained the strange lights and memories she had of shadowy figures around her bed. Unk simply comforted her by telling her that he felt these were angel-like beings protecting her and Kirsten, and not to be alarmed. "The Nazis have no reason to spy on you, and if they were involved, they would have just taken you away instead of slipping around in the dark looking for who knows what. Think about it, Olga. Isn't that true?"

"Well," Olga replied, "I guess you're right, at least about the Nazis. Oh, is there any news of the war? Did Dr. Brandt say anything?"

"Well," Unk hesitated, "he did say the Americans have bombed parts of Germany and it has become increasingly dangerous for all Germans. Also, food supplies were scarce. I attended a rally last week and previewed a new film showing a different story. It implied Germany was still having success on every front, but after talking to Dr. Brandt, I'm just not sure. Don't worry my dear. You and your family will always be safe." Unk stood and slid a box toward the kitchen. "I have brought enough staples to last for quite a while. Keep our conversation to yourself, I'll see what else I can find out for you."

"Oh, thank you," Olga whispered as she hugged the old man and said her goodbyes.

Part Six

Days dragged into weeks in the secluded forest that Dr. Brandt called "nowhere.". Elin and his colleagues began to wonder if they would ever receive word from the officials in Berlin. Sometimes, Elin would walk deep into the woods, carefully following the little waterway so he wouldn't get lost. Late one afternoon while walking, he happened upon a man kneeling by the water. Both men froze in position, surprised to encounter another person so deep in the woods. Elin waved his hand in a friendly hello. The man stood and walked toward him. "Hello," Elin called out in Norwegian. The man didn't respond. Elin then repeated his greeting in German. The man replied in German, "auf Deutsch, nicht so gut."

This is confusing, Elin thought, *what language should I use to communicate with this person?* But before he could speak again, the man abruptly turned around and disappeared into the darkness of the trees. *What a strange experience,* he thought. *I'll have to ask Heinrich about him and the safety of being out here alone.*

In an accelerated pace, he rushed back to the lodge, anxious to share the encounter with his colleagues. The door had just closed behind him when Dr. Brandt approached and disrupted his thoughts. "We have guests," Dr. Brandt announced with an excited expression. "Hurry, come in."

The ongoing conversation paused as Elin and Dr. Brandt entered the room. "Hello again," said one of the visitors. "Remember me; Dr. Omsbaugh?"

"Oh yes," Elin replied. "Nice to see you again. Are you here about the Project?"

"As a matter of fact, we are. I'm sorry about the delay, but the war has gotten complicated with American and British attacks. We've had to take more precautions."

What? Elin thought, *American and British together. The rumors must be true. Maybe Germany isn't winning every battle like we've been told.* The evening proved to be even more informative. Elin listened closely to the conversations of this Berlin envoy. The more wine was served, the more the information flowed. It almost seemed as if the visitors felt a great relief in sharing their concerns and frustrations over the war. It was an eye-opening insight into what really was happening. The men talked openly of the Jews and their demise. Elin knew nothing of this and was horrified. They also disclosed the struggle Germany was having in Africa and Russia. This was contradictory information to what Norwegians were being told even now by the Nazis.

Olaf and Elin once again visually connected, dipping their heads in a hopeful nod. *Could this be the beginning of the end of the war?* Elin thought. *I pray so.*

Dr. Brandt and Dr. Omsbaugh both appeared to be drunk by the end of the evening and had not taken the time to inform the men of the arrangements for their upcoming trip. Dr. Keiser, who had remained very quiet most of the evening, asked Dr. Omsbaugh's driver, Ben, about the arrangements. He replied that he didn't know. Dr. Brandt mumbled, "Let's talk tomorrow. Time to go to bed." And with that remark, all the men retired to their rooms.

That night, there was no comfort for Elin. He tossed and turned, weighted down by the heavy coverings on his bed and constant thoughts of home. He missed Olga and Kirsten. He worried about their safety and emotional stability. It had been weeks since he had last seen them, and he had not received any communications from Oslo. Olaf, likewise, had no contact with home. It was a lonely time for both men, and the stress of waiting around the lodge had begun to take its toll. Tonight, he thanked God that the Berlin officials had arrived. At least he would be free of the boredom that had overwhelmed all of them.

Unable to sleep, he decided to rise early and visit with Heinrich before breakfast. It would be a perfect time to discuss the encounter by the water, he thought. Quietly, he dressed and waited until he heard activity downstairs. Heinrich was re-stoking the fire.

"Good morning," Elin politely remarked. Heinrich was surprised by the early visitor and asked if everything was alright. Elin assured him things were fine, but that he was a little restless. He then asked Heinrich if they could talk for a moment. Heinrich sat down, and Elin joined him. Prefacing his remarks, he began with an apology. "I know it's hard for you to discuss things out of general knowledge, and I don't want to impose on you for information, but if you could help me understand something, I would appreciate it."

Heinrich looked a little puzzled, "What is it?" he questioned. Elin explained his adventure into the woods and the strange man he had encountered. Heinrich listened with undivided attention, occasionally looking directly into his eyes. Elin finished his story and sat back in his chair, waiting for a response.

There was complete silence.

Heinrich folded his arms and also sat back in his chair. It was obvious he was contemplating his answer. Elin patiently waited. Heinrich broke the silence, "You know this is classified information." He then asked Elin a forbidden question. "How concerned are you about this project and involvement with the Nazis?"

Elin found himself in the same position in which he had just placed Heinrich. It seemed that they both were talking about classified information. Both men returned to their silence, apparently not knowing what to say next.

Elin could no longer stand the suspense and whispered, "I am not a

Nazi; are you?" Heinrich seemed a little surprised and said, "Neither am I. Well, can we trust each other and talk in private as two friends?"

Elin responded. "I see no reason why not, as long as it stays just between two new friends."

"Agreed," Heinrich whispered, "No one else will hear of our conversation."

Elin spoke first. His story was not complicated, and he had no knowledge of the Berlin Project to report.

Heinrich appeared to understand his limited access to information. He had dealt with the Nazis for years and still didn't know their secrets. But he did know about the strange man in the forest. His family had lived in this area for hundreds of years and there were no secrets the woods had kept from them. Heinrich asked Elin if he had ever seen a "Weisse Haut" before. Confused by the term, he asked for its meaning. Heinrich explained it to him.

"It means 'white skin'—that's what our family always called them."

"I can't answer your question for sure," Elin continued, "because this man was heavily clothed with a hat and gloves, but I do remember his piercing blue eyes and pale cheeks, almost albino. He also reminded me of a woman I met in Oslo. She worked in a place we called The Facility: a genetic laboratory."

"So, you have seen them with the Nazis?" Heinrich questioned.

Once again Elin tried to explain. "I'm not sure about the relationship, but I didn't sense she was a Nazi, even though there were Nazis around. Strange now that you ask. I should have been more observant."

"It's okay'" Heinrich commented. "It really doesn't matter."

Elin's curiosity hadn't been satisfied, and he pushed for more information on the Weisse Haut. Heinrich continued his story which had been handed down from generation to generation within his family. "No one knows for sure the first time they were noticed in the woods, but they are a friendly people who stay to themselves. They speak their own language and grow their own food. I have never been invited to their homes nor talked at length with any of them. I don't think there are very many of them, and they don't or won't associate with outsiders. The strange thing is that the area they live in is a protected wilderness, secured by the German Government. Very few people know about them. The only reason I know anything is because our ancestral lands border theirs. Oftentimes they cross over to our land to be near the water. It seems to fascinate them."

Elin questioned his story. "How is it that they could remain hidden from the German people for so many years?"

"All I know," Heinrich explained, "is that the area is vast, dense, and foreboding. I wouldn't want to venture into it alone, and I suggest you not wander alone either. It is said there are devices that alarm them of any intrusion into the area. You could get hurt."

"How long did you say they've been there?" he asked. Heinrich answered with certainty that they had been there for hundreds of years. Elin expressed his thanks, excused himself, and returned to his room.

Part Seven

Intrigued by Heinrich's story, Elin couldn't dismiss certain questions. Who are these people? Could they possibly be his ancestors? Those born with blonde hair and blue eyes—are they a race older than the Nordics? So many questions and very few answers. He wanted to learn everything about these mysterious people and possibly make contact with them again, even though Heinrich had clearly warned him of the consequences.

Heinrich's story dominated Elin's thoughts for several hours after returning to his room. Nothing seemed clear. He pondered every possible scenario for the existence of these people, but there was no explanation. He also fretted about the promise he made to Heinrich not to share classified information with his colleagues.

He knew that sharing this information would certainly risk his relationship with him and maybe jeopardize his family. The only honorable thing to do was to keep silent.

It seemed like only minutes had passed when a soft knock distracted his thoughts. Olaf whispered, "Are you up? breakfast is ready."

Elin no longer had an abundance of energy and was reluctant to get out of the warm bed. Olaf continued to knock, forcing him to answer the door.

"You don't look so good. Are you sick?" Olaf inquired.

"No," Elin snapped, "just tired. I'm not sleeping well. I miss Olga and Kirsten. I need to know if they're okay."

"I know," Olaf replied. "I feel the same way. We need to get on with this project and go home."

Most everyone was seated when the two men finally entered the dining room. "Guten Morgen," Helen cheerfully greeted. "Coffee?" *Coffee?* What a pleasant surprise, a rare treat, Elin thought—a Nazi gift once again. Dr. Brandt explained that Dr. Omsbaugh had brought the coffee from Berlin, a hard-to-get luxury right now considering the shortages of food.

Elin spoke loudly with a bold question. "And how are the food supplies in Norway?" Dr. Brandt looked a little irritated and simply said not to worry about Norway or his family. Things were being handled.

Dr. Omsbaugh and his driver Ben approached the table and sat down, curling his hands around the hot coffee cup. "We have prepared the car, and after breakfast we leave for Berlin. It's only a short drive to the city, so leave your belongings here. We will return tonight."

Helen served the men a hardy breakfast, and they left for Berlin. The mood in the car had changed. They were like children going to camp. The waiting was over. They were on their way to a new adventure, and they were both excited and apprehensive. Dr. Omsbaugh talked about the faculty and some of the projects. One could tell by the things he said that he was a scientist first and a Nazi second—politics were really not on his agenda. But like the rest of the men, he altered his life to accommodate the prevailing powers.

The gravel road soon gave way to a paved highway, and after passing several villages in an hour's time, the outskirts of Berlin appeared. Elin found himself more relaxed than before. He actually felt comfortable. Dr. Omsbaugh was not the devil he had assumed, but a man interested in new ideas and the progression of medical technology. Elin actually became excited, as did his colleagues.

Part Eight

Oslo was a city in a state of uncertainty with little if any outside communication—rumors abounded and military presence had heightened. Food became still harder to get, and Olga now saw more and more people near the water's edge, apparently fishing. The city had taken on a sorrowful feeling, so it seemed to Olga. Or, maybe it had always been so. Perhaps she had been too busy to notice. Now, she wasn't. Now, she noticed.

Sonja worried about her child and grandchild and moved in with them temporarily which helped relieve the boredom and increase the feeling of safety for both women. Sonja delighted in the companionship of her granddaughter and encouraged Olga to teach Christina's children to play the piano. It seemed to please Olga and gave her a sense of usefulness. She also helped Christina with home schooling her children and several of another of Christina's friend's children. She had to admit that Dr. Brandt had been right when he said the two families would need each other. It was almost as if he had known.

Unk continued to visit weekly and tried to keep Olga's spirits up with stories of better days as well as brief updates of Elin's whereabouts. Just knowing he was alive and well gave her great hope and courage.

Part Nine

Before arriving in Berlin Dr. Omsbaugh remarked that they must stop by SS headquarters and register. "It's just a formality in case you get stopped. You must show proper papers when visiting Berlin."

The building was amazing. It looked more like a museum with polished marble floors and statuary on elevated pedestals. Brightly colored flags flanked the second-floor balcony giving the impression of a grand walkway. SS soldiers paraded in black boots polished til they looked like mirrors. The sound of leather shoes hitting the marble echoed like heavy rain: tap, tap, tap. Midway into the long entrance stood a gilded desk. Seated behind the registration desk was a blonde woman. "May I help you?" she inquired.

"I'm Dr. Omsbaugh; here are my papers. We are here to register my colleagues."

"Third door on the right," she instructed. Elin was impressed by the formality. The feeling was almost ritualistic or church-like. A great deal of respect for this institution was apparent.

Elin and his colleagues entered the registrar's office. Two young men quickly stood and addressed the assemblage of visitors. Dr. Omsbaugh requested the necessary papers, and as easily as that, they left.

"Where to?" Ben asked. "We'll stop for a short break and then proceed to the facility," Dr. Omsbaugh instructed. "Is that okay with you Dr. Brandt?"

"Perfect," the Doctor answered, who up to this point had taken a back-seat approach and acquiesced Dr. Omsbaugh. After all, Berlin was his project.

The city was alive with activity, almost an arrogance. No signs of war were here. Shops were open, cafes were busy. *What a difference*, Elin thought. Oslo was dead by comparison. Ben, the driver, pulled into a driveway leading to a small, private hotel. "Comrades, we'll rest here. The SS have several private rooms near the dining hall. Wash up and meet us for lunch in about half an hour," he instructed. Dr. Omsbaugh preceded the men down the hallway, opening each door personally. Olaf, Elin, and Dr. Keiser entered first. Dr. Brandt and Dr. Omsbaugh disappeared into another.

"Dr. Keiser, what do you make of this?" Elin asked.

"Typical SS," he replied. "Only the best—a great facade for a paranoid government. The people of Berlin have no idea of what's really going on. The Nazis are the great deceivers, liars, and murderers. I don't know when, but someday my people will learn the truth and they will be embarrassed by the trickery of the Nazis."

Elin then recalled the conversation from earlier, at the lodge. "What about the comments Dr. Omsbaugh made about American and British bombings?"

"If that is true," Dr. Keiser replied, "We'll know soon enough. Germany will be the number one target, and I pity my people for the wrath they will surely suffer at the hands of Russia and allied countries."

"Better wash up," Olaf reminded his friends. "Adventure awaits."

After a brief respite and an early lunch, the men were once again on their way to experience the unknown. Signs of the new order were everywhere. Flags, posters, flowing banners and flowers were commonplace. The appearance of a culture experiencing a renaissance was apparent. Public buildings modeled after ancient Greece were intimidating, and courtyard gardens with public seating were most impressive. Elin sensed no stress in the population: happy children and old people alike shared smiles and friendly exchanges. All was well in Berlin, a city of peace and harmony.

Dr. Keiser sat silently near the window with a sad, forlorn stare, watching the procession of bikers and shoppers juggling for a position on the walkways. It was obvious Ben and Dr. Omsbaugh had picked a route to the Facility that had exposed the best of Berlin. But the enjoyable tour turned dark as the car drove out of Berlin and back into an area all too familiar to Elin and his colleagues. It was the same well-guarded situation they knew in Oslo. Deep into the woods on narrow roads, heavily patrolled. The excitement from earlier suddenly turned to dread as the men approached the mountainside compound of the Genetic Research Facility.

The car slowed at the guard gate, and papers were presented. Dr. Omsbaugh asked the men to refrain from comments and to stay close.

Dr. Karl greeted the visitors and invited them to join him in the briefing room. Elin was confused. It looked the same as Oslo. If so, why come all this way to experience the same projects. He felt the visit was premature.

Part Ten

S S guards opened the inner locked door revealing a long dark corridor. This was not like Oslo. The air was misty and paneled lights illuminated the hallway with a strange green glow. "Just around the corner," Dr. Karl explained. "Just a few more steps."

Elin was relieved when they entered the brightness of a normal office, just off the hallway. He commented that he hadn't expected the strange hallway. Dr. Brandt likewise appeared to be surprised. This was his first visit, and he wasn't bashful in asking Dr. Karl what was going on with the depressing hallway. Dr. Karl assured the men everything was in order. The green glowing lights were simply a new method of killing any unwanted bacteria or germs. The mist in the air was a deterrent. Elin felt better and the others also seemed relieved.

"Now," Dr. Karl continued, "Let's talk about your involvement in Angel Hair. Your jobs in Oslo prepared you for the next phase. Now we are asking you to use your expertise as doctors to assist us in delivering live-birth babies."

Dr. Keiser seemed angry and challenged the speaker. "Anyone can deliver babies," he said. "Why us?"

Dr. Omsbaugh snapped back, "They're special with special parents.

We can't trust just anyone with this project. You have been selected and have proven yourselves to be trustworthy. You have qualified for this project by being loyal and professional. Dr. Keiser, you are probably the finest pediatrician in Germany. We require only the best. Elin, you and Olaf have been watched for several years. We know your qualifications. This project has to be kept secret for the sake of Germany. You were told that originally. Have you forgotten? We maintain a limited number of doctors in order to keep this project quiet. That's why you were brought here. You are the special doctors; do you understand?"

Dr. Brandt was quick to answer. "Yes, we understand, you can't blame my colleagues for inquiring. We didn't understand the scope of our responsibilities. We understand now and you have our full cooperation."

Dr. Karl accepted his apology. "I have not been briefed on the entire Angel Hair Project, only on a need-to-know basis. But what I know I will try to share with you. It gets quite complicated, so feel free to ask questions. If I can answer I will, and if not, I have another source that might be agreeable to assist us.

"As you probably have heard, the Nazis are obsessed with the concept of a pure race, and they have spent hundreds of man hours in their quest to find it. The ancient legends and history of the German people tell them they came from a great civilization of advanced and beautiful people. Blonde haired, blue eyed, and pale skin were the outstanding features of both males and females. Hitler is determined to re-populate his people with their rightful heritage. German scientists and eugenic personnel have been working on genetic research in Germany as far back as the late 1800's. Now it seems they are advanced enough to fulfill Hitler's dream and that is a portion of what the Angel Hair Project provides: genetic manipulation and breeding of a new race."

Elin was stunned. It all made sense. The babies, the young women, the secrets, the security. This was the way it had to be. The German people would never agree to altered genes and engineered babies. *Oh my God*, he thought. *My colleagues and I are making this happen. No wonder we've been kept in the dark.* Elin debated whether he wanted to continue in the service of the Reich, but flashes of Olga and Kirsten rushed his memories. He and his colleagues were in too deep to escape now.

Dr. Brandt broke the silence with a question on how advanced this project was. Dr. Karl again explained he only knew of things he himself had experienced and had participated in. Dr. Brandt followed up. "Would you refresh us on the steps we've already experienced up to this point, from your perspective?"

"I believe you have experienced everything I have up to this point, but I will briefly update you on what I know. As I remember, you were briefed in Oslo when I visited the Facility there a few months ago. Basically, nothing has changed, but let me explain the agenda I received as an update.

"First, A segment of the Germans population was profiled and separated, meaning they had to pass the following criteria: young, fertile, blue eyes or green, fair skin and blonde to white hair. Second, candidates were interviewed to determine intelligence and heritage. At that time, they were placed in a hypnotic trance and tattooed with the Angel Hair Emblem. Third, arrangements were made with their families to send them to a campus where they were schooled, etc. This also allowed us access to them at all times. The hypnotic suggestion was easily delivered and most of the time there was no memory at all of their encounters with our scientists. Fourth, and I think this is where I think you became involved, you examined the selected candidates to determine their physical conditions and extract sperm from the young men. Is this correct?"

"Yes," Dr. Brandt answered for the group.

Dr. Karl continued. "Then you were sent to the Eugenic Facility in Oslo where you monitored the babies and performed extractions."

"That's right," Dr. Brandt again answered, "but we were never told what the extractions were for nor the circumstances that put the babies in the metal boxes."

"May I answer?" Dr. Omsbaugh interrupted.

"Yes, of course." Dr. Karl nodded.

"The young women under hypnotic control were impregnated with genetically altered sperm prepared by our leading geneticist. We have not been told what this sperm is or who it came from. That's a secret so closely guarded that only a few of Hitler's closest inner circle know. I happened to find out that all extractions came from Oslo. We do not perform the basic steps here, and that's why you are so important to us. The population in Norway is much purer and more abundant than any of our other sources. It was decided that the first stages of the project should be initiated in Oslo and then finalized in Berlin. The new fetus requires only a three-month term. It is then removed and placed in a special laboratory until about the second trimester at which time it is placed inside the boxes you saw at the Facility. These babies are the future of Germany. They have been genetically altered in such a way that they will automatically excel in whatever they choose."

"How is that possible?" Dr. Keiser questioned.

Dr. Brandt quickly replied, "If you remember earlier, I told you to forget what you were told and embrace a new, advanced technology. Where it came from is not for us to know. We are here only to help the Project progress and help it succeed. This is the dream of the Fuehrer—a new super race—a new Germany."

Part Eleven

D r. Karl again addressed the group. "What I've told you is the past and present. The future for you is to assist in full-term live births, not babies destined to boxes. These babies are even more important than the others. Their parents are special as well. After we visit the medical facility, I will explain their importance. Any questions? No? Then follow me,"

"Oh," Elin interrupted, "I have a question."

"Yes?" Dr. Karl replied.

Elin continued, "How are they able to control patients with hypnotic suggestions? This is something new to me. I guess I don't understand."

"From what I understand," Dr. Karl answered, "the technology is very advanced. It's not a parlor game antic you've probably heard about, but a sophisticated system of light beams. I've heard once the patient has been programmed, contact with a special light beam activates the suggestion. They say initially Hitler perfected this system for crowd control. I can't begin to imagine all the technological resources the Nazis have. It's frightening. Do you have any more questions?"

Elin shook his head and stepped into the misty hallway.

The contrast between the brightly lit office and dark hallway temporarily blinded him, causing him to step directly into the path of a darkly cloaked individual. He panicked Dr. Brandt quickly took his arm and moved him aside.

"I'm sorry!" Elin called out to the passing figure. "I didn't see you."

The cloaked figure simply bowed slightly and moved on. Olaf and Dr. Keiser, also blinded, stood along the wall waiting to hear Dr. Brandt's explanation.

"Who was that?" Elin asked. "Why is he cloaked?"

Dr. Brandt turned to Dr. Karl and asked him to answer.

"He's a member of our special assignment personnel. He doesn't answer to us, just to his superiors. You will see them occasionally. They wear robes because they are light sensitive and work in the laboratories."

"Who are their superiors?" Dr. Keiser questioned. "I thought the only power here was Nazi."

Dr. Karl searched for words to explain. "I've been told this is a collaborative project between Hitler and another source. I've only heard stories about the other source. Some say at one time it was Russia. Now that we're at war with them, I seriously doubt any contact exists. So, I'm not sure who the robed ones answer to. Hopefully we'll all be briefed in the near future. But now, as I've said before, everything is on a need-to-know basis, and I suggest you abide by the agenda and not push for answers. Please follow me into the maternity wing."

Part Twelve

The long space was like a typical hospital ward. Ten beds lined the walls on each side of the room, each featuring pull-around curtains, an assortment of medical supplies, and a woman lying, apparently asleep. The room was not brightly lit. Soft, glowing lights over the beds were very relaxing, quiet, and peaceful. Elin felt strange with the uncommon calm. It was unlike any maternity ward he had ever visited. He couldn't understand why each woman had a strap on her head with a cord leading to a box.

Dr. Karl proudly invited the men to participate in one of his examinations. "This is the procedure we expect you to follow, so pay attention. It's simple but important."

The men gathered around the first bed and Dr. Karl turned on a lighted panel. Immediately, numbers appeared. "This box is a monitor," he explained. "This number is the heart rate of the mamma, under that number is the heart rate of the child. All her vitals are on top and her baby's underneath. It is a fantastic machine. Are you wondering why she is still asleep? Let me explain. When her term is near, the mamma is placed in a hypnotic trance. She is kept asleep until someone turns off the instrument on her head, at which time she will awaken immediately. If she goes into labor, this machine will alert the authorities, and delivery will follow. You will be asked to assist in the delivery. She will feel no pain and no artificial medicines or anesthetics will enter her body or the baby's. The delivery is to be natural, and she will be awake. Any questions?"

The men were speechless. What could they possibly ask? It all seemed so well planned.

Dr. Omsbaugh asked if they would like to meet the patient in bed number one.

"Is that possible?" Olaf questioned.

"Of course; let me show you how easy this is." First, he checked her vitals; all were normal. He then turned off the cord connected to her head strap. Almost immediately, she opened her eyes.

"Hello," Dr. Omsbaugh said. "How are you today?"

She looked up at him with eyes so blue that they seemed artificial. "I'm fine," she said.

"Any discomfort?" he continued.

"No," she answered. "it's a wonderful experience. I'm so rested."

"Very well," Dr. Omsbaugh replied. "We'll wake you when it's time. Until then, enjoy your rest." With that, he turned on the head plate, and she closed her eyes.

"When is the 9-month term due?" Olaf asked.

Dr. Omsbaugh speculated that all of the women would begin labor in about a week.

Dr. Keiser questioned the timing of the pregnancies. "Were these women artificially impregnated or sexually exposed? Is that why they all deliver at about the same time?"

"Well, yes and yes," Dr. Karl remarked. "Some were impregnated artificially and some were not, and as you well know, it's not always what you want in terms of timing. Some will start early, and some will go long term, but we will guarantee all will deliver within a 24-hour period, even if we have to induce labor. We usually don't like to do it, but we will if we must. Angel Hair is a project on a strict schedule, and we must not delay, otherwise there be consequences. So, comrades, in about a week you all will be busy delivering 20 babies. How do you feel about that?"

Dr. Brandt expressed an opinion for the group saying his colleagues looked forward to the experience.

"Good," Dr. Karl acknowledged. "Now that we're here, let's check the vitals of our little mammas and send you on your way home."

All of the women appeared dead with pale skin, white hair, and perfect stillness. However, checking their vitals revealed that all were healthy young women under no stress. Elin was relieved and attempted to absorb all that he had just seen—quite an experience, he thought.

Dr. Karl and Dr. Omsbaugh walked the men back to the entrance where Ben was waiting beside the car. "We'll continue tomorrow," Dr. Karl advised. "See you then—Heil Hitler."

Part Thirteen

The ride back to the lodge passed quickly, with the men engaged in deep conversation. Question upon question fueled the conversation. So many questions became confusing. No one had definitive answers, only speculations. *This is invigorating*, Elin thought.

As they neared the forest road, everyone paused to catch their breath. It gave Dr. Keiser a chance to ask about the visit with his family.

"I will arrange it and let you know," Dr. Brandt replied.

"You know," Dr. Keiser continued, "I get the feeling that this project is going to be longer than we anticipated. Do you have any timeline on our stay here, Dr. Brandt?"

"Not exactly," he answered. "I was told we'd stay until we understand the mechanics of the project. How involved we get is still undecided. As Dr. Karl always says, it's on a need-to-know basis. When we need to know, they'll tell us. I just hope we get to go back to Oslo soon and return to our work there. I think both Elin and Olaf are anxious to return to their families."

The soft lights of the lodge appeared in the distance. The men, tired from the long day, changed the subject to Helen's dinner and an early bedtime before the trip back to Berlin.

Almost before they knew it, they were back at the facility for another day. Dr. Karl arrived early with a cheerful hello.

"You seem to be in a happy way," Dr. Brandt commented.

"Oh yes," Dr. Karl replied. "We've just been told the Fuehrer is planning a visit to the facility. He wants to see firsthand the progress we're making. This will be his first inspection and we're all excited."

"You mean he has never visited this facility before?" Dr. Brandt asked.

"That's right," Dr. Karl replied. "He's seen the beautiful people, but never bothered to venture out this far to see the process. You've met the Fuehrer haven't you, Dr. Brandt?"

Dr. Brandt paused and glanced at his colleagues before he answered. He appeared uncomfortable with the question. He then explained that he had met him and his staff during the transition of power from Keiser Wilhelm's government to the Nazi regime but had had no contact since then. Elin was puzzled. He had assumed that Dr. Brandt was a newly recruited Nazi and had not been a part of the traditional government. *Interesting*, he thought. *I wonder how he managed to survive the change of power. He must be more important than we know.*

"Today, comrades," Dr. Karl advised, "we'll visit the nursery and school. You may be called on to comment about the physical condition of the children, so observe carefully, as your input will be noted. As outsiders, you may notice things that we don't see. Since we are here every day, we might not catch subtle changes."

Elin was looking forward to seeing the children and getting out of the menacing hallway.

"This first nursery is called Alpha," Dr. Karl continued. "The babies here are up to one year and were all artificially implanted with select sperm. This is the beginning of the new German population." Elin was surprised at the variety of children. They all had the required visual features; blond and blue eyed, but they all looked different from one to the other and it was easy to tell them apart. Each was truly an individual. Some had curly hair, some straight and some had little or no hair. Elin chuckled to himself. They almost looked like little chickens running around on the floor with heads bobbing up and down.

The room was cheerful and open. No walls divided the newborns from the older children. Young women sat along the side wall near the newborns, feeding them from their full breasts. Dr. Karl explained some of these mammas had several children. Oftentimes two of their offspring shared the same space. "It is important," he continued, "that these children have affection and bonding time with their mothers. All of these young mammas have volunteered their services to the new order and all are well cared for. They have been told only that they and their children are a critical part of the new Germany, and they are accepted into the program with enthusiasm and purpose. We're very proud of their commitment. I would like for you to take time now to observe and interact with the children. Tell me what you think."

Elin was unsure of what he should do, so for a little while he just stood and watched. Noticing that Olaf and Dr. Keiser were sitting amongst the little ones, playing on the floor, he looked around for something to do. In the far corner of the room a small group of children, appearing to be about 5 to 7, gathered at a little table. He picked up a chair and approached them.

"Hello," he said. "I'm Elin, may I join you?"

The children looked up at him and appeared to be totally at ease with his intrusion. Then something happened that almost made him fall off his seat. One little tyke smiled and said in perfect German, "Yes, we'd love to visit with you."

Once again, Elin was speechless. It seemed this entire project had become one shock after another, and he began to question if his heart could continue to take the stress.

"I'll be right back," he said to the little boy, and rushed over to Olaf. "Come with me," he said. "I need you to see this."

"What is it?" Olaf inquired.

"You'll see," Elin whispered. "I can't believe what is happening."

Elin and Olaf quietly approached the table where the little children were busy working puzzles. "Hello again," Elin said, "This is my friend, Olaf. Would it be okay if he watches you work these puzzles?"

Another little tyke looked up and said, "Okay."

Elin looked at Olaf. "Did you hear that?" he questioned.

"I didn't hear him," Olaf answered.

Elin looked at the child and asked how old he was. Again, the little boy looked up and told him that he was 11 months and 21 days old.

"There," Elin insisted. "You heard him, right?"

"No," Olaf repeated. "I did not hear a word from that child's mouth; you are hearing things. Are you okay?" Olaf became very worried about his friend and considered calling Dr. Keiser over.

Elin stepped back and stared at the little boy. When the little guy asked if he wanted to play, Elin lost it. "Tell me please, Olaf, that you heard him ask me to play."

Olaf stared at him. "That does it, you need rest. We need to talk to Dr. Brandt, NOW." He took Elin's arm and attempted to pull him away. All of the children took notice and, in unison, simply said, "Thanks for sharing time with us."

Suddenly Olaf stopped, looking surprised. "I heard them talking," Olaf said. "Did you hear them?"

"No," Elin answered. I did not."

Olaf was now totally confused as well. "What is going on here?" They both stood and stared at the children who were all laughing and holding their hands over their mouths.

Unable to understand, both men quickly returned to the entrance where Dr. Karl and Dr. Brandt stood waiting. "Back so soon?" Dr. Karl asked. Both Elin and Olaf quietly stood, waiting for Dr. Keiser to join them, refraining from any conversation about their strange experience.

"Very well," Dr. Karl remarked. "We'll move on." The next room was a gymnasium with about 30 children who appeared to be 1 to 3 years of age. Elin, still confused by his prior experience, hung back behind the group. He wasn't quite ready for what might be in store for them next. Dr. Karl pointed out various activities taking place at this particular time. All of the children were actively involved in dancing and gymnastics, advanced in both areas. Little boys and girls who should barely have been able to walk waltzed to classical music in part of the room. The rest tumbled and applied sophisticated moves to floor exercises.

Dr. Karl commented, "music and gymnastics are important for mental and physical well-being. We start them early. Are you impressed? The Fuehrer hopes to have several Olympic champions from his new race." Elin and his colleagues sat for about an hour marveling at the agility and stamina of these special children. "I've much more to show you," Dr. Karl boasted. "I think you'll be even more impressed."

The next room they visited had the ambiance of a library and was perfectly silent. Dr. Karl whispered, "we must not interfere with the training going on in here. After you observe, the instructor will brief you on the project and let you participate." The men sat in the back of the dimly lit room. Three long tables with six chairs per side were centered at the opposite end. The participants at the first table were only boys, the second only girls. The third table had children of each sex opposite each other. The instructor approached the men and informed them that the first lesson was on levitation. The children worked as teams. "We're trying to determine which sex is stronger in this category." He then placed small boxes on one side of the table in front of the children. They were instructed that they were to physically move the boxes across the table to their partner on the opposite side when the buzzer went off. They were not allowed to use their hands, only their minds. "Impossible," Elin thought, as he glanced over at Olaf and frowned. But to his surprise, when the buzzer sounded, the boxes began to move, some slowly, some faster. The first team to accomplish this at each table stood up. The rankings were then noted from first to complete, to the last in sixth place. The instructor paired the winners against each other until one team remained. The other children were then shuffled, and the test began again. After about an hour, two children emerged, both girls, one four years and one five. You could tell the children were invigorated. Competition was second nature to them, and they excelled. Elin was exhausted just watching. When the instructor suggested a break, he stood, eager to exchange words with his colleagues.

"How is that possible?" Dr. Keiser asked.

Dr. Karl suggested they visit a lounge nearby and talk more freely. "There are powers here even I don't understand," he said. "It was all in training and genetic programming. I've heard rumors that the Nazis searched for the most powerful psychics known in Europe and extracted genetic material from them. Whether this is true or not, I don't know, but with everything else going on, I wouldn't be surprised. They tell me when the mind is pure and young, you can accomplish many things. The proof seems to be in the putting, I've heard them say. The Nazis became interested in levitation because ancient monuments were said to have been moved by the power of the mind. Seems to make sense—these children can already move small objects. Just think what could be accomplished with advanced training. Shall we return? I can't wait to see what comes next." Dr. Karl was evidently highly enthusiastic.

The children were already seated, eager to start the next lesson. The instructor again addressed the men. "The next session will require the children to tap into what we call the mind's eye. This is very difficult to do, but a few may actually get it on the first try. They will be given coordinates of latitude and longitude and by using their own power of perception, tell us what is there. Or better yet, draw a picture taken from their mind's view. Are you ready?" he asked the children. They all smiled their approval. "Latitude 29°, 58', 34" E / longitude 31°, 7', 52' 'N. What is it? Focus and draw."

The children became very still with eyes closed. Some began immediately, others took longer and when all were finished, they signed their names on the drawings and passed them to the instructor. He then distributed them in random order back to the children. One by one, he had the children stand with another child's drawing and explain what it was and if the information was correct in their opinion. It was an amazing, eye-opening experience. Elin and his colleagues had never been exposed to anything like this. They had never heard of the mind's ability to connect with the type of outside influences demonstrated here. Most impressive was the ability of several children to correctly identify the proper image located at the designated coordinates. After all the children had time to express their opinions, the instructor held up a picture with the latitude and longitude of the location. It was the great pyramid of Egypt. "Those of you that have the correct answer, please stand up and show us your picture." Elin's mouth dropped as did his colleagues. Approximately three fourth of the children stood and presented drawings of a large triangle. *I can't believe it*, he thought. How can little children do this? Dr. Karl, obviously pleased, congratulated the instructor "Most impressive," he complimented.

"Okay children, put your heads down on the table and close your eyes," the instructor ordered. "We're going to rest for a few minutes. Clear your minds—you know the drill. The next lesson is the last one for today and it is equally impressive," he commented. "Best for last," he chuckled.

Elin and his colleagues sat respectfully silent as the children prepared themselves for the next lesson. "As a special treat for our guests, we're going to involve them in our lesson. Is that okay with all of you?" the instructor asked. The excited children giggled approval. "Very well," he said. "This is how we'll do it; I think it will work. Children, line up and count off one, two, one, two. All of the ones sit on this side of the table, and all of the twos, on the other. Now, our guests will write on two sheets of paper several questions and sign their names. Team one, please pick up the first page of questions from our guests and take your place again behind the table. Team one will relay the question to team two and they will repeat the question and answer it as clearly as possible. Each child on team one will ask one question and any child in team two may answer. Do you understand the procedure?" he asked. Everyone, including the visitors, agreed that they understood but it was obvious that the visitors didn't understand the delivery. After writing their question they just looked at each other in confusion.

A child from team one stood facing team two, apparently silently reading a question from the guest. Several children on team two stood. "Very good," the instructor commented. "Now let's see how well you've done. He then asked the little boy who had jumped up first, "Who is the question from?"

The little guy said, "From Dr. Keiser."

"And what is the question?"

The little boy continued, "He wants to know if we're happy here."

"And the answer?"

"Yes, we're very happy."

The instructor walked over and took the sheet of paper from team one and showed the visitors the question Dr. Keiser had written. "Is this your handwriting?" he asked the doctor. Dr. Keiser just held the paper in his hands, unable to comprehend what he had just participated in. "Yes, it is my writing, but I didn't hear her read it. Did I miss something?"

"No," the instructor answered him. "Don't be alarmed if you feel that way, most people react the same. The truth is our children are telepathic, meaning they can converse with each other telepathically. Once you master the ability, most people can do it. They can also block it. There are a lot of people who can pick up telepathic conversations, but don't understand the process. They think it's their own mind talking to them and sometimes it is, but there are also times when they meet a practicing telepath and the voice inside their heads is actually telepathic. Does that make sense to you?" he questioned.

No one answered. Elin personally felt unsure of his own reality at this point and was afraid to venture forth with any comments.

The children continued with the lesson until all of the questions had been answered and at the end of the class time, came over to personally meet Elin and his colleagues. The children appeared normal in every way physically, but it was apparent they were not normal mentally. As a matter of fact, it was frightening. Dr. Karl thanked the instructor and the children for sharing their talents with him and his colleagues then bid them goodbye. The little ones waived and marched out of the room. "Comrades," Dr. Karl whispered, "The new German Super Race—Heil Hitler."

Dr. Brandt addressed the group, "I am astonished at what I have seen today. We must learn more about their training."

The men were asked to followed Dr. Karl through the same exit the children used. There was a long, winding path separating the buildings.

It was park-like with beautiful flowers, fountains, and benches to sit on, a startling contrast to the building they had just left. At the entrance stood two guards. Dr. Karl flashed his papers. The men said nothing. They opened the doors and closed them behind the group. Inside appeared to be administrative rooms, occupied by SS and female personnel. Dr. Karl waved and was acknowledged. "This is where they live: apartments. The larger units are on the ground level—noise control," he laughed.

Inside was a very comfortable, pleasant living space—spotlessly clean. It consisted of a sitting room featuring two desks, a sofa, and a chair. A small kitchen was located off the end of the room. There appeared to be one bathroom and two sparsely furnished bedrooms. All lighting was in the ceiling. There were no lamps.

"Very nice, don't you think? Dr. Karl remarked.

"Yes, yes of course," Dr. Brandt answered.

"Upstairs are the one-bedroom units which are the same as this, minus a room. Now, follow me." Elin and the men obliged, and Dr Karl opened a door, revealing a huge lounge area filled with children and comfortable furniture. Large dining tables lined the far wall opening into a kitchen. "This is the heart of the living facility. It is where everyone can be a part of an extended family. We are just in time for the reunion."

Elin looked around and saw nothing more than children playing, closely watched by nursemaids. Suddenly a bell rang and a stampede of beautiful, blonde women flooded the room. Children scattered and women wrapped their arms around what whoever was apparently their child. It was indeed an event that everyone looked forward to. Laughter was deafening.

"Where have they been?" Elin asked. Dr. Karl explained. "The mammas stay here with their child until the child reaches the age of 6 years, then they are matched with an arranged male and marry. The young family will then move to a home of their own. But for now, the mammas have duties. They leave the apartments early in the morning for school and training. Every afternoon at this time they return. These are daily routines, but in the evenings both mother and child share critically important bonding time. It is necessary for a healthy mental state.

Everyone needs love. They are free to do what they want, as long as they don't leave the facility."

Well done, Elin thought. *Total dependence on the Nazis.*

The room quickly cleared out with children pulling their mammas outside to a play park. The men walked over and peered into the world of a perfect society—happy children, happy parents, happy government. How convenient. Olaf asked Dr. Karl about the women in the maternity ward. "Will they live here as well?"

"Oh yes," Dr. Karl remarked. "All that come here stay here until their child is 6, then they have to assimilate into the general population. That's how it is to be. Of course, we'll keep a close eye on them for a while to make sure all is within the scope of our agenda. Comrades, I don't know about you, but I think it's time to leave. I'm sure you have much to talk about and I'm pleased you have been so polite and cooperative. We'll meet again tomorrow. Heil Hitler."

Part Fourteen

Once again, Ben was waiting at the entrance. Dr. Brandt and the men climbed into the car, eager to discuss the events of the day. Dr. Keiser was the most vocal of the group, ranting about brain washing and the manipulation of the young women and children.

"Calm down," Dr. Brandt ordered. "I know you have no love for the Nazis," he continued, "but it's dangerous to criticize them in this manner. I can only protect you so much, and I'm not willing to get myself killed doing it. I'm warning you to keep quiet."

Olaf looked at Elin and said nothing. It was obvious that they had to refrain from sharing with Dr. Brandt. How could Dr. Kaiser have let down his guard and gotten so comfortable with him? He may be their guide and companion, but he was still SS.

The events of the day were rolling around in Elin's head when he had an epiphany. He sat straight up in his seat. "Olaf," he sputtered, "I know what happened this morning when I sat down with the little tykes at the table. Remember I called you over?"

"Yes," Olaf answered.

"What do you think happened? Don't you see?" he continued. "Our conversation was telepathic. That's why you couldn't hear him—that's why I didn't hear him talk to you. That's why they were laughing. They played a trick on us, and it was funny."

Olaf wasn't so sure. "How could they have heard the little boy so clearly?"

Elin hesitated, "I don't know. It felt like we talked, but now I'm not so sure. Could there be a possibility that we received his messages telepathically? It has to be that. Thank God I'm not going crazy," Elin whispered.

Olaf, not knowing how to react, sat quietly. Dr. Keiser listened, but didn't comment, afraid to upset Dr. Brandt again. Dr. Brandt turned around in the front seat of the car and said to Elin, "Oh, it's probably just your imagination and stress. I wouldn't worry about it."

The men returned home earlier than usual. Helen, unprepared for dinner, apologized and excused herself. Heinrich welcomed his visitors. He was anxious to hear about Berlin and updates on the war. The men settled in around the warmth of the flickering fire as Dr. Brandt produced more wine. The evening became agreeable again with a friendly exchange of ideas.

Shortly before bedtime, Heinrich took Elin aside and told him that his friend from the forest was standing at the edge of the woods, watching the house. Immediately, Elin went out to greet the mysterious man, but he had returned to the darkness of the trees.

"I felt he might be looking for you, because I have never known them to come here to the house for any reason," Heinrich whispered when Elin returned.

Elin was a taken back. "What do you think he wants?" he inquired.

"I wouldn't know; maybe he's just curious about you, like you are about him. You do have a similar appearance with the light hair and skin. Maybe he thinks you're his long lost brother." Heinrich teased.

"Thanks a lot," Elin laughed. "Maybe soon I'll walk again in the woods and look for him."

"Just be careful," Heinrich reminded him.

"I'll see you in the morning," Elin replied.

Sameness dominated the next few weeks, observing the children and keeping an eye on the maternity ward, basically a repeat of the original visit with the exception that Dr. Keiser was allowed to spend the nights with his wife. Its pleased Elin that Dr. Brandt kept his promise to the aging physician, allowing him this time with his family. It also pleased him that Dr. Keiser's wife would likely be more informed about the status of the war, so he and Olaf would have information not readily available to them from their SS hosts.

Elin and Olaf were extremely homesick and restless. Dr. Brandt was disappointed with Berlin. He had expected to be more involved in the project and often pushed Dr. Karl for more information. The weeks were boring, but passed quickly. Dr. Karl had suggested that they all relax this weekend because the following week was the time for the planned deliveries in the maternity ward. All physicians would be on call 24 hours a day and expected to stay in the sleeping rooms provided by the facility. He insisted they rest and clear their minds of any problems. He warned that they must be physically and mentally alert.

Elin was thrilled with the suggestion. It gave him an opportunity to return to the woods and hopefully connect with his obsession—the tall stranger. Dr. Keiser would be free to stay in Berlin and Olaf, an avid reader, would catch up on an unread book he had been carrying around. Dr. Brandt chose to stay in Berlin and visit friends which also pleased him. It freed him from the watchful eye of the SS.

Elin arose early the next morning, slipped on his boots, and headed into the woods just as daylight broke over the lodge. After a few yards, he realized it was still too dark in the heavy crop of timber for him to safely negotiate the winding streams, so he turned back to the lodge porch and waited until the sun rose a little higher.

This was a new world for Elin, these pristine vistas in uncanny silence. He saw things he had never taken time to appreciate before. He had never observed the simple act of the sun peeking over trees, or the of casting of light over frozen, sparkling ground. When the small ice crystals sparkled like diamonds, he smiled and wished Olga could see this. It was so beautiful. Suddenly he sensed that he wasn't alone. He stood and looked around. He couldn't see anyone.

"Hello. Hello again," a voice echoed. Still, he saw no one.

The voice echoed again, "Hello, over here, near the woods."

Elin turned slightly and saw the stranger standing at the forest edge. His heart beat faster and faster; he was excited, but afraid. *Is this safe?* he wondered.

Hearing the assuring voice again and the words "Come, walk with me," made the whole experience surreal. He heard the voice, but whether it vocal, or only in his head, like at his visit with the children, he couldn't tell.

The stranger waved his hand and motioned for him to come closer. The shock and fear were now subsiding, and he walked toward the tall stranger.

"Hello," Elin said in German. "I'm so happy to see you. I've been very curious about you since we met in the woods."

"I know," the stranger acknowledged in Norwegian.

Elin looked surprised. He actually heard him speak, and in his native language. "I didn't realize you spoke Norwegian."

"I speak many languages," the stranger continued, "but I'm selective about sharing that information with others."

"I understand," Elin remarked.

"If you like," the stranger offered, "we have a shelter some distance from here. You could walk with me for a while, then we can sit and get to know each other."

"I would like that," Elin answered. "It will shorten the long walk I was planning to take and give me a chance to make a new friend."

The stranger smiled and stepped into the trees with Elin close behind.

"My name is Elin. What's yours?"

"You may call me Alta."

"I don't think I've ever heard that name before," Elin commented. "Where does it come from?"

Alta didn't respond and began to walk faster. The sound of his walking stick cracking the frozen leaves eventually broke the silence. "I love these woods," Alta said, "and I'm glad to see that you enjoy them too."

"These brisk walks help me focus," Elin admitted, "and help relieve the separation anxiety caused from leaving my family in Norway."

The pace became even faster, requiring Elin to focus only on his steps as Alta moved further ahead. He struggled to keep up. Alta was a perfect specimen, obviously adapted to walking quickly in the dense forest. Elin was not; soon he stopped and bent over, gasping for air.

Alta, several paces ahead, stopped as well. "I'm sorry," he said. "I was so engrossed in thought I momentarily forgot you."

"I'm okay," Elin assured him, "just out of shape. I need to do this more often," he laughed.

Alta slowed down as the men approached the bubbling stream, near the spot they had originally met. "This looks familiar," Elin remarked.

"Yes," Alta replied, "it is near the shelter and the boundary to our lands." Elin looked around for the signs of security Heinrich had talked about, but he saw no fences, gates, or postings. One tree was just like another. It didn't seem so ominous to him. Maybe Heinrich was wrong.

He carefully followed Alta along the water's edge until the taller man held up his hand in a manner that said stop. Elin froze. *What's he doing?* he thought. *I see no reason to stop here.* Alta turned and explained that they were now entering private land, and he had to alert his people that he was approaching with a visitor. Once again, Elin looked around for some type of security—no guards or devices were visible.

Alta stopped, pulled a little black triangle from his pocket ,and pointed it into the woods. Elin jumped in surprise as Alta turned, grabbed his arm, and asked that he stand still.

"What is that in your hand?" Elin questioned.

Alta, in a reassuring voice, told him it was a security system, and they were being scanned. "If we entered the land unannounced, the authorities would quickly seize us and demand an explanation."

Elin watched in amazement as the red beam streaked across the front of him, emitted a deep humming noise, and turned green.

"We can go now," Alto advised. "We've been cleared."

"I can't believe what I've just seen," Elin said. "How does that work?"

Alta just smiled and said he wasn't sure. Elin now realized Heinrich was indeed right. There was security and technology far beyond anything he could ever imagine.

Part Fifteen

Just beyond a small clearing stood a shelter. The front door and chimney were visible; the rest of the shelter was covered with ancient sod and moss. Alta entered first. The small room was sparsely appointed with a long wooden bench and a table. Several buckets and cups for drinking sat in a handmade cupboard. The place reminded Elin of stories is mother told about elves and fairies living in the woods.

Alta excused himself and picked up a bucket. "I'm going for water," he said. "I'll be right back."

Elin sat down, tired and thirsty, but eager for a conversation with Alta. He was now more curious than ever. Alta returned shortly, bringing water and wood for the fire.

"Let me help with the fire," Elin offered. "I'm very good at that chore."

Alta handed him a few logs and carried the water bucket to the table. Piling the logs in a perfect arrangement, he looked for something to fire it with. Elin appeared perplexed. Matches were nowhere in sight.

Alta seemed amused. "Let me assist you," he suggested. "I have a fire starter." Pulling out a strange instrument, he immediately lit the fire.

Elin again was a taken back with the technology and asked if the advanced instruments were from the Nazis.

"Oh, no," Alta said emphatically. "These devices have been in our culture forever. To us, they're antiques. I'm surprised you haven't encountered them before. We gave the technology to the Germans many years ago."

The room warmed quickly, and the men settled on the old wooden bench. Alta poured cold, sparkling water into their cups. Elin was hoping to ignite a productive conversation but was hesitant. He didn't want to appear eager or offend his host with personal questions, so he quietly sat there warming his hands, hoping Alta would initiate the exchange. Shortly Alta did so, and Elin burst into a deluge of questions that even Alta found hard to keep up with. As the shelter became warmer, Elin removed his outer coat. Alta also removed his outer clothing.

The glowing fire lit the dim interior, and for the first time Elin could see his host well. His hair was almost pure white. His skin was the same, very pale and a little thin, unusual for a person of the outdoors, Elin thought. But the thing that captured his attention the most were his eyes. They looked like glass—pure blue in color with a silver halo around the pupil, almost like mirrors as they reflected the dancing fire. He was fascinated.

"Is something wrong?" Alta questioned.

"No," Elin replied. "I've been admiring your eyes. They're very interesting. I don't think I've ever encountered anyone with eyes so blue."

Alta smiled. "Family trait," he answered. The exchange of questions continued for hours. They talked uninterrupted. Often, Elin would gasp and express disbelief at what his new friend was telling him, but still wanting more, he pressed for new information.

I was near midday when their conversation was interrupted. Dogs barking in the distance prompted Alta to stand and open the door to listen more closely. "Someone is in the woods," he cautioned.

Elin jumped to his side and quietly listened too. He heard horns blowing, dogs barking and voices calling his name.

Alta looked concerned. "I think they're looking for you," he said. "You better go before they enter our lands. Hurry," he insisted.

Elin quickly dressed and Alta pointed him in the direction of the stream. "Hurry," he repeated. "They're not far. You'll be just fine. I enjoyed our time together, and you will hear from me again, I suspect very soon. Try not to be alarmed at your new knowledge; rejoice in it. It's part of your future."

Elin said goodbye to his friend and jogged back toward the stream.

He could hear the dogs getting closer and walked in the direction of their barking. "Elin, Elin," voices called.

"Over here," Elin answered. "I'm here."

Suddenly he was surrounded by dogs, three of Heinrich's pets all jumping and wagging their tails. Olaf, Ben and Heinrich soon followed. "Thank God!" Olaf exclaimed. "We've been worried about you. Were you lost?"

Elin decided it was in his best interest to say yes. It would excuse his long disappearance and eliminate any explanation. "I must have turned the wrong way," he mumbled. "This is a vast forest."

"I'm glad we found you before night fall," Ben added. Heinrich looked at Elin with a knowing glance and suggested they go back to the lodge.

After the men devoured a small plate of bread and cheese, Olaf recommended they rest. "You must be exhausted," he insisted. "Go to bed and we'll wake you for dinner."

Happy to oblige and needing time to absorb the volume of information he had just been given, Elin agreed. "Thank all of you again," he said, and ascended to the second story retreat.

Lying quietly in bed, he sensed that his life as he knew it was over. He felt different, empowered with new knowledge and a feeling of connection with something unbelievable: a new direction, a new identity, a new life. He would never be able to see the world in the same way because it isn't the same world he knew. He now had a clear picture of what the Facility was all about and what Hitler and his circle of warped elites were attempting to do. He was very concerned, but Alta had assured him that Hitler's plan would never reach fruition. Thought after thought raced through his mind until, out of pure exhaustion, he drifted off to sleep.

Part Sixteen

Monday morning, the men reunited in the Facility briefing room. Dr. Karl, who had kept watch over the maternity ward over the weekend, advised all was as planned. Several of the women were dilating and birth was expected shortly. "Please prepare yourselves: change your clothing and scrub. We'll meet in the maternity ward."

Just inside the doors, the temperature had dropped. It was rather cold. "Have a seat," Dr. Karl recommended. "It shouldn't be too long now."

Elin was nervous. Olaf and Dr. Keiser stood by and were obviously nervous as well. Dr. Brandt appeared calm, but that's what you'd expect from an SS officer. Suddenly, out of the silence, an alarm sounded. Elin almost jumped out of his skin. He wasn't expecting it even though he had been briefed earlier.

"Let's go!" Dr. Karl advised. "Bed number five is ready."

The men surrounded the bed as Dr. Karl removed the head strap from the woman's head. She immediately opened her eyes. He took her hand and in, a comforting voice said, "It's time; we're here to assist you." He then checked the screen on the monitor. "Yes," he said, "we're ready. Relax and remember what we taught you: breathe and push."

The men watched closely. There appeared to be no stress. She performed as instructed, and soon the baby's head broke through the vaginal canal. Dr. Karl carefully pulled it out, cut the umbilical cord, and handed the little boy to an awaiting nurse that had joined the men unnoticed.

"Before you take him, may I see him?" Dr. Keiser requested. The nurse hesitated, but at a nod from Dr. Karl, she handed the baby to Dr. Keiser. Elin and Olaf were also eager to view the first baby to be delivered. But when the blanket was opened, Elin gasped. The little guy had no color. His skin was stark white, and every vein and ligament was visible through it.

"What's wrong with him?" Dr. Keiser asked.

"Nothing," Dr. Karl answered. "I told you these were special babies that have been genetically altered."

"For what purpose?" Dr. Keiser questioned.

"I don't have the answer," Dr. Karl replied. "I just oversee the deliveries. I'm hoping to be informed soon. I too find it interesting."

"How could I possibly know if this child is in danger? I have nothing to relate it to," Dr. Keiser pleaded,"

"We'll visit the nursery, and you'll learn," Dr. Karl assured him. "If the child had been in danger, the instruments would have alerted us. As I said: fantastic technology."

Elin stepped back to his chair. He knew what was going on. Alta had explained it to him, and he knew this child had a special place in Alta's culture. What worried him was whether it was the property of the Third Reich or Alta's people. During the next several hours, many of the alarms sounded. Sometimes two or three at a time. The doctors split into teams, and by following Dr. Karl's instructions, were able to deliver all twenty babies by the following day. It wasn't hard work, but the lack of sleep and random intervals between deliveries made it impossible to relax.

Operation Baby went perfectly. No major problems were apparent.

"Good job," Dr. Karl complimented the men when they were all scrubbed out and clean. "Now, go home and rest."

As they walked down the dim hallway, there was a flurry of activity. Robed personnel scurried in and out of the room, excited about the babies.

Part Seventeen

The drive back to the lodge found the men unable to converse about the day. Dr. Brandt was there, but what more could they ask him? He evidently was not aware of anything else. If Dr. Karl didn't know, it seemed impossible that Dr. Brandt would not be kept in the dark.

Elin already knew many secrets but couldn't share what he had been told by Alta, at least not yet. Alta had told him that he could confide in his colleagues. He also suggested that Dr. Brandt was not what he appeared to be and that he could be a strong ally. This information piqued Elin's curiosity and he wondered just who Dr. Brandt really was. Time would tell, he thought.

The drive home proved to be boring, filled with small talk, chatter, and more speculation. It wasn't until evening when the men sat around the fire that stories began to surface.

Ben had new information. Dr. Keiser shared his stories and surprisingly, Dr. Brandt supplied a few stories of his own. Elin sat quietly, mentally taking notes and trying to connect the dots. He was still pondering the question of: *Who is the real Dr. Brandt?*

Near the end of the evening, Heinrich joined the group. He was interested in news of the war. Ben shared his story of the British bombing at the hydro plant in Weimar.

"What?" Elin exclaimed. "They bombed the plant; did they bomb anywhere else? Is Oslo safe?"

"Dr. Brandt," Olaf asked, "did you know about this?"

"Yes," he replied. "They only attacked the plant, and I didn't want to worry you."

"If they can do that, they can target anywhere. Where are the Germans? They occupy Norway but don't defend us. This worries me," Olaf lamented.

"Norway is not a prime target," Dr. Brandt said softly. "The country is isolated from main battlegrounds. The Allies aren't interested in satellite countries. They want Germany. Informants say the water at Weimar has properties used for some kind of bomb making. That's why they destroyed it."

Dr. Keiser repeated a story he had heard and asked Dr. Brandt to respond. "I've been told," Dr. Keiser continued, "That the German Army in Russia is surrounded and many soldiers have surrendered. Is that true?"

"It depends on who you talk to," Dr. Brandt answered. "But, personally, I think it's true. My sources say it's been a hard winter and Germans are starving and freezing to death. If that's the case, they wouldn't be able to hold back a large Soviet offensive. Germany is also having problems in Africa. I think they've spread themselves too thin."

Dr. Keiser inquired about rumors of mass murders of the Jewish people, particularly in Poland where he had heard rumors of death camps and gas chambers.

"I have been told," Dr. Brandt explained, "that Hitler is conducting a mass cleansing of the total populations in all of the occupied countries, including the killing of the Jewish, 'undesirables,' gypsies, homosexuals, and mentally impaired persons. He wants only a pure race to occupy his land. That's the purpose of Angel Hair—to produce replacements for the many killed. I don't know anyone in the governments inner circle, so I can't validate any of this, but if it's true, it's a tragedy. This is not the Germany I know, and I pray for its people."

Elin spoke up. "Is Germany losing the war?"

"I don't know," Dr. Brandt speculated. "If we are, we'll be the last to know. Hitler will keep us at war until the last man falls. God help us!"

Elin was beginning to see what Alta was referring to. Maybe this was the real Dr. Brandt, a softhearted man with the facade of a hard-nosed SS officer. Elin now realized Dr. Brandt really had attempted to be an ally to him and his family. *Yes*, he thought, *this is what Alta meant.*

"Well comrades, I think I'll retreat to bed," Dr. Brandt yawned. "Enough talk of rumors. Have a good night, and we'll meet in the morning?"

The following day proved to be a day of surprises, not all good ones. As the car approached the facility guard gate, they were stopped. On previous visits they had been waved through. "Yes?" Dr. Brandt questioned. "What's wrong?"

The guard said there had been an accident and they would have to obtain clearance to continue. The guard went inside and appeared to be making a call. "Go ahead," he called out, and the gate opened.

Ben was alarmed and the men sat on the edge of their seats, looking around with anxious stares. "This is a very secure facility, what could possibly happen here?" Dr. Brandt questioned.

Surrounding the front doors were a multitude of SS soldiers forming a blockade. Dr. Brandt and the others approached cautiously and then stopped. "We work here," Dr. Brandt explained. "What is going on?" Dr. Karl pushed his way forward from behind two soldiers and addressed his colleagues. "You must go back home. Someone has taken the new babies, all twenty of them. The facility is on lock-down. You cannot enter."

The men were speechless.

"I'll be in touch; Heil Hitler!" Dr. Karl shouted.

The surprised men stood in shock for a second, then returned to the waiting car, trying to make sense of the scene. A truck pulled up. Soldiers guarding the entrance opened the truck doors and forced several robed personnel into the vehicle.

"Let's go, Ben," Dr. Brandt ordered. "Hurry!" Ben turned the car toward the exit road and sped away. "This is not safe," Dr. Brandt declared. "I'm not exactly sure what happened, but I have an idea, and there's going to be big trouble here." Elin too had an inkling, recalling pieces of what Alta had told him.

The men were visibly shaken. Ben wanted out of the area as soon as possible. "Stop at the next village pub," Dr. Brandt ordered. "We need a break."

A few miles away, Ben pulled into a roadside tavern. "Is this, okay?" he inquired.

"If they have beer? Then it's okay," Dr. Brandt said in a sarcastic tone. Dr. Brandt's mood had changed from confusion to fear, anger, and then sarcasm in a short period of time. Everyone kept quiet, not knowing what emotion he might display next. It seemed safer that way.

Jerking open the car door and slamming it shut, Dr. Brandt charged the front door of the old tavern and held it open for his colleagues. Elin looked at his friends. The mood wasn't sarcastic anymore. It was obvious to them that Dr. Brandt was more than angry.

The little tavern was near empty. A few older men sitting at the bar stared at the men with a suspicious glare, unaccustomed to strangers, especially SS officers. Dr. Brandt gathered the men around a table in the corner and yelled at the barmaid to bring five glasses of beer. Elin could tell he frightened her. She fumbled around, clanging glasses and nervously pulling at her apron. Quickly, she served them and walked away. "Don't go far," he ordered. She dropped a little curtsy and returned to the bar.

Dr. Brandt drank half the glass in one swallow, then looked at his colleagues. "Friends," he said, "may I call you friends?"

Elin could tell that everyone was surprised by the question.

"Of course, we consider you our friend," Olaf answered.

"Can I trust you to keep quiet about what I am going to tell you?"

The men looked at each other, answering yes.

"Good," Dr. Brandt replied. "Listen, I'm sorry for my behavior, but I'm extremely angry at the Nazis. What happened today may change

Germany forever. They are fools: stupid, self-centered idiots. What I want you to know is something I've never shared with anyone, and I warn you if the Nazis find out you have information regarding what I'm going to tell you, they will kill all of you. Do you understand? If you don't want to be involved, please leave now."

The men looked at each other again. No one rose to leave.

"Very well," Dr. Brandt continued.

"When I was a young doctor after the first war and after Kaiser Wilhelm II abdicated, in 1918, the country was basically run by the military. My family was friends with one of the leading generals. One day he sent for me and swore me to secrecy. He said he needed a liaison to work between Germany and Legacy, a powerful society. He again stressed the importance of secrecy. Of course, I was flattered and immediately accepted the position. He told me only a few very select people in the government knew of this special agreement... treaty. I'm telling you now because I'm afraid our country has broken this treaty.

"Do you remember when I told you Angel Hair Project was a collaboration between two parties and I couldn't disclose who the second party was?"

The men nodded affirmatively.

"Well," he continued, it's Legacy, a genetically produced group of people called the mixed ones. They are the offspring of an ancient, highly advanced, pure race living in the mountains. The Legacy group lives as an open society among the general population and are carefully monitored. I was told that the pure race has been around thousands of years, basically living in secret.

"I was told, in the mid 1800's, there was a large explosion deep in a forest. The German Kaiser sent a select group of men to investigate. When they returned, they told him a story that was unbelievable, which later led to a treaty.

"It appeared the soldiers had discovered the original highly advanced pure-bred population living deep underground in a mountain range. They were told it was a crash which caused an explosion, some type of equipment failure. When the soldiers got there, they helped put out the fire and met their leader. This group insisted they must be left alone, and in exchange they would supply technology to the German people. They asked only for a section of the forest be set aside for their privacy. In return, they would not interfere in the German government or their people. It seemed simple enough, and the old German Kingdom embraced the alliance. Since the beginning of the treaty there has always been a liaison, and at this time, it's me.

"When Hitler and his thugs took power, they obsessed over the creation of a pure race. While they were searching files on the legends of a highly evolved race, they found my name in former government files regarding eugenics. I was called in and questioned, or rather interrogated, about my role in the program. I told them I didn't know any more than they did about these people. I only knew the old German empire had a special relationship with them, but I was never told exactly what it was. I was never able to contact them, and I've never seen any of them. If they need anything, they send someone to talk to me. I'm the only one they will communicate with, I'm told, maybe because all the other people who knew about the treaty are now dead. I feel that's why the Nazis give me a little freedom to do what I do; they can't make contact.

"My colleagues, this is why we're involved with Angel Hair; it's part of the original treaty agreement, and I have a responsibility to protect these people from the greed of the Nazi Party. Though I know they could eliminate Germany with the stroke of a stick."

Elin couldn't believe what he was hearing. Part of the story Alta told him corroborated Dr. Brandt's story. More now than ever, he could see the real Dr. Brandt. He was the liaison to Alta's people.

Dr. Keiser spoke softly. "These advanced people have been helping German scientists as well as supplying them technology?"

"Yes," Dr. Brandt replied. "They started teaching them eugenics in the late 1800's so they could cure many illnesses in the German people as well as their animals. They are innocent and naïve, but now they're really upset. Hitler has demanded they assist in the development of his pure race using their advanced technology. They refused because his reasons are dangerous and dark. These are unique people, both physically and intellectually, and they will not share their genes with him."

"What do they look like?" Olaf questioned.

"They supposedly are the beautiful people Hitler is looking for: white hair and skin with piercing blue eyes, possibly the original race of highly advanced people that is reported to have been here for thousands of years."

"Has Hitler ever seen them?" Olaf continued.

"No," Dr. Brandt answered. "As I said, they refuse to meet with anyone but me. And I haven't seen any of the pure race either, only the mixed ones. If they should find out that Hitler knows where they are, they'll leave Germany, and we will lose our greatest gift."

Elin ran his finger around the rim of his glass. "What do you think happened today at the facility?"

"Those babies we delivered," Dr. Brandt explained, "were children of the Voltar people. Their females are having trouble carrying full term babies, and it was agreed that twenty of the facility's women would act as incubators for the implanted fetuses. They all volunteered, and the experiment was a success, as you witnessed. The Voltar people were most appreciative and promised more technology to the military. They have already given them rocket power beyond our expertise. That's why Hitler is so sure of his success. He has an ally that is technologically years ahead of any other government. But now I fear his greed and thirst for power have pushed Germany over the edge and today sealed our fate."

"Are you saying the Nazis took those babies?" Dr. Keiser whispered.

"Yes, that's exactly what I think. They would now have the genes of the pure super race and the genetic ability to reproduce them. The Voltar people have been duped, and I know they won't let this pass. Germany is sunk."

"Oh my god," Elin sighed. "Those were Voltar babies. I feel so bad; is there anything we can do?"

"No," said Dr. Brandt. "I'm sure they will try to contact me, and I'll ask what they want me to do. I'll let you know. Now let's go home before World War Three starts."

Section Three

Part One

The men again sat in other worldly silence as the car carried them into the forest, trying to absorb what they had learned.

Dr. Brandt turned around in his seat, striking sadness in his face. "If the SS comes for me, I will protect you as long as I'm able. Please, do not volunteer anything. They don't know what you know, so for your own sake, keep quiet. I'll refuse to take them to the mountains, and I'll probably be killed. So, be safe my friends, and keep your eyes and ears open. Be on guard."

Later in the evening, Elin heard Alta call his name. *Fate has a funny way of surprising you*, he thought as he ventured to the window to peer out.

At forest edge was Alta. A small light glowed in his hand. Elin hurriedly put on his boots and coat.

"Where are you going?" Heinrich asked as Elin rushed past him and out the door.

"Be right back," he called over his shoulder.

Elin felt the need to embrace Alta like friends. "I'm so sorry about today," he said.

"It's okay," Alta responded. "We expected something like this and were prepared."

"What do you mean?" Elin questioned.

"After you left the facility, we surrounded the building and took our children away. We also retrieved our nurse maids from the soldiers. Then we destroyed the facility and all that was in it."

Elin didn't breathe. "What about the children and women that lived there?"

"They were puppets of an evil regime and genetically flawed. They were also destroyed along with the scientists and military."

"You know they'll come for you, don't you?" Elin warned. "

Yes, we know, but we will be gone. They'll never find us. I wanted you to know we will be watching you and your family. If need be, we'll come for you."

Elin didn't quite understand. Why would they care about him?

"I must go now," Alta said. "Tell Dr. Brandt goodbye. We'll miss him, but possibly will see him again soon."

"Goodbye," Elin said sadly. "Keep in touch."

Alta turned and walked into the darkness. Soon after, a yellow glow emanated from the woods, and all became quiet.

Elin slowly returned to the lodge. Heinrich met him at the door and asked if he had seen his friend. "Yes. He said they have gone. Where, I don't know, but away from here."

Dr. Brandt, sitting on the sofa, up. "Where did you go?" he asked.

"Out for a breath of fresh air and to say goodbye to a friend."

Dr. Brandt looked puzzled.

"He told me to tell you goodbye, that you are a good man. By the way, the facility has been destroyed, no survivors or buildings left, but the Voltar babies and nursemaids are all accounted for. I'm sure you understand."

Dr. Brandt put his face in his hands and cried. The rest of his colleagues lowered their heads in respectful silence.

Helen, standing in the doorway, asked if it was ok to serve tea. Dr Brandt raised his head, and Helen quickly turned away.

Elin, unsure how to respond, simply said what was on his heart. "I'm sorry, Dr. Brandt. This is so very personal. You have bared your soul and solidified the trust and friendship of all of us; what shall we do now?"

Dr. Brandt's voice was unsteady. "I think we should wait twenty-four hours, and if Dr. Karl doesn't contact us, we should head for Oslo as soon as possible. Is that something we all can agree on?" He paused, mulling something over in his mind. "I'm interested to see if the facility in Oslo has been compromised. It may have survived because the project there was primarily genetic manipulation and the transfer of genes. My biggest fear now is that they will try to expand the Oslo project to include the mental aspects as well, because they can't continue in Berlin without the Voltar people.

"Hitler has a taste of what could be and won't stop with just beautiful people. He will demand that they must also have superior mental abilities. And since Oslo is already involved in Angel Hair and is probably functioning, it stands to reason that the whole project will shift from Berlin to Oslo."

The remainder of the evening, the men tried to enjoy each other's company, talking about their families and playing cards. It was probably the most relaxed and intimate time they had spent together since they had met.

Elin hoped to spend time alone with Dr Brandt. Alta had spoken of things that puzzled him, and he was confused. He felt that Dr. Brandt knew the answers but wouldn't voluntarily discuss them.

He didn't have to wait long. Olaf broke the ice, asking Dr Brandt about the Voltar people. Dr. Brandt confessed he had limited knowledge about them. They were a very private and secret society. "I think their leader's name is Alta, but I have never met him. I've only had contact with their liaison. His name is Eno and is what I call mixed."

"Mixed? What do you mean?"

"I mean he is different than what I have been told about the appearance of the pure Voltar. This man fits the description of Hitler's new race: tall, blond, and blue-eyed, but my understanding is that the pure Voltar have almost white hair and very pale skin, much like the babies we delivered. I also believe the nursemaids that were cloaked were probably Voltarin."

"I've never heard that name before," Dr. Keiser commented. "What language do they speak?"

"It's their own language," Dr. Brandt continued, "but Eno told me their name means 'dedication to a particular pursuit'"

"How strange," Dr. Keiser remarked. "I mean, how strange that they have been able to isolate themselves for so long. It's almost like finding a new species. Do you know how long they've been in Germany?"

Dr. Brandt paused, "Eno told me they came into what we call Mid-Europe after the last big glacial period. Evidently, they were forced south by ice and cold weather. They were already highly civilized when they encountered stone-age people and chose to protect themselves: hence, their isolation. Now they're threatened again and have moved on to who knows where."

"Have you been told what their particular pursuit is?" Elin inquired. "I know they wish to maintain a core society of pure Voltarians and a satellite society of an integrated population that populates the known world. I've been told you can usually distinguish them from the general population by their blond hair, fair skin, and blue eyes. Much like you," Dr. Brandt joked.

"But you haven't told me about your visitor," Dr. Brandt inquired. "I can only conclude from the message you gave me it was a Voltar; is that right?"

"Yes," Elin answered. "I met him a week or so ago in the woods. Very interesting man."

"Did he mention his name?" Dr. Brandt asked. "As a matter of fact, he did, and unless there are more than one with that name he is as you have said: their leader, Alta."

"Was he mixed or pure?" Dr. Brandt questioned.

"I'm pretty sure he was pure. He had the white appearance and the most intense eyes I've ever seen."

"How special you must be for him to personally interact with you. It's most unusual," Dr. Brandt remarked. "Well friends, it's that time again. Sleep well, and I'll see you tomorrow."

The next day, word came from Berlin in a closed envelope from Dr Karl. "Friends and colleagues," it read, "I regret to inform you that the Angel Hair Project has been shut down due to the violence yesterday. I will make arrangements for you to return to Oslo as soon as possible, hopefully tomorrow morning. Security is tight, so make sure your papers are in order. Spies everywhere. I'll plan to see you soon." It was signed, Frederick Karl.

The men were not surprised and celebrated the prospect of going home to Oslo. But what they didn't expect was the news the young SS officers brought from Berlin.

He said, "I am to tell you today was a big day for the Nazi Party. They had prepared major propaganda speeches about the war in several Berlin locations. At 11 o'clock, one of Hitler's inner circle confidants was scheduled to deliver a major speech. As the people gathered, the British bombed the area. Panic erupted among the crowd, and they dispersed. But that wasn't the end. Later in the afternoon, another speech was planned by one of Hitler's other high officials, and that was also disrupted by bombing. So much for being safe in Berlin. But don't worry, Dr. Karl will expedite your departure and ask Ben to return you to the train by early morning."

Dr. Brandt thanked the young man, fed him, and sent him back to Berlin. "Well friends, it's official. We're going home. Pack your bags."

Ben and Heinrich were also listening to the news. "We must prepare for the worst," Heinrich said. "This is not good news—no matter how they try to cover this up, we know the war is not going well. I fear for your safety," he said sadly.

Elin and Olaf had a hard time containing their excitement. They had been gone from Oslo just over a month, and it seemed forever. Dr. Brandt appeared anxious to return as well.

Dr. Keiser, however, was reluctant to join in the jubilation. It meant he had to leave his wife and family in a very uncertain and dangerous time.

Heinrich assured him that things would be okay. "I'm sure the Nazis will keep them safe. They have too much to lose if something happens to her." Dr Keiser tried to smile, but it just didn't come. Elin felt bad and sobered up a little out of respect for his old friend.

The night was a short one. Elin hardly slept. He worried about the trip; would they be able to slip under the watchful eyes in the sky—British bombers—and return to Oslo in one piece? It certainly was going to be dangerous.

Carefully, he packed his bag, dressed in his fisherman's disguise, and joined the rest of the men in the kitchen for a quick breakfast.

Helen, a truly good soul, packed a food basket with extra bread for the men she had become so fond of. "We'll miss you," she said. "I'll pray for your safety." Each of the men hugged her as if she were their own mother and headed into the darkness of early morning.

Ben kept an ever-watchful eye on the sky as well as on the surrounding woods. If the news had gotten out about the bombing, the resistance might just be brave enough to stop the car. Luck, however, was on their side, and no signs of the resistance were seen.

The sky had just started to drop its shroud of darkness when they arrived back at the lonely platform. Ben took out a milk-colored cloth and hung it on a nail about 100 feet ahead of the platform. Then they waited. It seemed forever. Suddenly, there was vibration on the tracks. The train was nearing. Ben quickly lighted a fuse and stabbed it into the side of the tracks. The red glow and smoke could be seen quite a distance, and the engineer would be able to stop the train and pick up his passengers. Another signal would be the milk-colored cloth. If it was not there, the train would not open its doors. The signal had to incorporate both signs; this insured the engineers that the waiting forms weren't partisans.

A few minutes later, the train rumbled into sight, slowed, and stopped.

"Hurry," Dr. Brandt ordered. "Get aboard."

Elin thanked Ben and quickly joined his companions aboard the camouflaged train. Now all they had to do was to survive the next few hours and board the ship for home.

Part Two

Dr. Brandt engaged the engineer in a brief conversation regarding the situation in Berlin.

"It's intense," he said. "Security is tight and the military on high alert. We are constantly changing schedules and personnel. We have all been briefed on the status of the war, but the citizens of Berlin have no idea of how bad it's becoming. Every day I expect to be bombed, but so far, we have been able to elude the Allies."

Dr. Brandt thanked him and joined the group in the next passenger car. Elin was nervous and sat quietly, only on brief occasions, when the train hit a rough spot or ripped off an overhanging tree limb, did he make any noise at all. It was as if he feared someone might hear him.

The scenery began to change. Trees were thinning, and the incline sloped toward the sea. Finally, they reached the water and the men rushed toward the fishing ship.

"Welcome back aboard the Legacy," the captain called out.

A sigh of relief rolled out of Elin's mouth. He had made it this far and was confident the rest of the trip would also be successful.

He and his friends again entered the little cabin, sat down, and enjoyed Helen's fine food. Dr. Brandt, finding a bottle left over from the first trip in a closet, remarked how lucky fit was or them the wine hadn't been drunk. "No one dare steal anything from this ship," he laughed.

Olaf questioned the comment. Dr. Brandt explained that this ship belongs to a powerful group of people, and that no one would dare offend them, even Hitler. "This ship is also free to travel wherever it likes. It is considered a neutral vessel, of course at their own risk since we're at war. The captain is employed by a group called, 'Legacy', thus the name of this ship."

"But what of Walt and the other Germans on the ship?" Dr. Keiser questioned.

"Only for convenience and ease of getting in and out of the occupied ports. They answer to the captain."

"I see," Dr. Keiser said.

"Well friends," Dr. Brandt advised, "you know the routine; sit back and relax. It's going to be a bumpy trip,"

"I'm curious," Elin remarked, "who is this 'Legacy' group you're talking about? I've never heard of them."

"I'm not surprised," Dr. Brandt answered. "They are probably one of the most secretive organizations I've ever encountered, even more secretive than the Nazis. There are rumors that they have supported Germany and other countries at different times but are neutral in this war. I don't know that myself—just hearsay. All I know is that they have influence world-wide and no one knows their agenda. Supposedly, it's a large group controlled by a few select individuals. No one seems to know who they are, but I personally think that both of our Kaisers had working relationships with them."

"Really," Dr. Keiser whispered. "I can't believe that. How old is this group anyway?"

"It's been said, they go back as far as recorded history and have been called many different names in the past, depending on the language spoken. Right now, I think they're using the name Legacy. Tomorrow it may be something else. Friends, I'm tired, let's talk later."

With good reason, Elin thought.

Part Three

T he cold wind whipped across Elin's back as he and his colleagues trudged down the pier from the ship to the land. In an emotional moment, both Olaf and Elin knelt down and kissed the ground. It was their beloved Norway. It was home, and they were safe.

Standing in the twilight of morning, hidden by the dark, was a joy even more powerful. It was Unk with his charges: Olga and Christina.

Screams of joy vibrated across the wooden platform and the open sea. Uncertain who was charging them, the men stood silent.

Then Elin recognized Olga's voice calling his name. He raced toward her voice.

Tears mixed with salt spray from the sea and tumbled over Olga's chapped cheeks. She didn't care. The thing she felt the most at this moment was happiness. He was in sight, almost in reach. Her prayers were answered. They embraced as if it was the first time. The moment was magical. Deep, long, lingering kisses and intertwined fingers proved it was no dream.

They were home.

"Unk, with security so tight, how did you know we were coming home?" Elin asked.

"Dr. Karl informed us of your approximate arrival time and as the ship neared the harbor, the captain alerted us. We've been waiting patiently here for your return."

Dr. Brandt's driver was also waiting and suggested that Unk take the two young families home together. He would take Dr. Keiser and Dr. Brandt.

Elin and Olaf were told to take time off and be with their families. "I'll contact you within a few days," Dr. Brandt said and in leaving, raised his arm. "Heil Hitler," he said, apparently a show for his driver.

The two young couples were like newlyweds, clinging to and groping each other, casting shadows as one along the narrow path to their car.

"It seems things are not going well in Berlin," Unk remarked. "When Dr. Karl contacted us regarding your return, he gave us news of the bombing and implied that the war was not going as well as hoped. Today, I heard that the Russians have all but decimated the German Army in Stalingrad. It's just a matter of days before Germany will lose its position in that area. Also, the resistance has been capturing German commanders along the coast."

Olga put her hand over her mouth and gasped. "Does this mean the war's going to be over soon?"

Unk answered as any good spectator would. "I don't really know."

"How are things in Norway?" Elin asked.

"About the same," Unk answered. "Food and such are harder to get, but we are managing. I've heard on the streets that local government officials are putting pressure on the Germans to remove some of their soldiers from Norway. I haven't seen any compliance with that request yet. I think the Russian victory in Stalingrad is just one of the casualties of war for Germany. It doesn't mean Germany has surrendered the war or anything like that. It's just a setback. I don't expect the Nazis to abandon Norway or any occupied country in the near future."

"Thanks for sharing this information with us," Elin responded. "We appreciate the update. Will we continue to see you?"

"I believe Dr. Brandt is planning to convene the orchestra again. It seemed to bring a lot of pleasure to those involved. So, I'll be around to drive Olga for a while longer, if that meets with your approval."

"Oh yes," Olga cried out. When will we start?"

"Soon," Unk answered. "Dr. Brandt will let us know."

Olga was elated. The love of her life was home and the love of her heart, the piano, was also promised. She held Elin tight, basking in a state of bliss.

The short, glorious reprieve ended abruptly when Dr. Brandt appeared at the door early one morning. "I'm sorry for the short notice, but we need you at the Institute today. The hospital is full of injured soldiers, and they desperately need help. It seems the Resistance and the Dutch were busy bombing while we were gone."

"What about the Eugenic Facility?" Elin questioned. "Is it still there?"

"We'll talk about that soon, but for now, we must comply with orders." Dr. Brandt cautioned.

"I understand," Elin replied. "I'll get my coat." As he turned to explain to Olga, Dr. Brandt stepped next door to Olaf's home to reiterate the request.

Elin was surprised to see Unk standing beside the open car door. Dr. Brandt explained that there was a shortage of available drivers, so Unk had volunteered. Inside the black sedan was Dr. Keiser. "Good morning." he said, "Happy to see you again. Did you enjoy your time with the family?" He was in such a jovial mood for so early in the morning. Elin wondered why. The last time he saw him he was severely depressed at leaving Germany. Dr. Brandt settled into the front seat next to Unk and turned around to face his colleagues.

"Dr Keiser, would you like to share your good news with your friends?"

"Indeed, I would," he replied. He was like a child with a secret, and now he had permission to share that secret with everyone in the car. "My wife is here in Oslo," he blurted out. "She arrived the day after we returned. It was a total surprise to me and her. Dr. Karl intervened on my behalf and the Nazis apparently agreed. I think the argument put forth by Dr. Karl was that I couldn't do a good job for the Reich if I was constantly worried about the safety of my wife in Berlin. They accepted his concern and sent her here by plane. I can't wait for you to meet her."

Elin and Olaf expressed their surprise and happiness for the couple and thanked Dr. Brandt for any part he had played in accommodating their friend.

Unk slowed the car and stopped at the front door of the Institute. They were back at the place where it all started, back to the basic medical procedures of stitching and patching war wounds, back to routine days of hard work. Johanna was the first to approach the men and welcome them back. Elin had actually forgotten her, but she hadn't forgotten him. She appeared very pleased to have them back, walking and chatting with them on the way to the operating room where several young soldiers lay in various semi-conscious states.

In the next few weeks, things returned to a more normal state. Elin went to work, and Olga resumed her duties with the children and orchestra. Dr. Keiser and his lovely wife, Wanda, were frequent guests at the Svenssons' home along with Dr. Brandt, Olaf and his family. They had all become very close, more so than just colleagues. Times had become harder, and friendships had deepened. They needed each other.

Sonja began frequenting Olga's home on a regular basis, often inquiring about Dr. Brandt. Olga, suspecting her mother had become infatuated with the charming German officer, began teasing her about her girlish crush. Sonja would laugh it off and say, "What's wrong with a little romantic excitement once in a while?" It pleased Olga to see her mamma in this light. It had been a long time since she had seen such a twinkle in her eyes, and Dr. Brandt certainly encouraged it, flirting with her at every chance. Elin, on the other hand, didn't quite know how to react. After all, Dr. Brandt was German, not Norwegian, and even though he had proven himself as a friend, and was endorsed by Alta, he was still a Nazi. It was hard for him to overcome his suspicions, but after closer analysis, he decided it could be to his advantage. He would have access to the progress of the war and political information not available to the general population. *Yes,* he thought, *this may work.* Sonja wasn't marrying Dr. Brandt; they were just having fun. He had jumped to conclusions regarding the seriousness of their relationship. Dr. Brandt was a powerful ally and friend. Sonja was his mother-in-law. Let them enjoy each other. It is just a fling.

Many of the sick and wounded men at the Institute began to heal and go home. Most were young Norwegians who had volunteered to fight for Germany. As the war slowed down, so did the days at the Institute. There were no young, beautiful people for Elin to examine, no sign of Angel Hair. Even Johanna, who had experienced the invasive experiments, had no updates. It was if it all had been a bad dream.

The only exception was the room in the back with frosted glass. Cloaked individuals who were not Voltar still mulled around inside, casting shadows onto the lighted windows. Elin often inquired about the activity, but Dr. Brandt said it was classified. Still, Elin was curious and had a difficult time containing his suspicions. It felt sinister, and having experienced firsthand the abilities of the Reich, he knew in his heart it was just that: pure evil.

It was near the end of a workday when Dr. Brandt called his colleagues into a nearby office for a meeting. "Thank god," Elin whispered to Olaf, "maybe we're getting out of here." It was indeed good news. They were going back to the Eugenics Facility, but it was not going to be the same. 'Angel Hair' had changed. Its focus now would change from genetic research to just reproduction and insemination. It was under total control of the Reich. There was now no collaboration with previous partners.

"May I ask what happened?" Dr. Keiser asked.

"I can only tell you what I've been told," Dr. Brandt explained. "Do you remember the incident in Berlin when the babies were taken and the facility was destroyed? It seems the same thing happened here in Oslo, except the facility here survived, but all the high-technology equipment and special assignment personnel have disappeared mysteriously. No one knows where. Speculators say the collaborative partner is responsible. What I'm now trying to tell you is that the facility is just a baby-production facility, creating the beautiful new race for

Germany. No special talents needed, just pure, ethnically manipulated children."

"Are you postulating the Voltar people are the mysterious partners who have taken the babies here in Oslo as well as the equipment?" Elin questioned.

"Yes, exactly," Dr. Brandt commented. "I'm just sharing an idea of what might have happened, and because we've had access to privileged information, we must keep it to ourselves."

"It's so hard to imagine how a small group of people living in the mountains could accomplish a feat such as this." Elin commented.

"I only know they are very advanced," Dr. Brandt said. "Germany has now destroyed the partnership and trust given by these peaceful people. Our longtime ally has disappeared and furthermore, they're upset. It's anyone's guess what will happen now."

Elin smiled to himself. The fact that Oslo had been targeted and not destroyed meant to him that the Voltar people had moved from Germany to somewhere in Norway. It pleased him greatly that he might once again meet his mysterious friend.

Elin had drifted off in his own thoughts and fantasies when Olaf nudged him. "Are you coming?" he asked. The men were all standing, apparently waiting for Elin to join them.

Embarrassed, he jumped up and joined his colleagues. "So much to digest," he laughed.

"Tomorrow we'll learn more," Dr. Brandt explained. "Keep your eyes and ears open and don't push for information. Let things unfold at a safe pace."

The timing was right for Elin to quiz Dr. Brandt, and in a blatant way he asked, "Dr. Brandt, we've been colleagues for some time now and I feel there are things we should know. Is there a connection between the Voltar People and Legacy?"

Dr Brandt replied. "We know a little. I've had the privilege of meeting one of them, but there are many unanswered questions."

Olaf quickly interrupted, reacting to Elin's question. "How do you know about the Voltar?" he snapped. "And if you know things, why haven't you told us?"

Elin was on the defensive. "Yes," he said simply. "I met Alta in the forest at the lodge and again when they left. He basically warned me about the Nazi agenda and told me about Angel Hair."

"So, you knew who those babies were when we assisted the birthing?" Olaf continued. "Yes," Elin said, "but I was asked not to interfere with their agenda or discuss our conversation. Sorry."

Olaf became very quiet, almost sulky.

"Dr. Brandt, will you share what you do know with us?" Elin requested.

"I know this sounds like a broken record, but I have limited knowledge about the Voltar or Legacy," Dr. Brandt explained. "I was told by their liaison, a mixed one, that a small colony of the highly advanced Voltar People have been around for thousands of years. He told me they originally lived in the far northern part of the world and as climate changed, they were forced south and established a colony in what is now an area of Germany. Their goal was to maintain a portion of their population as a pure race, but to selectively bred a new mixed race.

"That's where I think Legacy comes in. It is the genetic foundation, the gene pool, for the mixed ones, and consists only of the genetically manipulated blonde-haired, blue-eyed people. The gene pool was specifically selected by the Voltar years ago so the race could survive in harmony with the rest of the human race, who they originally called the dark-haired. For hundreds of years, the races were segregated, then they began to inter-breed with other races. This was a problem for the small colony of pure Voltar. If discovered, they feared the race would be forced to integrate into the general population. They have been successful in isolating themselves for thousands of years, and with their advanced technology, been able to survive unnoticed until Hitler discovered the former treaty with the Kaiser and files on the genetically manipulated mixed ones. So, in short, the Voltar are the pure race, and the mixed ones are Legacy.

"Most of the technology we enjoy today started as gifts of the Voltar or Legacy people: medicines, livestock, food, and education have all been influenced by this purely humanitarian, non-political, secret group.

"I've also heard it rumored that Legacy/Voltar has its home base deep in the southern hemisphere near the South Pole. Germans have been trying for years to find it, and the Nazis have sent many U-boats along the coast of South America to try and discover their secret base."

"So," Dr. Keiser interrupted, "all the beautiful young people we've encountered are not just for Germany, but also for the mixed-breeding project of the Voltar."

"That's what I understand," Dr. Brandt continued. "Those tattooed with the 'Angel Hair' emblem had been genetically altered for the Legacy population. The gifted children are also Legacy trained. That's why the project was so secretive, but now with the Nazis trying to steal Legacy babies, the Voltar have broken all ties with Germany. They have abandoned the project and broken the treaty. Maybe they've gone South to their home base, but for sure you can expect a major turn in the war. These people will not tolerate what the Nazis are doing. Hitler's agenda is not compatible with the peace-loving Voltars. Germany will not succeed in winning this war."

Strong words, Elin thought, *coming from a Nazi*. It made him nervous knowing he had to continue in the service of the Reich and worried about what might happen to him and his colleagues.

Dr. Brandt suggested that it was time to leave and reminded his colleagues that it was imperative that they keep this meeting quiet.

Unk, patiently waiting to drive the men home, smiled when Olaf asked, if anyone was up for a card game, obviously over his snippy attitude.

"I'm in," Dr. Keiser said.

"Me too," Elin answered. "What about you Dr. Brandt?"

"I can't tonight. Someone special is cooking dinner; rain check?"

"Whoa," the men teased. Unk was invited as the fourth. He looked pleased.

Olaf smacked his knee in satisfaction. "Then it's set. Elin's house,

7:00, hope that's okay. Sorry Elin, I have too many children to deal with," he laughed. All was forgiven.

Part Four

E xcitement faded after the meeting with Dr. Brandt. Without all the fantastic technology, the Facility would be like any other hospital. Elin's idea of excitement definitely wasn't delivering babies all day. Olaf and Dr. Keiser echoed his nonchalant attitude.

Dr. Brandt tried to elicit conversation. He failed. Finally, totally frustrated, he yelled "Colleagues, we are still under orders and until something changes, we are required to serve the Reich. Have you forgotten your families? Their safety depends on your cooperation. So, get a grip and drop the attitude." He was right; Elin and his friends had become accustomed to their privileges and had taken for granted their freedom.

Times were rapidly changing, and as Germany struggled to win the war, the situation became more serious and dangerous. The men needed to be more aware and alert during a time of desperation and failing in the Nazi Party.

Dr. Keiser and his wife arrived a little early for the card game and asked if Olaf could come over early as well; he had news to share and didn't want to involve Unk. After all, they practically knew nothing of him. As kind and loyal as he appeared, he had never shared his personal life with anyone.

The women, including Wanda, gathered in Christina's house and sent Olaf across the garden to the Svenssons'. Olaf arrived quickly, anxious to hear the news. Dr. Keiser told the men that he had heard from his German friend who told him that the Nazis had accelerated the killing of undesirables at the death camps. The slaughter was like nothing he had ever heard. Children, women, old people: it didn't matter. He had also heard that they had increased the birthing project, involving many more Nazi soldiers. He said they were literally mass-producing the new super-race in institutions or homes. He also said the German Army in Stalingrad had all but surrendered. But the propaganda machine continued praising the loyal German soldiers, bolstering the idea that the final victory would be German— "lies, lies, lies," Dr. Keiser whispered. He also said Hitler's Allies in Italy were near defeat, and that the Allies had increased the bombing of German cities. "This is a terrible time for mankind," Dr. Keiser commented. "So many innocent people are dying and suffering. I pray it will be over soon."

Elin and Olaf sat quietly, almost in disbelief.

"That must be why Dr. Brandt was so upset about the facility. It's like Europe has become an incubator for the German race," Elin commented. "I guess, as bad as it is, we should be thankful. Norway's remote location, has made it easier for us; at least they're not bombing us yet."

Dr. Keiser agreed. "I'm so thankful to be here with my friends and colleagues and not in Germany. I'll keep you updated as news comes in, but for now, be careful."

Promptly at 7:00, Unk arrived and opened the door. "Game's on!" he laughed.

A good evening of cards relaxed the minds of a worried group of men and released volumes of paralyzing stress.

The drive to the Facility the next morning was fraught with apprehension. Trying to escape the boredom, Dr. Keiser asked Dr. Brandt if he had ever heard of radar. "Since you're a military man, I hoped you could explain it to me."

Dr. Brandt turned and looked at Dr. Keiser. "Where did you hear that term?" he questioned. "I heard it on the ship coming home," Dr. Keiser explained.

"Oh, I see," Dr. Brandt continued. "It's a device used to determine the location, distance, and speed of distant objects. It uses a new technology with high-frequency radio waves. Actually, it was a gift from Legacy in the early 1900's. It helped to avoid crashes in foggy seas. Now the Allies are using radar to track our missiles and planes. That's why I was surprised to hear you use the word."

"Is it working for or against Germany?" Dr. Keiser questioned.

"Well, our long-range rockets, also developed from Legacy mathematics, were not successful at avoiding radar and they were often shot down. Now we have a new rocket that cannot be detected by radar and has the ability to strike great distances, possibly as far as the United States itself."

Elin gasped, "You're kidding, aren't you? Dr. Brandt?"

"Well, I've not seen it personally, but I've heard it is possible and I wouldn't be surprised if Hitler tries to use it, along with the super-bomb his scientists and engineers are trying to develop. As long as we're talking, I might as well tell you one reason Norway was so important to Hitler. The country possesses what's purportedly an important component in bomb making: something called heavy water. That's one of the reasons the partisans targeted the hydro plant and the British bombed it: to slow down the process of developing a super-bomb. Scary, isn't it?" he continued. "Knowing what you know now, just pray we are not going to be totally destroyed."

"Oh my God," Olaf whispered. "I had no idea. No wonder the Nazis have kept this information quiet. It would cause total panic among the population."

"That's right," Dr. Brandt continued. "So, like everything else we discuss, keep it quiet. This is highly classified privileged information."

Part Five

U nk slowly approached the facility. It was heavily guarded. They obviously were not taking any chances. The soldiers cautiously approached Dr. Brandt for clarification of their papers before allowing the men to access the building. It seemed different; armed guards lined the hallway and stared suspiciously at Dr. Brandt and his colleagues. "Wait here," Dr. Brandt ordered. "I'll announce our arrival. I'm just not sure of the new procedures."

Elin was surprised when Dr. Brandt returned with Elisa and a SS officer. "Hello again," she greeted. "Welcome back. First let me introduce you to Walter. He is now in charge of the facility." Walter quickly snapped his shining jack boots and stabbed the air with an aggressive 'Heil Hitler.' Dr. Brandt responded with his own aggressive salute. Elin and the others were not quite as enthusiastic and drew a glare from Walter.

"Elisa, can you validate that these are in fact the doctors they say they are?" Walter demanded.

"Yes, they are the same," she confirmed.

"Good. You may proceed with your duties and show the good doctors our new facility. Dr. Brandt, will you join me in the office? We have some business to discuss,"

"Very well. Colleagues, I'll catch up with you later."

Elisa guided the men into the former nursery. There were no strange boxes, no monitors, nothing technical, only rows of baby beds and what appeared to be nursemaids. "This is the new project," Elisa said. "Babies, babies, and more babies." Elin was not prepared for the massive onslaught of crying children. "As you can see," Elisa continued, "we've been very busy. Many of the children were bought from Germany to protect them."

"Is Dr. Niniva around?" Elin inquired.

Elisa snapped a short response, "No, no, no, she's gone. Only German personnel. No more outsiders, except for you and Olaf. Let's continue into the medical facility."

The podium was gone. There was no more extraction equipment, only young women in various stages of pregnancy. "This is your area now where you will assist in the delivery of our new race."

"What about insemination?" Olaf asked.

"Not your problem," Elisa responded. "Right now, your only concern is to treat and tend to the medical needs of the mothers and newborns".

Elin looked around and noticed there was still activity in the old lab area and shadows were still looming in the frosted glass windows.

"What's going on in the lab?" he questioned. "Highly classified operation and dangerous," Elisa responded. "Do not go there under any circumstances."

"Are the living quarters still in back?" Dr. Keiser inquired. "Yes," Elisa said. "The apartments are still being used for housing as they were before. Now, shall we join Dr. Brandt and prepare for your first day back to work?"

The men washed up, changed clothing, and began the routine, mundane job of caring for the newest members of Germany's population.

It was an exhausting day and Unk, waiting outside to take them home, was the highlight of the day. Outside the gates and beyond the shadow of the facility, Dr. Brandt asked the men what they thought of the new operation. Dr. Keiser was first to congratulate Dr. Brandt on his insight. "It is as you suspected; an incubator, a baby-producing facility. I saw very little of the old facility at all."

Elin was quick to remind them of the lab and the shadowy figures.

They all speculated that something sinister was still taking place. "You're right," Olaf said. "It is very suspicious, and Elisa warned us about the dangers inside."

"Dr. Brandt, did you learn anything?" Elin inquired.

"Nothing," Dr. Brandt whispered. "Walter was very guarded. He mostly talked about home and the war and how happy he was to have another SS officer at the site. Our meeting was mostly social. But go with your instincts and be alert."

Weeks passed. It was springtime again, and Elin was in a rut, his colleagues were in a rut, but at least the weather allowed them the pleasure of being out of doors. Kirsten was a lovely little 2-year-old, full of happiness and energy and very attached to Dr. Brandt and Sonja. Olga continued teaching piano, of course for free. The children in the neighborhood looked forward to the lessons and some of them became very accomplished. It helped pass time and gave Olga a sense of pride. The orchestra got together weekly, but no public concerts had been given since the Gala. The people of Oslo seemed to be suffering from depression, and the occupying Germans had become lethargic. Everyone was war-worn. Occasional news of the war continued to give Elin and his friends hope, but the end seemed in no way forthcoming.

Spring quickly became summer. Elin and his colleagues were still unable to discover the secrets in the lab at the facility. The doors were always heavily guarded, and activity seemed to have increased. Often Elin would see the robed figures entering or leaving the lab, but he could never see their faces. However, he could sometimes discern what looked like a face mask. *Very strange indeed*, he thought. *What are they hiding?*

Late one sultry summer night, Elin became restless. He could sense a presence; a feeling of someone watching him. It wasn't Olga, she was sound asleep, and the city was quiet. But the feeling was overwhelming.

Unable to sleep, he checked on Kirsten and found his way to the sitting room. The silence was amplified to unbelievable heights. He could hear his own heartbeat. He was completely intrigued. He had never allowed himself the luxury of just sitting quietly and listening.

Unexpectedly, a soft voice broke his silence. Jumping up, trying to focus his eyes in the darkness, he could see nothing. He stood listening. The voice spoke again. Quickly turning, he still couldn't locate the direction the voice was coming from. Again, the voice spoke to him. "Elin, come to the garden. No harm will come to you."

Then a memory rushed into his head. He had heard this voice before. It was in his head, not a distant vocalization. *Could it be*, he thought, *could it be my friend, Alta?*

The voice clearly responded. "Yes." he was stunned. The voice again asked, "Please, come to the garden."

Elin made his way from the darkness of his home into the grayness of the garden. Standing nearby was a shadowy figure holding a familiar stick light, the same light Alta had held in the forest.

"Alta," Elin whispered, "is it you?" The shadow moved forward, and the silhouette of a man with outstretched arms appeared. It was Alta. Elin embraced his friend and they sat talking in the garden until just before daybreak.

"I must go," Alta said. "Remember what I've told you, and we'll meet again soon." Exhaustion slowly overcame Elin, and he fell fast asleep on the sofa.

The sun peeked through the window; he was awakened by Kirsten touching his face. Olga, standing nearby, smiled at the little one's eagerness and expressed her surprise at finding him on the sofa. "Thank God it's Sunday," she said. "Otherwise, you would have been late for work. Do you want to go back to bed or have breakfast with us?" Elin, also amused at Kirsten, chose to stay up and enjoy his family. It was a pleasant day, but by afternoon exhaustion began to tug at his body again.

"Olga," he asked, "would you be up for a nap when Kirsten takes hers?"

"Of course, I would," she responded. "We can cuddle."

"I'm ready now if that's okay with you," Elin yawned. Kirsten didn't fuss and promptly fell asleep.

The two young lovers wound their bodies together and after making love, fell into a deep relaxed sleep.

Elin opened his eyes refreshed. Olga, resting close to his body, opened her eyes when he tried to move his arm from under her neck.

"Is Kirsten awake?" she asked. "I don't think so; it's still quiet." he whispered, "Let's take advantage of the quiet time and talk. I'm always so tired and you're so busy, I don't think we've really had a good talk for some time. Why don't you tell me about your life?" he teased.

Olga filled him in on all she knew and updated him on the budding romance between Dr. Brandt and her mamma, Sonja. He was amused.

He then asked her a strange question, "Do you ever wonder if your parents are really your actual parents? You know they were older when you were born, and you really don't look like either of them."

"Don't be silly," she said. "Why would you ask such a question?"

"Well," he continued, "Every day I take care of children that have been placed in homes with non-birth parents. These children all think of their adoptive parents as their biological parents. It seems so easy. I just wondered how often it really happens to regular families."

"You know, I could ask you the same." she quickly pointed out. "Maybe you're not really a twin. You don't look like your sister."

"Got me there," he laughed. "I'm gorgeous and she's just good-looking with brown hair."

"Oh, stop," Olga giggled. "You're thinking entirely too much."

"Maybe so," he whispered, "but what I know for sure is you're my wife and Kirsten is our daughter and that's what is important to me. Nothing else matters, agree?"

"Yes, my love, as long as we have our little family, that's all that is important to me as well."

Kirsten, now awake, fussed to be included, calling insistently for her mama. "Quiet time over," Olga laughed. Elin lay for a while, sorting all the information he had received from Alta. He needed to share with Dr. Brandt some of what he had learned, per Alta's request. Dr. Keiser and

Olaf were also to be informed, but with limited information. His dilemma was how to separate his colleagues so that they received only the portion of information Alta had recommended for them. This would call for some adept maneuvering on his part, but he was more than up for the challenge.

"Dinner is served!" Olga called out.

The next morning, loyal Unk was waiting with Dr. Keiser to drive the men to the Facility. *Another boring day*, Elin thought, but Dr. Keiser had news. After talking with Alta, Elin wasn't surprised, but it still was good news for him and the others.

"It's confirmed," Dr. Keiser announced. "The Soviets have won the battle at Stalingrad and what's left of the German army has surrendered. This happened a while back, but what's interesting is the joint invasion of Africa by Italy and Germany has also failed. I believe they have also surrendered. Dr. Brandt was right again when he said Germany would eventually lose the war, but I'm not holding my breath just yet. I fear something horrible happen before Hitler and his Nazis finally concede. He's not going to go down easily."

"Unk, what do you think?" Elin asked. Never before had he engaged Unk in such conversation, but his own curiosity compelled him. Unk simply stated, "I don't think about such things. I have no interest in war or politics. I use my energy thinking about how I can help those around me. It's that simple."

Elin didn't know how to react to such a selfless comment, but managed to say, "Thank you, Unk, for choosing us as your beneficiaries. I'm sure I speak for all of us, but especially for Olga. She adores you." Unk's face lit up and a soft smile crossed his otherwise somber face.

Part Six

The day came and went. Dr. Brandt had not been seen the entire day. It seemed somewhat unusual, but it was not yet alarming. After all, he still had duties with the SS. Elin, still unsure of Unk's allegiance, chose not to engage his colleagues in conversation about Alta's information in Unk's presence. Alta had said nothing of including Unk and he didn't want to presume it would be okay. In his heart he felt safe, but thinking with the heart could prove to be dangerous. Choosing to refrain, he hoped to find another approach.

Unk, as usual, delivered the men safely home and bid them a good night. Elin and Olaf sat briefly on the porch and talked about the man, Unk. No one knew much if anything about him. How could he not be interested in what was happening in the world and especially the war? It was like nothing affected him except his service to Dr. Brandt. He basically did what he was told and in a most agreeable way. What a wonderful demeanor. Elin decided not to discuss his meeting with Alta at this time with Olaf. He felt it should be done when Dr. Keiser was also present. So, after the small talk, the men retired for the evening.

Several days passed before Elin had the opportunity to approach Dr. Brandt. Sonja had come to visit and shortly after, Dr. Brandt appeared, apparently preplanned. After a light dinner, Sonja helped Olga with Kirsten and Elin suggested he and Dr. Brandt take a short walk. *Perfect,* he thought. *No one is the wiser. I'll deliver the message as promised.*

Dr. Brandt was confused when he told him of Alta's visit. "Why is he coming to you?" he questioned.

Elin explained that he was shocked to see him in Oslo, but felt they had a strong bond for some reason or another. He then repeated Alta's message to Dr. Brandt: Alta wanted to meet with him on a serious matter, and Dr. brandt should not be alarmed when the liaison appeared at his home some night soon.

Dr. Brandt looked at Elin with a perplexed stare. "Do you have any idea what this is about?"

"No," Elin answered. "I haven't a clue, but I need to give you some of the other information he gave me to share with you and the others. He said the war would soon be over and that all of us were in danger. It's just as you've always said: If we have too much knowledge of the projects, the Nazis will eliminate us to protect themselves. He also told me that the strange, hooded individuals at the Institute and Facility are scientists and biochemists who have been and still are working on chemical warfare for Hitler's army. He also told me of atrocities a man called Dr. Death has been committing on infants at the facility, behind the frosted glass windows. Those areas are contaminated with highly contagious, very dangerous infectious diseases that the Nazis plan to use in case they lose the war; a type of plague, he said. So, he asked that I warn all of you and advise you to stay clear of those areas. He also mentioned that the Voltar are monitoring the situation and would, if necessary, take action to protect themselves as well as the general population. He said his people have never involved themselves in conflicts such as this. They were always taught to let societies and cultures rule according to their own desire. A non- interfering position had to be adhered to by his people, or they would spend their entire lives fighting battles for other's causes. But this is different. The Nazis have the potential with the new rocket technology to arm warheads with biological material and, in a matter of minutes, spread these deadly diseases over the entire world, wiping out millions of lives, including the Votar and Legacy population. This will not be permitted. The Voltar are humanitarian and will act accordingly if they see any signs of this happening. Again, he warned to be extremely careful around the facility. It is a biological time-bomb."

Dr. Brandt, for the first time, appeared frightened. "Oh my God, how are we going to deal with this?" he pleaded, not as a soldier or physician, but as a frightened human being.

"I don't know," Elin replied, "but at least we've been warned. Alta also asked me to tell the others, but I haven't had the opportunity without Unk being present." Elin paused. "Who is Unk anyway? He is so mysterious. Can he be trusted?"

Dr. Brandt stood in silence for a second before answering. "Yes, you can trust Unk. He is a loyal member of Legacy."

"The Legacy we've been talking about?" Elin questioned. "Yes," Dr. Brandt confirmed. "That's why you know nothing of him, his history is secret." "Does Unk know the Voltar?" Elin asked. "Oh yes," Dr. Brandt answered. "He has always known them."

Hundreds of questions tumbled through Elin's thoughts, rendering him momentarily speechless.

Dr. Brandt posed a question. "Elin, do you remember hearing the term 'mixed ones?'"

"Yes, you told us about it in reference to Angel Hair and the Voltar people's involvement in the breeding project."

"Well, our friend Unk is a 'mixed one,' which simply means either his mamma or pappa is of Voltar lineage. In some cases, individuals like Unk are raised by Legacy and assume a life of service, somewhat like a monk or Buddha. When they reach a certain age, they can choose. Unk chose to become a benefactor, a person who basically is a humanitarian. An empath, if you will. The Legacy community contacted me shortly after I became a liaison for them and assigned Unk to me because I could protect him and his mission during the war. But make no mistake, if he were ever in danger, Legacy would rescue him even from me."

"Help me understand," Elin replied. "The Legacy Project has also been going on for some time, right?"

"Yes," Dr. Brandt confirmed. "Remember the Voltar are a pure race, limited in numbers, but still pure. Over time, thousands of years ago, they were forced to go outside of their community because of in-breeding problems. Now, with the mixed ones, they can genetically manipulate the genes and produce a pure Voltar again, but they need diversity in genetic material to do so. That's basically the reason for the new mixed race of blonde-haired, blue-eyed people. Today there are many variations of the original mixed ones, but now only a select few are actually genetically linked with the Voltar. Other races of humans have also evolved. Over time these races have infiltrated the gene pool of the mixed-ones and have become a new race of their own. Descendants of the original Voltar are still found in the field of professional humanitarian causes. We still assist the genetic improvement of present and future Voltarians. For example, Elin, you are a doctor—a great humanitarian profession. Science and medicine would have been your focus. Olga, the arts and music, etc. Do you get my gist? The Voltar and their people, humanitarian themselves, excel in all these fields. They would never encourage warriors, soldiers, or any violent behavior or profession. They hope, in time, the world will become a place of peace and beauty for all. But as you see, we're far from that at this time. All we can do is hope and try."

"What a beautiful story," Elin remarked. "I had no idea that was the Voltar agenda. No wonder Hitler is so obsessed with the concept. He also wanted a utopian world, but with himself as king. I am surprised at your knowledge of the situation, Dr. Brandt."

"I have been able to piece together parts of the story from Unk and my liaison, but no one actually sat me down and explained it to me," Dr. Brandt remarked. "Maybe someday I'll know for sure."

"I'm with you," Elin chimed in. "I'd love to understand these remarkable people."

"You know, it's getting late, Elin. We better get back to the house before the women begin to worry. I really don't want to try and explain our delay to them tonight," Dr. Brandt commented.

"You're right," Elin agreed.

After a restless night, Elin emerged from his bed tired and worried.

He felt an urgency to inform his colleagues about the danger facing them, and after a quick breakfast, he rushed to the waiting car, only to be surprised by Dr. Brandt sitting in the driver's seat along with his first passenger, Dr. Keiser.

"Good morning," Elin commented. "What a surprise to see you driving, Dr. Brandt."

"Well, I happen to be a very good driver, and Unk was going to be busy with Olga and the orchestra today. I also used that as an excuse to allow us to discuss certain subjects in private. Understand?"

It took Elin a minute, then he got the idea, and filled in Olaf and Dr. Keiser on the new information. The men were horrified and, like Elin and Dr. Brandt, unsure how to handle the news. They all had known something sinister was happening behind those frosted glass windows, but never in a million years did they dream it involved biological warfare with babies being used as lab rats. "That explains the strange appearance of the infants we saw," Dr. Keiser remarked. "It also explains the little child they requested I examine in Berlin. Those children have been subjected to horrible experiments and they are almost unrecognizable as human."

"You're right," Olaf said. "And the heavy robes are to protect the scientists and whatever else is there. For all we know, all of them could be infected workers. We have to steer clear of the area and avoid all contact in the halls with those robed personnel.

"The other thing I need to tell you," Dr. Brandt interrupted, "is we will have to go back to the Institute every other day to assist in the hospital. There have been many casualties and they need our help. So today we'll go there. Please be cautious—keep quiet and don't arouse suspicion. The SS are very nervous. They will react or over-react at any suspicious comment."

It turned out to be a long and feverish day. It took all the doctors and nurses working together to achieve success. Many lives were saved, some lives lost, but the teamwork was beyond anything Elin expected. It was as if a new energy had come over the entire staff. Maybe they just sensed the beginning of the end of war gathered from all the stories the soldiers were telling. Whatever it was, something was excitingly different.

Elin and his colleagues joined Johanna and others in the lounge for tea at the end of the day. Johanna purposefully sought out Elin and sat next to him. She made a few remarks about her prior experiences and then informed him that the pregnancies had not been repeated. Further, the 'AH' tattoo had completely disappeared from her leg. "One day it was just gone, as mysteriously as it had appeared. What do you think happened?" She asked. Elin was just as confused. He knew now that the tattoos were just for select individuals who were chosen to be a part of the Voltar breeding program. But he couldn't figure out why they would remove their mark. He must remember to ask Dr. Brandt about this.

"I really can't say," he finally replied. "Tell me, have there been any strange things going on here since I left?"

"No, not really," she replied. "We've been too busy to notice, but for sure there has not been the parade of young people coming in for physicals. We only get wounded, sick, and dying now."

"What about the room at the back with the frosted windows?"

"Oh, it's still there—same-old," she whispered. Feeling he had asked enough questions, he turned his attention to other conversation.

Part Seven

The next few days back at the Facility were routine. After three days passed with no sign of Dr. Brandt, Elin and his colleagues became worried. They looked around the Facility often, but he was nowhere to be seen. Maybe he had been discovered and taken away, the men speculated. They all began to develop a case of paranoia and became even more cautiously, afraid someone would hear or see them talking among themselves.

As usual, Unk was waiting and midway home, Elin asked about Dr. Brandt, trying to present his question in a normal, calm way. He just inquired if he was ill. Unk didn't appear offended by the question and simply said he was temporarily out of town. Dr. Keiser and Olaf looked at Elin for clarification, but he said nothing more. Elin knew in his heart that Dr. Brandt was with the Voltar liaison but couldn't share that information with Olaf or Dr. Keiser. It was not in the best interest of Dr. Brandt.

By the end of the week, Dr. Brandt had returned. No explanation was forthcoming, just a sober expression lingering on his chiseled face. His demeanor had somehow changed, and it worried his colleagues. Again came speculation and paranoia—the unknown was their enemy.

The week was finally over. Elin looked forward to spending time with Olga and Kirsten. It seemed that time had accelerated and summer was nearly over ,and he had missed the pleasure of it all. He was tired. They were all tired. How much more could they physically and mentally endure? In his head he carried these thoughts but, in his heart, he knew they would endure anything to protect their families and themselves.

It was late Sunday afternoon. Olaf and Elin were in the garden watching the children play. The women were busy trying to pull together enough food for dinner when Dr. Keiser and Wanda walked up unexpectedly carrying food from their pantry and a new bottle of wine, a gift from Dr. Keiser's German friend.

"What a surprise!" Elin shouted. "Welcome."

"I hope we're not intruding, but it is such a wonderful day, Wanda and I decided to take a long walk. We thought you might share this wonderful gift with us. It's not much, but we'll savor the last drop together.."

Wanda joined the women inside and Olga returned with three glasses. "What about you?" Elin questioned. "We women decided to let you men enjoy the wine. You certainly deserve it. Don't worry about us, we'll survive," she giggled.

"What a wonderful day this turned out to be," Elin remarked.

"It's going to get even better," Dr. Keiser remarked. "My friend told me he had heard that the Allies had landed in Sicily and bombed Rome. It's rumored that Mussolini's days are numbered. If that happens, Hitler's close ally will be defeated. I'm hopeful that the rumors are true and the war will soon be over."

"We can only pray it's true," Olaf commented.

Still, the days ran together, always the same, back and forth between the two institutions, treating the sick and delivering Nazi babies. Only three things were different: the caution the men exercised around the robed personnel, the area surrounding the back room, and Dr. Brandt. He had not been the same since returning from his mysterious disappearance. He no longer spent time with his colleagues or Sonja. As a matter of fact, he avoided them. It was a great concern to Elin, because he knew of the connection between Legacy and Dr. Brandt. He could only assume Dr. Brandt had an important reason for his actions.

Olga hadn't seen much of him either. One of his favorite things to do was listen to the orchestra, but it had been several weeks since he had come to enjoy the music. Sonja appeared hurt but shrugged it off, not wanting anyone to assume she had feelings for him. It certainly was hard for Elin to explain to his women the absence of Dr. Brandt.

Elin decided to try his luck again with Unk and asked "Is there something wrong between Dr. Brandt and me?"

Unk simply replied, "You will have to ask Dr. Brandt personally when he returns from Berlin." Elin glanced quickly at his colleagues for a reaction. Dr. Keiser's lips moved but did not vocalize the word 'Berlin'. Elin shrugged his shoulders in an 'I don't get it' gesture. Olaf sat quietly, watching the inaudible discussion going on between his two colleagues. Unk offered no more information, and the men spent the rest of the ride to work in silence.

Somehow news seemed to be becoming easier to get. Dr. Keiser's friend was a frequent source of information. The only problem was their ability to verify the truth. It still could be Nazi propaganda, but any news was welcome. And when Dr. Keiser told them Mussolini had been arrested, Elin and Olaf cheered out loud.

In the following days, Unk struggled to provide enough food and milk for his adoptive families, and Dr. Brandt continued to be unavailable. It was a strange situation, but his colleagues and friends seemed to cope. Activity at the facility increased. More soldiers were visible, more shadows moved across the frosted glass windows, and Elisa always appeared to be on edge. No joking or laughter had been heard from her for weeks. Elin sensed an uneasiness among the nurses and Walter, the SS officer in charge. Something must be about to happen, he concluded, but what, was the important question.

Several nights later, Elin had another of his restless nights. Even the cool Norwegian air gave him no comfort. Unable to relax, he left the bedroom, took his pillow, and headed for the sofa. Just before lying down, he heard his name in a soft whisper.

"Elin, Elin."

Once again, he was uncertain whether he really had heard it or imagined it.

"Elin," the voice repeated, and he knew it was Alta.

Quickly, he headed for the garden. There the man was with his light stick and arms in his familiar outreached position. Elin was ecstatic. It had been so long since he had seen him that he had feared the Voltar had moved away.

"My friend," he whispered, "how I've missed you. Can you stay for a while?"

Alta assured him a visit long enough to update him on the condition of the war and other important issues. Elin again had a multitude of questions and Alta seemed most accommodating with his answers. He began to ask questions that had intrigued him from the first time they had met. Alta seemed amused and in the spirit of friendship, tried to answer what probably seemed to be some pretty absurd questions. Elin then focused his questions on more familiar subjects like Unk and Dr. Brandt. He told Alta that he and Dr. Brandt had briefly discussed the situation, but that Dr. Brandt had made it clear that most of what he knew was speculation and hearsay.

"Let me explain Dr. Brandt," Alta replied. "He is a good friend to the Voltar and Legacy. He basically was placed in his position in the SS to monitor them. You could almost say he is a spy. Unk is under the protection of Dr. Brandt."

Part Eight

"Elin, I need to tell you something that may upset you, it's time you know certain things. You'll have to decide whether share this with Olga."

"Elin, it is no coincidence that you and your family are in my life. We have been with you since birth. You know the process of insemination and extraction that we use in our own birthing process.

"Olga was born a Legacy baby. She is not the biological child of Sonja. Sonja and her husband had been selected as potential prospects for a Legacy child because of their high standards and musical abilities. Olga was predisposed to be in the arts, and this union was perfect.

"Sonja was older when she became pregnant, and we monitored her very closely. There were also other candidates, but as it happened, Sonja gave us the first opportunity to place Olga in a normal family environment. Unk had the new infant Olga already at the hospital, and when Sonja came to deliver, we already knew her baby would not survive. A Legacy doctor delivered the still-born baby and placed Olga in its place. Unk was there to oversee the placement and has shadowed the family from that time forward. That's why he is so protective."

Elin was speechless; that his own wife was a product of Legacy was beyond his immediate comprehension. Alta continued as Elin sat in incredulous silence.

"No one but you and Unk know of this. I'll leave it up to your discretion whether to tell Olga or not. To us, it makes no difference. She is and has become a beautiful example of your people and ours; this is what we strive for."

Elin spoke in a soft, choking voice. "Does she know anything?"

"No, as I said, only you and Unk know. Dr. Brandt knows nothing of this or anything about our Legacy population. And if I didn't trust you, we wouldn't be having this conversation either." Alta turned the little light about in his palms. "But there is more."

Elin looked straight into Alta's eyes, "More? More what?" he questioned.

"Have you ever wondered why I chose you to visit?" Alta whispered. "I have never met Dr. Brandt, and I have met very few people even from the Legacy community. Our visit and encounter in the forest was not happenstance. It was planned by Dr. Brandt and our liaison. I was waiting for you; I needed to see for myself the type of person you had become."

"Why is that important?" Elin questioned. "It's important because you are my son."

Emotions raged, and Elin tried to choke back tears. He couldn't. He sobbed uncontrollably, releasing months of built-up frustration and anxiety. This was almost more than he could handle. Alta put his arms around him and held him like a pappa would an injured child.

Alta himself appeared to be crying; it had been a long-awaited reunion for him. He had been patient for the exact time to divulge this to Elin. Now, with his entire family facing possible extermination, this was the proper time. Alta could wait no longer. A rescue was looming, and Elin needed time to prepare himself and the friends he loved.

Finally, Elin pulled himself together.

"But I have a mamma and pappa," he muttered, "or was I another Legacy baby?" Alta said in a reassuring voice, "You are a Voltar baby, and you were birthed differently than Olga. The difference is that your surrogate mother is a mixed one, but she never knew it. She was predisposed in science and medical, hence your disposition. Your twin sister is not Legacy, but the pure biological child of your mother and father, who are not mixed."

"How can that be? I am one and my sister is not?" Elin stuttered.

"When my partner was unable to have a child, we selected your mother to be our surrogate vessel. She is a remarkable example of high moral values and proven to be a productive humanitarian. We just felt she was the right one, and I'm glad we did. You are a remarkable person. We're very proud of you."

"Tell me how it was done," Elin insisted. "If not like Olga, then how?"

"You were placed as a fertilized egg into the womb of your mamma and shared the vessel with your sister. There again, we carefully monitored your mother and knew immediately of the pregnancy."

"But how?" Elin continued. "How could this be? You would have to been present every second."

"There are things you cannot not know at this time. You must trust that this is true. I will try to put your mind at ease with this information. Every Legacy citizen has a biological implant, and we can monitor everyone for illness and trauma. It is not an invasion of privacy, because we're only alerted when there is danger or if we need access to genetic material."

Elin appeared to accept the idea of his relationship with Alta and began to calm down.

"You know, Alta, I was just talking to Olga, and we were discussing the idea that we may not be the biological children of our parents. Of course, it was just a whimsy on both of our parts. We never really believed that it could be possible. So," he continued, "my biological mamma is your wife or partner. What do you call them in your culture?"

"We call them partner, but it is the same as your wife," Alta remarked. "She is very anxious to meet you." "She is a mixed one, right?" Elin questioned. "And she lives with the Voltar?"

"That's right," Alta confirmed. "It was her choice. There are several mixed ones in our community."

"It must be a pleasant place. Maybe someday you'll let me visit," Elin whispered. "Soon," Alta promised, "very soon it will be possible. Elin, I know what you have learned today is overwhelming, but there is one more important subject I need to discuss with you. For centuries, stories have circulated among many European and Middle Eastern tribes of an advanced race of people with light hair and skin. The same race Hitler and his comrades have been searching for. Elin, this race is our people, the Voltar, most recently called Aryans or Nordics. We have evolved over thousands of years and are highly advanced. I don't have time to go into detail now; we need to focus on the current situation; when we are safe, I will explain."

Alta continued, "Oh, by the way, Dr. Brandt was sent as a liaison to meet with the Allies in Britain, hopefully to arrange a new treaty for the Voltar. That's where he was recently. Now he is in Berlin. His mission there is to meet discretely with the leading rocket scientists, warn them about what's about to happen, and then direct them to an area of safety in the event that Berlin is overtaken. This is at the request of the Allies. Just know this is a dangerous assignment for Dr. Brandt because he is already under suspicion and being carefully watched. That's why he has been so evasive and unavailable to you and your colleagues. He is trying to protect you.

"Please, when it's time for rescue, and be assured the time is near. Unk and Dr. Brandt will come and take all of you to safety. You must be ready to leave; it will be spontaneous. Take nothing with you, just move as quickly as possible. Do you understand?" Alta asked.

"I do," Elin replied. "Should I inform Dr. Keiser and Olaf?" he questioned. "Yes, by all means; they are loyal friends, and we will not leave them behind. Invite your colleagues over tomorrow night and give them an update on what's going on. Also, instructions for evacuation. Keep it simple for now, the less they know, the safer all of you will be. Is that clear?" Alta demanded.

"It is," Elin confirmed.

Alta embraced his son and left.

Part Nine

E lin was mentally fuzzy; thoughts raced so quickly through his mind that he felt physically dizzy. He wanted to share all that he knew with someone, but he couldn't. He found himself in a lonely place— isolated with important information but unable to discuss it with Olga or his colleagues. He knew he had been placed in a position of trust and had to perform as a trustworthy confidant to his new-found father and the family and friends he loved.

The next morning, he asked Olga to invite her mamma over for dinner even though he knew food was difficult to come by. Olga questioned the invitation, but said she would honor his request. He also asked Dr. Keiser to bring Wanda and Olaf to include Christina and children as well. Of course, they were all curious and tried to elicit information, but he ignored their inquiries.

Much to everyone's surprise, near midday at the facility, Dr. Brandt finally surfaced. Businesslike, he and Walter walked the floor checking on various activities. As they approached Elin, his eyes locked with Dr. Brandt's and softly nodded his head in a non-conspicuous way. Elin got the message. Dr. Brandt acknowledging him in a personal way immediately made him feel more confident and renewed his trust. Now all he had to do was wait for evening.

Olga and Sonja greeted Elin together at the door. Olaf returned with Christina, and they all waited for Dr. Keiser and Wanda to arrive. Olga, on pins and needles, tried to persuade Elin to give them a hint about the meeting, but he was determined to hold his ground until Dr. Keiser's arrival. As they waited for their friends and laughed about this or that they were going to do after the war, Elin felt encouraged that they hadn't given up hope for a brighter future. So many Norwegians had long since conceded all hope for freedom from occupation. Thank God, he and his family had not.

Olga held Kirsten as the little girl dozed, trying to stay awake, but not quite able. Sonja sat on the arm of the sofa near her daughter and grand-baby, softly stroking Olga's hair. Elin watched and a new respect emerged for this loving grandmama. It was then he decided to keep secret the information Alta had given him regarding Olga and her adoptive parents. As Alta had said, it made no difference to him, and as Elin thought about it, he concluded it would make a world of difference to Olga, Kirsten and especially Sonja. It would dramatically change their lives and possibly their relationship. He really couldn't take a chance, and he couldn't bear the pain it would cause if they were to find out. *Sometimes things are better left alone*, he thought.

Dr. Keiser and Wanda soon arrived. "Greetings," Elin called out. Dr. Keiser had sensed the urgency and quickly asked the purpose of this gathering. Elin had to be careful with the information. He didn't dare include Dr. Brandt's missions or involvement with the Allies, but he knew his friends would push for more, so he needed to be on guard.

"Do you remember when I told you of a strange meeting I had at the Lodge?" he remarked. Dr. Keiser looked at Olaf, trying to recall the incident. As they struggled, Elin reminded them of the stranger in the forest. Olga, not knowing any of the story, immediately questioned the experience. Elin interjected that he would have to explain it to her later because now he had to discuss something more important. "Well," he continued, "that man visited me a couple of days ago with a warning that he asked me to share with you.

"Wanda, Olga, Christina, Sonja: I'm sorry that you have not been privileged to all the information that we have had, but it was for your own protection. So please trust me and your husbands at this time. It's for our very survival and you cannot discuss this with anyone. The Nazis are watching everyone, especially us.

"I was warned the war was practically lost and because certain people were a liability to the Nazis, their lives were in immediate danger. Those people are us. This man told me that arrangements have been made to evacuate us in the very near future. Be prepared for the coming rescue. This is what I was told; pack only those essentials you absolutely need: medicines, a few toys and a small amount of food—everything else must stay. They will have clothing for us. Unk or Dr. Brandt will come for you, leave with them immediately, whether we're with him or not: you will be taken to a safe place where we will all be united. This could be anytime: morning, noon, or the middle of the night. I'm not here to frighten you, but the quicker you act, the safer we will be. Right now, that is all I know."

Olaf questioned the relationship with Unk. "Are you sure we can trust him? Maybe it's a Nazi trick."

"I'm positive he is trustworthy." Elin assured them.

Dr. Keiser interjected his own thoughts. "My friend has told me of the decline in the German war effort and Dr. Brandt warned us in the beginning that we were in a dangerous predicament. I am really frightened, but I chose to believe this man and trust Unk. If we do not take a chance with them, we'll be killed for sure by the Nazis. I know the SS; they are ruthless, and they know who we are. If they think they will be exposed for their crimes, they will stop at nothing to eliminate the proof. We are witnesses."

Olga and the other women sat in disbelief. It was so unexpected. They wrapped their arms around each other and wept.

"Where will we go?" Sonja said in a voice of forced calm.

"I don't know," Elin replied. "Hopefully somewhere safe."

Christina asked, "Will we be gone long?"

"I don't know that either," Elin again responded. "I guess that will depend on the war."

"I saw Dr. Brandt today," Olaf remarked. "Will he be joining us?" Elin hesitated, and just said, "possibly. That's all I have to report right now; are we all on board with this?"

Even though there was anxiety and apprehension, everyone agreed they would rather take a chance escaping the Nazis instead of waiting for an inevitable arrest.

Elin quickly walked out of the room to the garden, hoping no one would ask anything else. There was a lot of chatter coming from the kitchen, then silence. The women, trying to absorb what they had just been told, focused their thoughts the familiar rhythms of preparing food. Dr. Keiser and Olaf joined Elin in the chilled air of the garden.

"My God," Elin said. "That was difficult. I was as evasive as possible, and almost forgot that our wives know nothing of all the dangers revolving around our lives. I'm glad this is over."

"Tell me," Olaf requested, "was that man you referred to a Voltar?" Elin had hoped that he wouldn't have to answer his question, but what was the use? He wasn't going to lie. "Yes," he responded. "That's why I said we could trust Unk, because I trust the Voltar."

"Elin, since you're the only one that has ever seen a Voltar, what do they look like?" Olaf questioned. Elin thought a moment and said, "You know in school when we studied ancient Greece and Rome? The Voltar look like one of those statues with very light hair. I've often wondered if they were the Greek Gods." he continued.

"Wouldn't that be a surprise," Dr. Keiser remarked. Elin laughed a little. "It certainly would," he said.

Part Ten

The next few days seemed like any other, but then a flurry of activities consumed the Facility. Strange trucks arrived. A small squadron of SS officers came with them. It was only midday, but all non-military personnel were asked to leave. A special bus was waiting to transport the personnel away from the grounds, escorted by SS on motorcycles. It appeared they wanted to make sure no one was left at the facility to observe their activities.

Elin and his colleagues were frightened beyond belief. They worried about being detained and unable to return home to their families. The entire bus filled with nurses and caregivers, anxious and confused. Elin and his colleagues had an idea of what was going on, but that was only conjecture.

As the bus arrived at Elin's and Olaf's home, the children and Olga were busy playing on the sidewalk. Olaf stepped off the bus first. Olga approached him and asked that he invite Dr. Keiser in for tea. It seemed to be an unusual request, but Olaf did so. The SS guards had long departed as escorts, and only a few people were left seated. The driver didn't seem interested at this point, so Dr. Keiser accepted the invitation.

Just inside the home sat Sonja and Wanda. Dr. Keiser walked in and was taken aback by her presence. "What are you doing here in the middle of the day?" he inquired.

"Following orders, she explained.

"Orders from whom?" he insisted.

"Unk," she said. "He came about 20 minutes ago and told me it was time. 'Bring only essentials', he instructed. So here I am, along with Sonja."

The little families entered the house.

"It's time," Dr. Keiser whispered.

"I know," Elin replied. Someone asked what they'd do now. "We wait," Elin answered.

Several hours passed; the children were restless, and the adults struggled to contain their fears. They had hashed out every possible scenario but were at a loss to predict what was going to happen. Olga began playing the piano and singing children's songs. It diverted attention away from the repressive atmosphere and gave the children a reprieve from boredom. The adults joined in, rearranging the deep lines of worry on their faces.

The sun had started its decline when there was a knock at the door. Olga was quick to answer. It was Unk and Dr. Brandt. Dr. Brandt was not in his SS uniform but was casually dressed as a civilian. Sonja greeted him with a hug.

"We don't have time to visit now," he insisted. "I have a truck waiting around the corner. I want each of you to casually stroll toward it, look around to make sure you're not under surveillance, and then enter the truck via the side door. Close the door and wait for the next person. Do not attract attention. Unk and I will bring along your belongings. Does everyone understand the procedure? Start leaving now. Wait in the truck. Remember, don't rush, make it seem as if you're going for an evening walk."

Unk and Dr. Brandt gathered the few belongings of their friends and waited inside until they were all in the truck. The streets were relatively empty except for a few neighbors walking by, glancing at the truck—more out of curiosity than suspicion. It seemed that the timing was good.

Dr. Keiser and Wanda walked with a natural, nonchalant pace. Elin and his family took one last walk-through of their lovely home and departed for the truck. Lastly, Olaf and his large family followed. Unk and Dr. Brandt closed the door to the Svenssons' home, checked to see if everyone was safe, and entered the truck.

Pulling down his trucker's cap, Dr Brandt drove onto the street.

The children were excited. The adults were stressed and unsure of the outcome of their decision to attempt escape. To keep the children quiet, they were told they were going on a great adventure but had to pretend they were sleeping until they arrived at the surprise destination. All was going well until sirens and bombs were heard. The truck picked up speed, flying out of town and toward the coast.

Dr. Brandt re-introduced himself with a friendly gesture. "Please don't call me 'Doctor' anymore. My name is Albrecht." Dr. Keiser mimicked his friend and requested his friends also call him by his name: Helmut. The new names took the formality out of the atmosphere and nourished a family-friendly feeling.

The road up the coast became narrow as the precious cargo continued toward a dense forest. "Where is our surprise?" the children kept whispering.

"Soon'" Unk would say, "soon." The terrain became more and more isolated, and Elin began to worry whether they would be safe hidden somewhere in this environment. Suddenly his thoughts raced back to the lodge in Germany. *Maybe we'll live in a place like that. That would be wonderful.*

His daydream soon faded, and he faced a different reality. The truck had stopped near a clearing not far from the sea. Unk suggested everyone should get out and stretch their legs. Several children headed into the privacy of the woods to relieve themselves as the adults surveyed the area for safety reasons. There appeared to be nothing special about this location other than its isolation. Why had stopped here? The road didn't lead to any known village or resort, just a country road running through the woods: maybe a logging road.

Softly, Unk called to his companions and asked that they gather the children and bundle near him in a close circle. Elin was perplexed. What a strange request! But they did as they were told.

Then they saw it: a light appeared in the distance. As it neared land it became brighter and larger, often shooting a searching beam into the water. *Strange airplane*, Elin thought.

Panic overcame the group, even as Elin attempted to keep everyone together by asking them to remain calm. Secretly, he too worried about what this light might be.

Was this a Nazi aircraft brought here to eliminate all of them? Where is it going to land? Had they been betrayed by Dr. Brandt and Unk?

The light slowly approached the shore not far above their heads, and multi-colored lights filtered through a cloud-like enclosure, circling the immediate area. Everyone froze, mesmerized by the quiet phenomenon. The children became excited, the women and men confused.

The object paused overhead again, showering a gentle glowing mist softly on their bodies. Fascinated, the children began to twist and turn, stretching out their arms like birds in flight. Of course, Elin and his medical colleagues examined the substance in a more analytical way.

"What in the world is this?" they asked.

"Don't worry; it's a disinfectant," Unk said in a comforting voice. "It will disappear when it dries."

Everyone had been so preoccupied with the glowing display of material they hadn't noticed the disappearance of the cloud overhead. Once again, the sky darkened, and the men were left questioning what just happened. "Everything is in order," Unk announced. "It won't be long now."

Elin asked if the strange silhouette overhead was some sort of advanced surveillance plane, or if they were waiting for a ship like the one they took on their earlier trip to Berlin.

Unk didn't respond. He watched the dim horizon.

Near the water's edge, a strange noise began to vibrate in the silence.

Elin called out, "It must be a submarine. Children, watch, it is a submarine."

Excitement overtook the little ones. They waited together. Slowly, the sea whipped up a froth with no sound of motors or machinery. The spinning of water like the center of a tornado became overwhelmingly powerful.

Suddenly, without sound or lights, the submersible emerged. A large shadow seemed to float on the surface of the moonlit water, creeping ever closer to land. Elin had never seen a submarine, but he was positive this was exactly what he was watching. Drawing near, the silhouette became visible in the graying night. It didn't look like the typical structure he had imagined. It was huge, much larger than anything he had seen in photos. But what was it, he wondered?

Unk asked that they all step back as the silent shadow crept ashore toward them. "This is not a submarine," Elin mumbled. The unknown image was frightening, and the children were now in a state of distress, clinging to the legs of their fearful parents.

"It's okay," Unk reassured them. "You'll see."

The structure, ominously quiet, released a soft spray around the perimeter. Elin, his colleagues, and family stood as statutes, frozen with fear and wonder as a soft green and yellow glow emanated from the underside and illuminated a set of evenly spaced supports. It obviously was not floating, and it certainly was not a submarine. No one dared make a sound or speak a word.

Quietly, a chard of light fractured the darkness on the surface of the unknown object. Lights, now pulsating in a symphony of color, exposed silver steps emerging from under the now glowing mysterious machine. The light shard continued to widen and produced an opening the size of a large door. Confused, the on-lookers, seemingly holding their breath, released a unified cry of relief when a voice called out.

"Welcome," Alta said. "You're safe, my friends."

Finis

About the Author

Yvonne Beck Cambray is an avid world traveler with a lifelong passion for ancient history, art, and civilizations.

Her interest in genealogy led her to discover the legends of her own "blue eyed - blonde haired" ancestry.

Yvonne has written and illustrated several children's books.

She is currently working on a compilation of poems as well as her second novel.

Yvonne, an interior designer, resides on a barrier island near the Gulf of Mexico with her husband Greg.